BORN TO SOAR

WELLES T BRANDRIFF

Copyright © 2012 Welles T Brandriff
All rights reserved.

ISBN-10: 1466480157
ISBN-13: 9781466480155

DEDICATION

To my wife, Maria, my sister-in-law, Karen Kukil, and my special friend, Hilary White...

With much appreciation and love for their enthusiastic support of my writing endeavors

I

August 23, 1944 2000 hours (8PM)

When Kelly Rossiter walked into the Officer's Club at Long Beach Army Air Field on Wednesday night, the jukebox was playing the latest recording by Glenn Miller's Army Air Force band, and there were several couples out on the dance floor. Rickert, the bartender, had spotted Kelly as soon as she walked in. He reached for two glasses and started mixing her usual Hurricane.

"Hi, Kelly. Someone tried to claim your favorite table tonight, but I put a reserved sign on it."

"Thanks," Kelly said, glancing around the room. It was more crowded than usual for a weeknight.

"Why the crowd? Who are they?"

"Not sure," he said as he shook her drink back and forth several times in a tumbler before pouring it into the glass, "but From what I hear, there was a lot of traffic today including a flight of Mustangs that landed late this afternoon. They're headed for the east coast."

Kelly nodded as she picked up the glass and started toward her table. After taking a couple of steps, she stopped, turned around, and asked Rickert if he had any snacks.

"Peanuts okay?"

"Sure," she said, reaching out for the basket he held out to her.

"Oh, almost forgot to tell you something, Kell."

"What?"

"There was a lieutenant colonel in here earlier asking about you."

"What did he look like?"

"Big guy. Kind of tough looking. Mentioned his name but it was so noisy in here I didn't catch it."

"Could it have been Singleton?"

Rickert shrugged as he wiped a few glasses and put them up on the overhead rack. "Yeah, I suppose. Said he'd be back later after taking care of some business."

✯ ✯ ✯

"Mind if I sit down?"

Kelly looked up from her drink and into the glazed eyes of a slender, youngish, blonde-haired first lieutenant who obviously had a few already. Her first thought was that he must be one of the Mustang pilots who had flown in a few hours earlier. And in her current state of mind she would take considerable pleasure in wiping the cocky grin off his face. But then it struck her: if he was a typical fighter pilot, that would be part of his stock in trade. It was probably etched on his face even when he slept.

"Would it matter if I did?"

"Nope. Not likely. My name's Maynard Magnuson. The guys that I fly with call me Maynard the Madman. Most of the women I know call me Maynard the Magnificent."

Kelly peered at him sourly from behind her raised glass but said nothing.

Lieutenant Magnuson was mildly disappointed at her lack of response. He always thought that to be one of his more clever lines. But for him challenges were the spice of life. A conquest that came too easily would invariably turn out to be a disappointment.

"You know," he said, gazing at her face, "you are, without a doubt, one of the most beautiful women I've ever seen!"

Kelly had no false modesty about her looks. As far back as her early teens, compliments on her natural beauty became commonplace. Her prominent cheekbones were likely passed down from Indian ancestors on her mother's side. They gave her face a fullness that was enhanced by shoulder-length, lustrous black hair that she typically wore swept up in a pompadour. Her cobalt-colored eyes evoked the beauty of a pristine wilderness lake, or so she had been told by one of her college English professors who couldn't decide if he was more enchanted by her startlingly good poetry or her extraordinary looks.

"Lieutenant," Kelly said, as she set her glass slowly back down on the table, "I'm just trying to enjoy a quiet drink alone."

As Magnuson considered his next move, Kelly's boyfriend, Lieutenant Colonel Kirk Singleton, walked in. Noticing Kelly at her table with a man he had never seen before, he sidled up to the bar, choosing a spot where he would be inconspicuous, yet within earshot of their conversation. Singleton was well over six feet tall and had the build of an athlete.

"I notice you're not wearing a ring on your finger," said Magnuson.

"You don't say," Kelly answered.

"Does that mean you're not married or just looking for a good time?"

Kelly, seeing that Kirk was starting to move towards their table, signaled him with a subtle shake of her head. I can handle this jerk, she thought. Ignoring Magnuson's rude question, she said, "I assume you're with that fighter group that arrived earlier this afternoon."

"Damn right, darlin'. And we happen to be the hottest bunch of Mustang jockeys anywhere."

"I am not your darling or anything else for that matter," Kelly snapped, while motioning to the bartender for a refill. Backing off a bit from her combative tone, she asked, "So, how many aces are there in your squadron?"

"There are ten of us altogether."

"Including you, I suppose," she said, offhandedly.

"Yep. I shot down eight Krauts. Six Me 109's and two Shrikes."

"Well, you've still have a ways to go to catch up with Gabreski and Preddy," Kelly said, deliberately stifling a feigned yawn.

"Yeah, but they've been at it a lot longer than I have. Anyway, you never answered my question."

"And what was that?"

"Are you available?"

"For what?"

"C'mon, you know what I mean. Why are you giving me such a hard time?"

"Giving you a hard time? Lieutenant, I made it clear right up front that I'm not interested. Are you really that dense?"

"Geez! What are you anyway?"

"What do you mean, 'what am I?'"

"What do you do? Why are you here?"

"How is that any of your business?"

"Wait a minute," he said, ignoring her comment. "Don't tell me; you're one of those women pilots aren't you? You're a WASP. Right?"

Kelly placed her elbows on the table, and cupping one hand over the other, rested her chin on the back of them.

"That's right," she said, with an edge to her voice that would have been a clear warning to anyone in full command of their faculties. "I'm a WASP. Is that a problem?"

"Hell yes! As far as I'm concerned, any woman who thinks she thinks she can handle a fighter or a bomber is a major problem."

"And why is that?" Kelly asked, trying to control her temper.

"Simple. They don't have the reflexes or the physical stamina and they're likely to panic any time they find themselves in a jam." His words were already starting to slur as he turned around and waved his empty glass at the bartender. "Hell, I could go on all night!"

"Don't bother. It's obvious you don't know what you're talking about, Lieutenant," Kelly said, raising her voice so that it could be heard throughout the room. "For your information, there are hundreds of women out there as we speak, ferrying military aircraft all over the country—to free you guys up to concentrate on combat missions." That's what the WASP program is all about: doing the grunt work so you guys can get all the glory."

At this point, most of the conversation in the room stopped as everyone turned and looked over at the table where Kelly and the lieutenant were seated. Although no one had intervened, it was obvious that most of the people sympathized with Kelly. Kirk Singleton, on the other hand, having witnessed her wrath, knew Kelly could take care of herself.

"Let me tell you something, lady. Most people aren't too excited about having a bunch of women cluttering up the sky. And I agree with them. I happen to think that a woman's place is at home in the kitchen or bedroom where she can put her unique talents to their proper use."

"And I think that you're just plain drunk and don't know what the hell you're talking about."

"It doesn't matter what you think," he said, knocking over his empty glass. "The war will be over soon, and then you dames will be permanently grounded. In the meantime, it might help if we lost a few more of you to a crash or two."

By the time the lieutenant was halfway through his last sentence, Kirk knew there was no way he could move quickly enough to head off what was about to happen.

"Why, you bastard!" Kelly growled. Reaching across the table, she grabbed him by the collar, and pulled him off his chair and onto the floor, landing on top of him. Fighting back tears, she began choking him with both hands, as a torrent of profanity poured from her mouth.

✯ ✯ ✯

II

When Kirk pulled Kelly off Magnuson, the lieutenant remained sitting on the floor for a moment, too stunned to move.

Kelly turned to Kirk and said in a thick voice, "I need you to arrange for the use of a Mustang. Can you do that?"

"Sure," he said, giving her a quizzical look. "What do you have in mind?"

"A little aerial competition. I want to show this bozo how..."

"Ok Kelly. When?"

"Tomorrow morning at 0800."

Turning to Magnuson, who was still rubbing his neck, she said, "My Mustang against yours, Lieutenant. You take off first and I follow. You use any trick you have up your sleeve to try and shake me off your tail, but if you fail, you will publicly apologize for your disgusting remarks."

Magnuson, eying her nervously, began in a halting voice, "And... and what if..."

"You won't!" Kelly snapped back at him, her anger swelling back up, "That is *not* going to happen!"

With that, Kelly turned away and stalked across the room toward the side exit. Kirk called after her and told her to wait for him outside.

Magnuson watched her walk away with a sense of relief, continuing to massage his sore throat. Standing next to him, Kirk could see the red marks from Kelly's fingers on his neck as well as several beads of blood where her fingernails had actually broken the skin. Shaking his head slowly from side to side, Kirk said in a voice lacking even a hint of sympathy, "Well, Lieutenant, I hope you learned your lesson."

"Who the devil are you anyway?" Magnuson asked, his voice still hoarse.

"Colonel Kirk Singleton of General Arnold's staff," Kirk replied. "And snap to Lieutenant, when you're speaking to a senior officer."

Magnuson instantly stood at attention, while Kirk, who towered over him, began pacing slowly around him.

"What's your name, Lieutenant?"

"Magnuson, sir."

"Well, Lieutenant Magnuson, it looks like you have a new mission in the morning."

"Colonel, we have to get to Newark tomorrow."

"Don't you worry about that. I'll take care of it. Whether you know it or not, you have accepted Miss Rossiter's challenge."

"Sir, I don't…"

"And," Kirk continued, raising his voice a notch, "I would *strongly* suggest that you call it a night and get back to your quarters. You've had enough and if you're going to fly in the morning you'd better sleep it off. Any questions?"

"Well Sir…"

"Then it's settled," Kirk continued, "I'll expect to see you on the flight line at 0800 sharp! Is that clear?"

"Yes, Sir," Magnuson said, saluting Colonel Singleton, before turning and leaving the club, his earlier swagger replaced by a noticeable stagger.

Singleton then walked over to the corner table where the remaining four Mustang pilots were seated and briefly surveyed them.

"Which one of you is the senior officer?"

"Well sir, I'm the flight leader."

"And you are…?"

"Captain Claiborne sir," he replied, standing up and coming to attention as the others followed suit.

"Well then Captain Claiborne, let me just remind you that your command does not end when you land." Pausing for a second, he continued, "You gentlemen are welcome to stay and enjoy your drinks, but you *will* behave like officers. Is that clear?"

"Yes Sir!" replied all four pilots, almost in unison.

"And Captain Claiborne, I am holding you personally accountable for the behavior of your men. Allowing Magnuson to behave the way he did was a dereliction of your duty."

"Yes Sir, but he doesn't usually carry on like that."

"No excuses, Captain!" Singleton snapped. "That kind of behavior is unacceptable, period! Is that clear?"

"Yes Sir!" replied Claiborne, hesitating for a moment then haltingly, "Not to be disrespectful, sir… wasn't Miss Rossiter's attack on Magnuson a bit… excessive?"

"Captain Claiborne, her best friend was a WASP who died in the line of duty," Singleton replied. "How do you think *you* would have reacted?"

Claiborne, pausing a moment to look at the floor, quietly said "I don't know Sir," then looking back at Singleton he asked, "How did it happen?"

"She was towing a target for air-to-air gunnery practice up in Dodge City," Singleton began. "They were about to call it a day, so her crewman started reeling in the target when some hotshot decided to make one more pass."

Claiborne's eyes widened, "Oh my God, you don't mean…"

"Yeah, he hit a wing tank instead. They never even had a chance to bail out. The shooter was a lot like your boy Magnuson, always griping about women pilots. Last I heard, the IG declared it an accident and the son of a bitch is still flying."

Claiborne and his men remained silent.

Singleton turned to leave, "Goodnight gent…"

"Sir," the captain said, somewhat tentatively.

The colonel stopped and looked back at him. "Yes?"

"Well Sir, I think I should point out that…um…Lieutenant Magnuson is an exceptional pilot."

"And your point is?"

Clearing his throat nervously, Claiborne continued, "Sir, with all due respect, I think Miss Rossiter may be a bit out of her depth…."

"I guess we'll know for sure tomorrow, won't we Captain?"

Clearing his throat nervously, Claiborne continued, "But sir, even if she is an excellent pilot, which I'm sure she is," he quickly added, "that doesn't mean she's ready to take on an experienced fighter pilot like Lieutenant Magnuson who already has established a superior reputation for his dogfighting skills."

Singleton looked at the captain with a faint icy grin on his face. "Tell me, Captain Claiborne, what do you consider the three most important qualities of a successful fighter pilot?"

The captain thought for a minute. "Well . . . superior flying skills, of course, total confidence in one's own ability, and a basically aggressive nature, I suppose, would be the three that first come to mind."

"I think I'd be inclined to go along with your choices," said Singleton, nodding his head thoughtfully. "Now, you'll have to trust me when I tell you she has no shortage of piloting skills. But let me ask you this: is there anything you observed here tonight that would suggest to you she's under-endowed with either of the last two qualities?"

A brief smile passed over Claiborne's face as he looked down and nervously rubbed his foot back and forth on the floor. "No, sir, she certainly displayed a lot of confidence and as far as aggressive behavior goes . . . . Well, I certainly wouldn't ever want to get on her bad side as Lieutenant Magnuson managed to do."

"I agree," said Singleton. "Let me ask you something. Do you know who David McCampbell is?"

"Well, sure. Everybody in the flying business has heard of him. That's the navy fighter pilot who shot down nine Jap planes in one dogfight. Next to Butch O'Hare and Pappy Boyington, he's probably the best known of the carrier pilots."

"Exactly," replied Singleton. "Well, Miss Rossiter's brother, Jack Rossiter, flies with McCampbell off the carrier *Essex*. Kelly actually learned to fly before her brother, but once he started flying, they spent a heck of a lot of hours in the air engaging in mock dogfights. And I've been a first-hand witness to their shenanigans. At the time, I was working on my grandfather's farm, which was only a few miles from the airport that they flew from. And I saw them upstairs many times in their Meyers or Steermans going at each other like they were out for blood. In fact, I was always amazed that they didn't tear the damn wings off those birds by the time they got finished putting them through their paces. My point is this: I never saw Kelly Rossiter bested in any of those dogfights."

Claiborne nodded appreciatively. "Pretty impressive, Colonel, but what I'm wondering is just how good a pilot is her brother?"

Singleton grinned like a card player who's been waiting for this moment to play his best hand. "Last I knew he had twenty-two confirmed kills."

The colonel's revelation triggered a flurry of admiring comments from the rest of the Mustang pilots while Claiborne let out a long, low whistle of respect.

"And those were mainly Zeros (Japanese fighter planes), so they weren't cheap kills.

"Now you can see why Lieutenant Magnuson might be in for a rough time tomorrow morning," Kirk said, as he turned to leave. "Goodnight, gentlemen, and remember what I said about your behavior when you're on the ground," the hard edge of authority returning once again to his voice. "I expect I'll be seeing you all on the flight line bright and early," he added and left without waiting for a reply.

Once outside, he looked around for Kelly, eventually finding her on the golf course, pacing back and forth at the first tee.

"How are you doing Kell?"

"I really need a cigarette."

Singleton produced a pack of Chesterfields from his shirt pocket, tapped out two cigarettes and handed one to Kelly. With her still trembling hands cupped around his, Kirk lit her cigarette with a brass Zippo lighter, and then his own.

"So am I going to be court martialed for attempting to strangle an officer?" she asked wryly.

Singleton grinned, "Well if so, you'll be the first civilian."

Flicking a bit of tobacco from the tip of her tongue, she continued, "What about my father. How do you think he'll take it when he finds out?"

"Kelly, I'd be a lot more worried about him catching you smoking."

"Seriously, Kirk, am I going to be in trouble for this?"

"I'm not going to lie to you Kell. This is the sort of thing that could get a girl thrown out of the program."

Kelly took a deep drag as her eyes began to tear up.

"Look, that's not going to happen," Kirk said, "You're too good a pilot and the program simply can't afford to lose you. But we both know this is going to get back to Hap Arnold so I should tell him before that happens."

"What are you going to say?"

"You tell me. What the hell happened in there Kelly?"

"I just lost my temper. That's all. It's as simple as that."

"This was about Elaine wasn't it?" he asked, then immediately answered his own question. "Of course it was. Kell, you can't go on grieving forever."

"I don't intend to go on forever, Kirk," Kelly replied curtly, "only as long as I need to."

"Well you need to put it behind you soon. General Arnold will not be amused by one of his WASPs getting into a barroom brawl."

"When are you planning to tell him?"

"The sooner the better. I'll be talking to him first thing tomorrow morning, so that'll be as good a time as any." They finished their cigarettes in silence.

"Don't worry," said Kirk, "Magnuson was way out of line. As far as I'm concerned, he got what was coming to him and that's how I'll present it to the general."

Singleton turned the remaining butt between his thumb and forefinger until all of the tobacco had fallen out, then balled up the remaining paper and put it in his pocket. He was taught how to field-strip a cigarette in basic training. The practice was to cover one's tracks and insure that no butts were left behind for the enemy to find. As with most other servicemen, the habit stuck with him. "Come on. I'll drive you back to your quarters."

As Kelly settled back in the passenger seat of the staff car, she asked Kirk, "What brings you to Long Beach anyway?"

"I've been dropping in on the ferrying groups, to see how things are going. I'll be staying long enough to have lunch with your CO tomorrow, then I'm flying out to Utah to check on a new outfit that's being organized at Wendover Field. And..." he looked at her with a smile, "...*you* are coming with me."

"What?"

"You heard me. We're flying to Utah together. I'll fill you in tomorrow. Right now let's just concentrate on getting you back for a nice hot bath and a massage. You really need to unwind"

"And?"

"And what?"

Kelly looked at him knowingly, "A massage and what?"

Kirk chuckled as they got out of the car and started walking towards the barracks, his arm around her.

"Tell you what," he said, "consider the massage a starter, then we'll see how interested you still are. Remember, you've got a hot date first thing in the morning, so you're going to need your rest."

As they entered her quarters, Kelly asked Kirk if he remembered her telling him about Ami Takahashi, Kelly's best friend in high school.

"Vaguely. Which camp is she in?"

"Minidoka in Idaho."

"Do you ever hear from her?"

"Sure. We exchange letters regularly."

"How is she doing?"

"She's worried about her father. He doesn't write often, but when he does he sounds depressed."

"They're American citizens for Pete's sake! Hell, between breaking up their families and throwing them into camps who *wouldn't* be depressed?" Kirk replied.

Kelly continued, "Well, she asked me to do her a favor."

"What kind of favor?"

"Oh just to drop by their house and see if it's being cared for."

When they got inside, Kelly began to undress. Kirk started her bath then returned to the bedroom, lit another cigarette and sat on the edge of the bed. When she returned from her bath, Kirk was lying on his back with his hands clasped behind his head, eyes closed but awake. Kelly lay face down, squeezing next to him on the narrow bunk bed. Rolling over on his side, Kirk began to massage the back of her neck. Kelly let out a soft moan as she felt the tension flow out of her body. Kirk had barely worked his way down to her shoulders when he heard the rhythmic breathing sounds of someone in a deep slumber.

No action tonight, Kirk thought wryly as he stood up next to the bed. Bending over, he kissed her bare shoulder, pulled the blanket up and slipped out into the night.

☆ ☆ ☆

III

August 24th 0800

    Despite the early hour, it was obvious that it was going to be another scorcher. Except for a few scattered cumulus clouds on the horizon, the sky was cloudless, visibility unlimited and the winds calm with only a steady two-to-three knot westerly breeze. As is typical of Texas summers, this bucolic picture would change by late afternoon, when those small cumulus puffs having grown into towering, cumulonimbus anvil heads, would bring isolated but violent thunderstorms with the inevitable rain, lightning and possibility of the dreaded wind shear.

    Kirk leaned over into the cockpit of the mustang and helped Kelly finish strapping herself in.

    "How's your confidence level?" he asked.

    "Reasonably high," she said while leaning down and pulling the pin near the base of the control column to unlock the flight controls.

    "You know, you really don't need to do this to prove a point. You put Magnuson in his place last night."

Kelly gave him a sharp look. "You don't think I can take him in the air?"

"No, that's not . . . ."

"Look, this is something I need to do. Attempting to strangle him was one way to vent my anger," she said. "But the question about my flying ability can only be answered in one way."

"Fine. Just try not to let him get between you and the sun."

Kelly squinted up at him. "Why? Is that a bad thing?" she asked, sarcastically.

Kirk recoiled, then broke into a laugh. "Okay. I'm going to shut up now," he said as he brushed his finger playfully across the bridge of her nose.

"Good. I'd better get going before you dig yourself any deeper," she said, grinning up at him as she slid the canopy closed and locked it shut.

For the next few minutes, she forcibly eliminated all outside distractions from her mind while concentrating on her pre-flight checklist:

Battery switch on.

Flap lever in up position.

Carburetor intake control set in filtered position.

Radiator air control switches in auto position.

5 degrees of right rudder trim for take-off.

Elevator trim at 2 degrees nose up.

Aileron trim in the neutral position.

Fuel mixture control Idle Cut-off

Fuel selector at main tanks and check each booster pump at Normal and Emergency and note fuel pressures.

Switch battery off; have ground starter battery plugged in.

When it was time for engine start-up, Kelly opened the throttle a half an inch, flicked the mixture control to the cut-off position, advanced the prop control forward to the fine-pitch position, switched the booster pumps on to pressurize the fuel lines, and after several quick shots on the primer, pressed the starter switch.

Following a few slow rotations of the blade tips, the powerful Merlin engine sprang to life with a throaty roar, shattering the morning silence and reverberating across the field.

After switching the mixture control to auto-lean, she scanned the oil pressure gauges and checked the magnetos. Then she confirmed that with the hydraulic system pressurized, the flaps had come up to the pre-selected position of 20 degrees.

Moments later, Kelly glanced over at Lieutenant Magnuson's Mustang. When he was ready, he signaled a thumbs-up to which Kelly responded with a tight-lipped nod of her head. Magnuson began taxiing and Kelly eased the throttle forward on her Mustang, pulled out of the parking spot, swung the plane 90 degrees, and began following him toward the end of the runway.

As she swung the nose-high plane back and forth in the familiar S-pattern to avoid any collisions with parked aircraft, her thoughts returned briefly to the events of the night before. It was true that the intense hostility she felt for Lieutenant Magnuson had evaporated overnight. The need to strike back at him, to humiliate him, to destroy his male ego had left her. But the will to win was still strong, if not stronger. It was no longer a personal matter, a vendetta. Now, it was a matter of proving that women were every bit as capable as men in all aspects of flying.

Kelly stopped briefly at the end of the taxiway for the engine run-up and final pre-flight check of her instrument settings and readings. The tower briefed them with traffic and weather updates, both of which were unremarkable. It being a Sunday morning, the base was all but closed for business, so with no traffic in the area they were cleared to take-off ad lib. As Magnuson began his roll, Kelly got into position at the end of the runway. As soon as the other Mustang lifted off, she released the brakes and advanced the throttle. Well before the half-way mark, the Mustang's tail wheel lifted off the ground and as she pulled back on the control column her plane virtually leaped into the air. Kelly found the Mustang to be the best aircraft in which to experience the pure, visceral sensations of flight. Despite having done it more times than she could count, taking off in a Mustang had never lost the thrill of the first time.

Her favorite routine was to accelerate as quickly as possible and once airborne, immediately retract the landing gear, maintaining level flight just a few yards above the ground while gaining more speed. Nearing the end of the runway, she would pull back on the stick and feel the g-force push her down hard into her seat as she began a near vertical climb. At altitude, she would gradually level off in a wide arc in which all sensation of gravity disappeared. So what began with a sense of fierce, unbridled power, ended with a serene sensation of floating in space. Years later, this last maneuver known as the parabolic arc would be performed using large aircraft to simulate weightlessness in the training of astronauts.

But there was no time for that this morning. With the landing gear fully retracted, Kelly banked sharply to the right and began a steep climbing turn in an attempt to catch up to Magnuson as quickly as possible.

As she continued her pursuit, Kelly briefly reviewed the pros and cons of her immediate situation. First and foremost was her assumption that Magnuson would greatly underestimate her ability, or, looking at it from the other side of the coin, overestimate his own. Another thing working in her favor was the fact that she and her brother had always flown the same aircraft with the exact same handling and performance characteristics, so neither of them could claim an advantage in that area. Magnuson, on the other hand, was used to flying an aircraft with certain performance advantages over its German counterparts, which Kelly assumed would place him at a disadvantage in attempting to outmaneuver an aircraft whose performance characteristics were exactly the same as his own. On the other hand, since he knew the Mustang so well, it could also work to his advantage.

One other advantage she had enjoyed when dog fighting against her brother Jack was her intimate knowledge of the way he thought and fought. After a while, Kelly found she could generally anticipate how he would respond in a given situation. Since she had only the sketchiest knowledge of Magnuson's thought processes, there was that element of unpredictability with which she would have to deal. But, of course, he would be in the same boat in terms of trying to outguess her.

All of these racing thoughts suddenly dissipated as Kelly realized that she was rapidly closing in on Magnuson's Mustang, and in the same instant he throttled back and entered a tight chandelle in an effort to quickly reverse his course. Kelly's complete attention was now on her flying as she closely pursued Magnuson through the turn. He then advanced the throttle and began a near vertical climb, rapidly losing airspeed and bringing the plane to a power-on stall. The Mustang appeared to be momentarily suspended in place then slowly spun one-eighty degrees to begin a steep, high-speed dive. Magnuson assumed that Kelly wouldn't dare push her P-51 to such treacherous limits.

Mustangs were well known to be prone to compressibility effects at very high speeds, the most dangerous of which was a tendency for the entire craft to begin vibrating. If the shaking becomes severe enough, it could result in structural damage to the airframe with catastrophic results. Kelly was well aware of this, but opted to stay right on Magnuson's tail throughout the maneuver, much to the lieutenant's chagrin.

From that point on, Magnuson's attempt to shake Kelly off covered several square miles of sky, and altitudes ranging from 20,000 to less than 500 feet. Magnuson tried every acrobatic maneuver he'd used in combat plus a few he improvised on the spot, taking Kelly through a head-spinning, airframe-straining series of maneuvers pushing both pilots and aircraft to their limits.

When he glanced back over his shoulder, she was still on his tail. He had to admit she was damned good. Hell, the last couple of maneuvers had thwarted Nazi pilots on more than one occasion. But Kelly had stuck with him.

A few miles out from the base, Kelly broke off the chase and put the Mustang into a shallow dive leveling off just a few hundred feet from the ground. Moments later, she came streaking across the field at full tilt, the airspeed indicator hovering just above the 400-mile an hour mark. As the Mustang approached the end of the field, Kelly nosed the aircraft into a vertical climb, doing a series of victory rolls until the plane ran out of momentum. Performing a stall-turn at the top of her climb, she reversed direction, descended quickly and turned on to final approach. At that point she lowered the wheels while being careful to maintain an airspeed of around 150 mph. Like most high performance aircraft, the Mustang was not very forgiving and allowing the airspeed to fall below 135 on final would risk stalling without enough altitude to recover. Just before she was to flare out for touchdown, Kelly encountered a sudden crosswind forcing her to quickly drop the left upwind wing while applying right rudder to keep the nose straight.

Almost imperceptibly, the left wheel touched down, followed by the right. As the plane lost speed, the tail wheel softly settled onto the pavement and Kelly applied gentle pressure on the brakes continuing a leisurely roll to the end of the runway and onto the taxiway. She then zigzagged her way back to her tie-down on the tarmac in front of the Operations Building, shut down the engine, slid back the canopy, and unbuckled the harness. As she pulled herself up out of the cockpit, she was surprised to see that a small crowd had gathered: pilots, mechanics, tower personnel, Operations staff. Even the Mustang pilots from Magnuson's flight were there, and they were all applauding. Not surprisingly, the loudest cheering of all came from a small group of WASPS standing nearby.

A few days later, the base photographer gave Kelly a couple of photos from the day of the competition. In one, she was stepping out of the cockpit while looking back over her shoulder toward the end of the runway. Kirk said it looked like one of the famous newspaper images of Amelia Earhart and that Kelly's gaze appeared other-worldly, as if she was looking into the future. On the other hand, he added, perhaps she was contemplating something a bit more prosaic. Like, what the hell was taking Magnuson so long to get back?

Kelly told him that she was actually thinking of her mother and Elaine. Wherever they might be, she was hoping they knew that her victory was theirs as well.

Later, Kelly was relaxing in the Ready Room with two other WASP pilots. Celeste Marino and Doris Delaney, were Kelly's classmates at Sweetwater and were awaiting their next ferrying assignments.

"You really put that guy in his place, Kelly," said Celeste.

Kelly shrugged. "All I wanted to do was let him know that we can fly as well as the guys."

"Well, I'm pretty sure he got the message," said Doris.

☆ ☆ ☆

Kelly's military flying career began on the first day of March 1944 when her father handed her a telegram from Jackie Cochran. In it were orders to report to Sweetwater, Texas the second week of March to begin pilot training with class 44-W-6. She had been accepted!

"This was addressed to me," she told her father slapping the telegram down on his desk. "What business did you have opening it?"

"I'm your father, so anything that affects your life is my business. And you damn well know how I feel about women flying military airplanes."

"No dad. Why don't you tell me again...."

"Don't get smart," snapped her father.

"Well I'm sorry dad, but it's my decision. For God's sake, I'm twenty-four! Last I checked that makes me an adult."

"Twenty-four is still young. You can learn from someone who's been around longer than you have."

"Yes, but I'd rather learn from my own mistakes."

"All I want is what's best for you, Kelly."

"I know Dad. But as I said, I'm not a child anymore. You really need to let go"

"Why are you so anxious to get away from me?"

"Because you're *smothering* me! After Mom died, I was glad to pitch in and do whatever I could to support you and the boys, but that was over six years ago. And now it's time for me to move on. Plus I'm tired of you interfering in my life.

"How did I ever interfere in your life?"

"How about the time you pressured me into attending a West Coast school when I wanted to go to college in the east.

"That's because there were plenty of top-notch schools on the West Coast. There was no need to go so far away," he said.

"See! That's exactly what I'm been talking about. Ever since Mom died, you've kept me as close to home as possible. And that's why you didn't want me to apply to the WASP program."

"Dammit, Kelly, you'll be a lot more valuable to the country if you stay here and help me in the plant than if you fly military airplanes. And a lot safer, too."

"My three brothers aren't sitting around fretting about their safety. They're off fighting the war—putting their lives on the line every day."

"Yes, but a woman isn't expected to do that."

"What about the nurses who serve in forward areas near the front lines?"

"They made that choice."

"And I've made my choice, Dad."

"Look, you can still fly while you work here with me."

"I give up. I don't think you'll ever understand," she said, snatching the telegram out of her father's hand. Leaving her father's office, she slammed the door behind her and collided with a tall Army Air Force colonel who was talking to the secretary.

"Well I hope I wasn't in your way," said the colonel.

"Mind your own business," Kelly replied.

"I beg your pardon?"

"You heard me."

"I was minding my own business, Miss. You're the one who ran into me."

Kelly paused a moment to size him up. He was quite tall and his face was a study in contrasts. It was as if some sculptor had chiseled the rough outline of his features but never got around to finishing the task, yet the twinkle in his eyes suggested someone with a sense of humor who wasn't taking this little skirmish too seriously.

At that moment, Kelly's father buzzed his secretary on the intercom.

"Yes, Mr. Rossiter?"

"Has Colonel Singleton arrived yet?"

"Oh yes, he's here," she replied portentously.

Bob Rossiter opened the door and briefly paused to survey the scene in his secretary's office. Colonel Singleton was standing by Ruth's desk, leafing through a copy of the annual report, his thoughts obviously elsewhere. Kelly, to Bob's surprise, was still there, arms folded across her chest, staring out the window at the distant mountains.

"Colonel Singleton!" Bob greeted him, with outstretched hand. "How good to finally meet you."

"And you, Mr. Rossiter," Singleton replied, shaking his hand.

"Have you met my daughter Kelly?

"Well our paths did briefly cross," Kirk chuckled, "but no. Not properly." Then turning to Kelly he smiled, "It's a pleasure to meet you Miss Rossiter."

"Likewise, I'm sure," she replied somewhat frostily, but her anger was quickly melting away. *Damn,* she thought, almost unconsciously, *the son of a bitch does have his charm.*

Kirk, turning back to Bob said, "I'm afraid I'm on a bit of a tight schedule Mr. Rossiter. Will we have a chance to meet with the Boeing folks today?"

"Yes, they're expected to arrive at the plant around ten. Have you had breakfast yet?"

"Just some coffee and a donut."

"Our executive cafeteria makes an excellent breakfast. I have to get a few things ready before the Boeing contingent arrives, so I won't be able to join you. But perhaps my daughter could walk you over there. Is that all right with you, Colonel?"

Singleton put the report back down on the desk and said "Sure."

Rossiter looked over at his daughter. "Kelly?"

Kelly nodded. Her anger had given way to fascination.

When they got to the cafeteria, Singleton invited Kelly to have breakfast with him.

She accepted. "What are you having, Colonel?"

"Thought I might give the eggs Benedict a try."

"Good choice." Pausing briefly, she continued, "Have we met before? You look vaguely familiar"

"I don't think so, but I suppose you could have seen me around town."

"What were you doing in Seattle?" she asked.

"I was working on my grandfather's farm."

"Whose farm is that?"

"Sal Locarno's."

"Locarno's!" she exclaimed. "That's barely a mile down the road from where I grew up. I used to bike down that road quite often when I was younger."

Singleton nodded. "Each year I spent most of my summer leave from the academy at my grandfather's harvesting fruits and vegetables."

"But you're not from this part of the country?"

"No. I was born and raised in Philadelphia."

"You couldn't have gotten any farming experience there."

"Nope. But both of my mother's brothers were farmers. One, Pete Locarno, stayed in Pennsylvania. He owned a farm out in the Pennsylvania Dutch country. When I was quite small, like around seven, I started spending a month each summer with him and my aunt Gladys. Then when I got into my teens I'd visit Uncle Sal in Seattle for a couple of weeks each summer. That's when I really began to pull my own weight on a farm."

Kelly's brief exposure to the virility that Singleton exuded was sufficient to trigger strongly sensual thoughts. And those thoughts set off corresponding sensations in parts of her body that had been virtually immune to such feelings for the past few months. She hadn't experienced anything like that since she had been with Christopher Steele. Kelly decided that she was strongly attracted to Colonel Singleton in spite of their initial conflict. She sensed that the attraction was mutual because every time she looked over at him he was staring at her.

After finding an empty table, Kelly asked what his parents did.

"My father was an attorney and my mother a grade school teacher."

"And you had no interest in following in their footsteps?"

"No. I knew from early on that I wanted to fly. And in the military, not as a civilian."

"How did you get your name? I don't know of anyone else with that name."

"It's Scottish and short for Kirkland."

"It's typically a surname, I gather."

"Yes, but my parents stumbled on the name when they were leafing through a genealogy record of my mother's family. She was Scottish."

"So what exactly does this WASP flying program involve, Colonel Singleton?"

"Please call me Kirk," he replied.

"Kelly," she smiled, holding out her hand.

"Well, Kelly, you'll be living in a barracks, military style, that is, six women to a bay. You'll be issued bedding, clothing, flight suits, and a parachute in the course of the first few days. Even though you're not technically a part of the military, you're going to find that you have to march in formation to wherever you need to go. And, believe me, in the first ten days, you'll cover a lot of ground—to the mess hall for your meals, the theater for briefings and lectures, the supply office for your equipment, the flight surgeon's office to get your shots, and so on."

"Ouch!"

"And at some point in those first few days, they'll give you a psychiatric exam."

"A psychiatric exam?"

"Uh huh. You know. Some character who might be a little crazy himself will ask you all kinds of weird questions."

"Like what, for instance?"

Kirk thought for a minute and then responded. "Well, like have you ever had a death wish, or do you hate your father. You know, stuff like that."

Great, Kelly thought, *I hope they don't give me a lie detector test while they're asking the questions.* "So tell me more. When does the real training begin?"

"Ground school will begin within two or three days after you arrive; flying training should begin a few days after that, weather permitting. How long have you been flying anyway?"

"I started taking lessons when I was fifteen and soloed shortly after I turned sixteen. I have more than 500 hours in my log, much of it in either a Meyer or a Stearman. My second-oldest brother learned to fly shortly after I did. Once he got his license, we'd chase each other all over the sky in mock dogfights."

Singleton nodded. "I remember seeing two Stearmans go at it when I was out working in the field. I hope you realize that your military flying will mainly involve moving planes from one part of the country to another. It's going to be anything but glamorous. No acrobatics or anything like that."

Kelly shrugged. "I love to fly, Kirk. Besides, my primary goal is to serve my country. Whatever they want me to do, I'll do."

Kirk gave her a hard look. "Are you sure you're going to be able to rein in your independent streak and submit to the limitations of military flying, Kelly?"

"I repeat I'll do whatever I'm asked to do and without complaining."

Kirk stared at her but said nothing in response.

"You don't believe me, do you?" she asked.

Kirk shook his head. "No. And it's not that I think you're lying to me. But, I think you're going to find it's more difficult to do than to say."

Kelly made a promise to herself that she would prove him wrong in his estimate of her.

✫ ✫ ✫

At her father's request, after the meeting with the Boeing reps was over, Kelly accompanied Kirk Singleton to the guard post at the entrance to the building to make sure everything went smoothly while going through the check-out procedures.

On the way down, Kirk asked her if she'd go out to dinner with him that night. Kelly said she'd already made plans for that evening but that she'd take a rain check until the next time he was in town.

When they reached the guard post, one of the two guards was about to turn Kirk's briefcase upside down and dump everything out onto the table until Kelly intervened and said that it would not be necessary.

"It's standard operating procedures, Miss Rossiter. Your father's orders."

"I'm aware of that. But Colonel Singleton has a top-secret clearance and is a personal assistant to General Arnold."

The older of the guards nudged the younger one and said, "Pass him through, John. If Miss Rossiter vouches for him, that's good enough for me."

The younger guard frowned but, after a cursory examination of the papers in the briefcase, he handed it back to Singleton.

Singleton held out his hand and said, "Goodbye, Kelly. Good luck with the program. And remember to watch your tongue."

"It's not something I'm likely to forget," she said.

✯ ✯ ✯

IV

Mid-March, 1944

    Two weeks after receiving the telegram, Kelly boarded a train in Seattle and enjoyed the trip to Los Angeles in the comfort of a Pullman. Arriving the next morning, Kelly transferred to an eastbound train which would reach Sweetwater in just under twenty four hours, so she opted to continue by coach.

    With LA well behind her, the landscape unfolded into a vast, arid expanse that reached out to the far horizon. Then something extraordinary began to unfold. As the sun gradually sank lower in the sky behind her, the bleached, inhospitable desertscape began to gradually fill with color. At first, the sand, rocks and mesas took on a subtle yellow which quickly accelerated to a deep red orange as the sun reached the horizon, perfectly complementing the now dark, blue sky. It was as if the world had come alive before her eyes. As the ever growing shadows turned into complete darkness punctuated by the occasional flicker of light from an isolated ranch house, Kelly's sense of awe was replaced by an unsettling feeling. For the first time since leaving Seattle, she realized that she was already homesick.

Three women sitting with her were also headed to Sweetwater for WASP training. A short while earlier, they had gone back to the club car for snacks and drinks, inviting Kelly to join them. Kelly declined, opting instead for a break from the incessant chatter of the two younger seatmates.

Elaine Goodrich, who was sitting directly across from Kelly, had winked when they got up to leave, indicating that she could well understand how Kelly would appreciate the break. A lawyer from Los Angeles, Elaine, like Kelly, was determined to do something other than serve coffee and doughnuts at a United Service Organization (USO) canteen or pack tongue depressors for shipment to the combat zone. The other two, Peggy and Louise, were both only twenty-one and had just made the cut-off with 35 hours of flying time.

Kelly heard them coming back when they were still half a car away.

"Hey, Kelly, you missed out on a car full of gorgeous guys in uniform. Every one of them was anxious to buy us a drink," said Peggy.

"Yeah, and they were climbing over one another to be first in line to light our cigarettes," Louise chimed in.

Kelly glanced at Elaine, who shook her head in a dismissive gesture. "As far as I can tell, Peggy and Louise have a thing for anyone in uniform."

Kelly smiled. "Well, they do say that clothes make the man. And I have to admit that all four of my brothers look great in their dress uniforms. But only one of the four would be considered handsome by the usual standards."

Kelly looked back out the window and saw her own reflection since the sun had set and the lights had come on in the coach car. She rubbed her nose between her thumb and forefinger. She had always been dissatisfied with that particular aspect of her features. It had always seemed to be a little too broad across the bridge, although no one else seemed to think so.

During Kelly's early teens, her mother would often find her daughter in front of the bathroom mirror, rubbing her fingers back and forth over the bridge of her nose as though the act could somehow reduce its thickness. Kelly could still hear the soft, gentle laughter of her mother as she wrapped her arms around her daughter and suggested in a light-hearted, teasing manner that the only thing Kelly was likely to accomplish was to wear the skin off the side of her nose.

Then Kelly experienced her first great loss: watching her mother's life slowly ebb away over a period of almost a year and, worst of all, having it come to an end on the eve of Kelly's sixteenth birthday. Eight more birthdays had passed since that terrible day, and although the pain had lessened, it had never really gone away.

As a grown woman, Kelly still missed her mother's presence and the nurturing, loving support she had lavished on her only daughter. To Kelly it had been a safety net in a world that seemed increasingly chaotic and dangerous. Even though Kelly had been the second-youngest of the children, she made the decision to take on their mother's role, which was hardly surprising, she being the only girl among five children. In addition Kelly felt as if she had became entangled in a web of mutual dependence deliberately spun by her widowed father.

"When are we due to arrive in Sweetwater?' Louise asked.

"Ten of ten," Kelly answered.

"If there are six of us to a bay," Peggy said, "we need to find two more women to share it with."

Elaine responded, "That shouldn't be a problem, Peggy. There will probably be a lot more women arriving about the same time as us. I'm sure we'll meet a couple of gals who will fit into our little group."

A half-hour later, the conductor passed through the car announcing their arrival at Sweetwater, Texas.

Kelly's first view of Sweetwater reminded her of the dusty old cow towns in Hollywood westerns. They got a ride in a beat up old taxi to the Blue Bonnet Hotel, the only place of its kind in town. Several small groups of WASP hopefuls had already arrived and informed all the newcomers that they'd have to wait until the following morning for someone from Avenger Field to pick them up.

"Does that mean we spend the night in the hotel lobby?" Peggy asked.

"I suggest we check into a room and try and get some sleep so we won't be total wrecks in the morning," Kelly said.

Although it seemed like a pointless exercise, Elaine volunteered to go and check availability.

"It looks like all the comfortable chairs in the lobby have been taken already," said Peggy.

"Who could fall asleep in the midst of this bedlam anyway?" Louise added.

The lobby was crackling with the sound of myriad conversations punctuated with gales of nervous laughter. Kelly surveyed the scene. She and

Elaine were the only two women who appeared to be totally relaxed and confident about their upcoming experience. From the comments Kelly had overheard, it seemed clear that most of the women present had a minimum number of flying hours and were, like Peggy and Louise, extremely anxious about their prospects for successfully completing the program.

When Elaine returned, she announced that the only room left was under renovation but was livable and had twin beds plus a couple of cots. Apparently no one else had wanted it.

After checking into their room, Kelly proposed they flip a coin to see who got to sleep in the beds. Peggy and Louise won the coin toss but Peggy said she was too wound up to fall asleep just yet.

"Besides, I want to hear what else this Army Air Force Colonel had to say about the program."

Kelly explained, "He said we should keep in mind there's a certain percentage of males that resent the idea of women pilots and would love to see us fail."

"How are we supposed to deal with that?" asked Peggy.

Kelly thought a moment. "He said the best way to deal with it is to bite our lips and concentrate on giving the program our best. If we do that we'll show our critics we can perform as well, if not better, than men."

"So," Peggy groused, "in addition to the demands of the program, we're going to have to deal with abuse from the men who are training us."

"Hopefully it's only a small percentage who fall into that category," Elaine interjected. "Besides, there's no point in getting all worked up about something that may never happen."

✯ ✯ ✯

The next morning, two more women joined them for breakfast. Vicki, who had been a fashion model for *Vogue, and* Sandy, a former elementary school teacher. All four of the original group immediately took a liking to Sandy, but it took Kelly a while to warm up to Vicki. Elaine, on the other hand, was immediately comfortable with Vicki's big city character, and Peggy and Louise were in awe of her status as a professional model.

The bus to Avenger Field arrived at the hotel around ten. With canvas windows and wooden benches for seats, it was informally referred to as the cattle wagon. Shortly after arriving at the field, a young lieutenant, the squadron adjutant, went out of his way to make the women feel welcome, then fingerprinted and photographed each one and marched them over to the hangar where they got their bedding and blankets. Following this, Kelly's group made their way back to the recreation hall where they received a stack of paperwork that kept them busy while awaiting the arrival of their CO (commanding officer).

Lieutenant Colonel Michael McGinnis was a good-looking guy who looked a lot like Henry Fonda. But that was where the resemblance ended. McGinnis made it clear that he had no use for the WASP program and claimed he was invariably surprised when some women from each class successfully made it through. Kelly knew that McGinnis was just trying to scare them. The washout rate up to that point was no worse for the women than it was for the men who went through pilot training.

After being subjected to McGinnis' spiel for several minutes, Kelly decided to speak up, despite Kirk Singleton's admonition not to.

"Permission to speak, Colonel," she said, raising her hand.

"Permission granted, Miss . . ."

"Rossiter, sir," Kelly quickly interjected. "Kelly Rossiter."

"Ye, what is it Rossiter?" McGinnis was clearly annoyed by the interruption.

"Excuse me, sir, but we've all been accepted to the program and we're here now, so what exactly are you hoping to accomplish by discouraging us?"

There was an audible gasp followed by the briefest smattering of applause that immediately ended as McGinnis harrumphed a couple of times and fixed his gaze on Kelly.

"Well, Rossiter, it's like this," McGinnis began with a sarcastic edge. However cocky you may feel about getting here, there are some very influential people who think the whole program's a waste of time and the taxpayer's money. So before you girls get your heads too far up in the clouds, just be aware that this could all end at any moment."

After a seemingly endless litany of the myriad ways in which the students could find themselves summarily dismissed from the program, McGinnis introduced Lena Davenport, the establishment officer and unofficial housemother. Lena promptly announced that she was always available to help with whatever their needs might be. Her genuine warmth and obvious desire to see each of the women do well in the program contrasted sharply with McGinnis's attitude and the tension in the room quickly lifted.

Lena told them to get into groups of six, each of which would share an open bay. Kelly's group quickly claimed one at the end of the barracks to avoid feeling boxed in.

Each trainee had a cot and an oversized footlocker that served the purpose of a closet, a bureau and a dressing table. The supply sergeant informed them that a contingent of RAF flying cadets had been stationed at Avenger Field until very recently, so there had been no time to make changes that would have helped the women to feel more comfortable. They quickly realized that the limited bathroom facilities could easily become a source of friction among them. Two bays, totaling twelve women, shared one bathroom with only two toilet stalls, two shower heads, two sinks, and one mirror.

As they unpacked their belongings and put their clothes away in the footlocker, Lena told them it would be okay to temporarily store their surplus baggage in her office. After everything was squared away in their bay, they marched back over to Hangar 2 and checked out their flight gear.

The uniform of the day was coveralls that they would wear for ground school and flight training. Unfortunately, the coveralls came only in men's sizes, so the shorter girls had to roll up the sleeves and pants several times. The coveralls were nicknamed zoot suits after the baggy style worn by men in Harlem.

Their final briefing came from Lieutenant LaSalle who would be both their calisthenics and drill instructor. After a full day of school and flying, the students would be required to spend an hour exercising under his supervision.

Shortly after LaSalle's talk, they fell out in formation and marched, out of step, over to the mess hall. They were pleasantly surprised by the food, but by that time they were so hungry that just about anything would have tasted good.

Back in their barracks, the new acquaintances spent more time getting to know each other as well as the trainees in the adjoining bay. They took turns using the bathroom facilities, and then, somewhat self-consciously, undressed in front of their bay mates and fell exhausted into their beds. Reveille would be at 0600.

✯ ✯ ✯

The next morning at breakfast, the squadron adjutant came to Kelly's table and told her to report to Colonel McGinnis's office immediately. Ten minutes later, Kelly was standing at attention in front of Colonel McGinnis' desk. He looked up from the papers he'd been studying.

"Rossitor, by now I would hope you're aware that you were completely out of order yesterday. As an officer, I am also obliged to be a gentleman, which is why I didn't publicly dress you down in front of your classmates."

Kelly refused to be intimidated. "With respect sir, I think your disparaging remarks about women pilots were out of order. Isn't it your job…"

McGinnis leaned forward, his face turning red, "First of all, it was *you* who was out of order! Second, I do not need you, *Miss* Rossitor, to tell me what my job is! And if you *ever* address me again with anything less than the respect incumbent to my rank I will not hesitate to send you up on insubordination charges, and you can kiss the program goodbye. *Is* that understood?

"Yes sir!" replied Kelly, somewhat shaken, but also suppressing the anger that was urging her to further engage.

"Good!" snapped McGinnis. "Dismissed."

✯ ✯ ✯

V

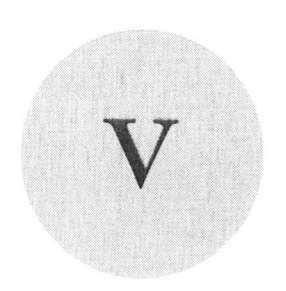

Kelly was the first in her group of trainees to solo during the primary phase of training. Once a student pilot soloed, they were allowed to take the aircraft and fly to auxiliary fields in the area to sharpen their flying skills.

Several days after her first solo, Kelly took the primary trainer up again. Since it was an unusually warm day in early April and the cockpit had no roof, she decided to enjoy some early sunbathing while she was up in the air a couple of thousand feet. Shortly after removing her shirt, she discovered company. Several other primary trainers from nearby pilot training bases were pulling in as close as they could to get a better view.

Kelly frantically tried to put her shirt back on, but the wind flowing by the open cockpit snapped it out of her hands, much to the delight of the male cadets. Once back on the ground, she was able to get the attention of a few of her classmates who brought her a blanket to wrap around her shoulders before getting out of the cockpit. Although word surely got around about it, nobody other than her fellow trainees ever asked her about it.

Kelly awoke one morning to a perfect flying day. There wasn't a cloud in the sky. Even the feathery tracings of cirrus clouds at the highest altitudes were absent. In addition, it had rained during the night, and the sky had been washed clean of the haze that had been building up over the past few days. Once in the air, she gloried in the pure joy of this type of flying. She was alone with no one to be accountable to and no pressure to be back at a particular time. As long as the fuel held out, she could stay out all morning.

She had decided to fly out to one of the auxiliary fields to practice forced landing approaches. The procedure was simple enough, and she had practiced it a lot when she was working on her private pilot's license. All one had to do was pull back the throttle, and when the engine dropped to an idle, proceed on the assumption that there had been engine failure and begin a quick survey of the area to find the likeliest spot to put the aircraft down. Then, after gliding to within a couple of hundred feet of the ground, the pilot would advance the throttle and break off the forced approach. The point was to avoid either overshooting or undershooting the chosen spot. Since the PT-19 was heavier than the Meyers in which she had accumulated most of her flight time, the problem became one of avoiding landing short.

After practicing several approaches to her satisfaction, Kelly decided to take a tour of the area before heading home. In sharp contrast to the region in which she had grown up, all of the ground in this part of the country looked pretty much the same from the air. The only variations were in the slightly different shades of brown, but whether it was light brown, medium brown, or dark brown, it was still bland and boring! Perhaps that's why she made the mistake to surpass all mistakes.

Out of the corner of her eye, Kelly spied something green on the distant horizon. Was it possible? Could it be that there was something alive and growing in this wasteland? She banked to the right and pointed the nose of the aircraft toward the green blur on the horizon. Within minutes, it grew in size until it assumed the shape of a field of grain; what kind, she wasn't sure, but it was exciting to find a spot that offered even a small reminder of the lush, familiar landscape of the Puget Sound area.

Deciding that the field would make a perfect point of reference for one last practice approach, she began a gradual descent from an altitude of a few thousand feet. If she worked it correctly, that would bring her into a perfect position to glide in over the edge of the field and then abandon the forced approach before getting too close to the ground. The closer she got to the field, the more entranced Kelly became with the fresh, vibrant color of the grain. At the time she began her final approach, she still had a few hundred feet of altitude.

As the altimeter continued to unwind, Kelly suddenly caught a whiff of the fragrance lifted aloft on some stray air current from the grain field. Transfixed by the fresh scent, her thoughts began drifting again until she was rudely shocked back to reality by the wheels knocking over the short stalks of grain and then settling into the furrows on either side of the rows. *Oh my God*, she thought, *how stupid could I be! How am I ever going to explain this one?*

As she taxied toward the edge of the grain field, a small glimmer of hope took form in her mind. If she could just get the plane airborne again, she could fly it safely back to the base without anyone being the wiser. That was Kelly's immediate problem, of course: managing to get the plane aloft again. Luckily, the ground was still fairly firm in spite of the rain that had fallen the night before. She was also fortunate that the grain was only several inches tall. If it had been late summer, the drag created by stalks of grain that were several feet high would probably have made a take-off roll impossible.

Fortunately, there had been no real damage to the crop and, other than wondering how the strange wheel marks got there, the farmer would probably never know what had happened.

After working her way to the edge of the field, she managed to swing the plane around in the tight space that was available and line up the wheels with the same furrows they'd created when landing.

Advancing the throttle slowly while trying to keep the wheels from bouncing out of the furrows, Kelly managed to pick up speed fairly quickly, and was actually off the ground and in the air before she had covered half the field. On the way back, She vowed to never again let her attention drift. One could get killed that way! She was fortunate to have gotten away with nothing more than shattered nerves and a slight setback to her self-confidence. But, unfortunately, fate had something else in mind.

Shortly after landing, she completed the paperwork and was walking out of the
Operations building when Kirk Singleton pulled up alongside her in a jeep and told her to hop in. She obeyed automatically—Kirk's voice had

the commanding quality that triggered an instinctive response in most people.

"What brings you to Avenger Field?" she asked.

"I came here to see you," he said. "So, how did you do with your forced approaches today?" They pulled away from the Ops Building and turned back toward the flight line.

"Fine. Why?"

"Just wondered," he said.

"Why are we headed back out to the flight line?"

"I want to show you something on your aircraft. I'll be damned if I can figure out what it is or where it came from."

Kelly had a sudden sinking feeling in the pit of her stomach. *Damn,* she thought, *he must suspect something. But why? And what could this thing he's referring to possibly be?* She hoped it wouldn't reveal anything about her unplanned landing in the grain field.

Her hopes proved to be short-lived, however, as they pulled up and stopped in front of the aircraft. Even before she climbed out of the jeep, she spotted the green film on the wheel struts and engine cowling. *Damn it!* she thought. It had never occurred to her to walk around and check the front of the trainer once she got back to the base; if she had, she probably could have cleaned it off before anyone noticed it.

She stared at the coating of grain particles on the front of the plane for a long moment, and then she turned and looked over at Kirk. He was leaning against the side of the jeep with a hint of a grin on his face. Obviously, he had already guessed what she had done but was going to enjoy making her explain how she had managed to get herself into such a mess.

"You seem to find this whole thing pretty amusing," she said, trying to walk a tightrope between sounding either antagonistic or conciliatory.

"Actually," he said, the smile vanishing from his face and his tone becoming very serious, "I don't find it amusing at all. I find it totally out of character that you would do what you did."

Kelly shrugged. "What's the difference? No one got hurt and nothing got damaged, except for my pride," she added, while squinting at the distant horizon.

"The difference is this. You were lucky this time. The next time you might not be so lucky. You know as well as I do that there can be no tolerance for mental lapses of any kind or duration when piloting an aircraft.

Take your mind off what you're doing for even a few seconds and it can kill you or someone else.

"Okay, Kirk. I understand," she said.

But Kirk continued. "Concentration. That's the name of the game—total concentration every minute you're in the air. Your younger brother, Cary, suffers from the same shortcoming, but it's more than just an occasional lapse with him. That's why he's being washed out of pilot training."

"Washed out! Are you serious?"

"Yes, I am. Do you think I'd make up something like that?"

"No. I can't imagine how awful he must feel. My father will be devastated."

"Better to be disappointed than to deal with the death of his youngest son."

"But my father has such high expectations for his sons. And Cary and my three other brothers have had that message drummed into them since they were children. He's going to feel like a failure."

"If that's the case, then your father has placed an unfair burden on your brother's shoulders."

"Why do you say that?"

"Because your brother's first instructor said he lacked the power of concentration that's necessary to be a good pilot. The check pilot who gave him his first check ride said he's a dreamer, that his mind wanders. None of this should come as a surprise to you, Kelly. You were closer to him than anyone else."

"I can't argue that point," she acknowledged. "But I never thought of that in relation to flying."

"Now, I understand you've got to get busy studying for a test tomorrow, but I thought you might like to see the inside of a real live B-17 before you get started. We've got one here that made an emergency landing about an hour ago. They didn't find anything seriously wrong with it, so it'll probably be taking off again in a couple of hours."

"Okay," she said, without enthusiasm.

As they drove in the jeep down toward the flight line, Kelly asked Kirk if he had ever flown a B-17.

He looked over at her and grinned. "There isn't a plane in the inventory that I haven't flown," he said "Except the new jet fighters that are under development at Wright Field. I haven't even had a chance to look inside the cockpit of one of those babies yet."

When they pulled up next to the plane, she was stunned by how large it was in comparison to the plane she had been flying. Entering the B-17 involved swinging up into the belly of the plane through a hatch just behind the pilot's compartment. Kirk swung up first and once inside he leaned down, and when Kelly obediently raised her hands over her head, he lifted her up through the open hatchway as if she were a small child. *He is so incredibly strong!* she thought. She had never before been in the presence of a male who made her feel so fragile and at the same time so safe and secure. Even her brother Cliff hadn't made her feel like that.

Once inside the plane, Kirk took her on a quick tour, leading the way along a narrow catwalk that extended back to the tail gunner's compartment.

"There's a lot less room inside than I expected from looking at the outside," Kelly remarked, as they worked their way back up to the front of the plane.

"Yeah, it gets a little tight all right. The Boeing engineers deliberately designed it that way. They skimped on the airframe so the plane could carry a heavier bomb load."

When they got back to the cockpit, Kirk motioned for her to sit down in the left seat while he took the copilot's seat.

Pivoting sideways, he crossed one leg over the other and wrapped his hands around his knees. "So how does it feel?"

Kelly took hold of the yoke with her left hand and moved the control column back and forth tentatively while resting her right hand on the throttle grips. She glanced out the side window at the left wing, which appeared wider than the entire wing span of the trainers she had been flying, then let out a long slow breath and turned back to Kirk.

"I can't imagine ever getting used to handling something this large. It's so damn big; it would be like flying a bus. And I'd be afraid to even attempt to taxi it for fear I'd ram another plane in the process."

Kirk just grinned at her. "Trust me. A lot of pilots who are considerably less skilled than you, have learned to handle this baby."

A growing conviction took root in her mind—Kirk had an ulterior motive when he invited her for a tour of the plane.

Before she could say anything, she heard the sound of wheels screeching on the pavement as a jeep pulled up to a stop next to the plane.

A moment later, a voice called up through the open hatchway, "Hello, up there! Anyone on board?"

Kelly looked over her shoulder as a pair of legs appeared in the hatchway, followed by the rest of the body. It was the flight engineer. He had come back to pick up the travel bag that was stowed in a compartment behind the flight deck. The look of surprise on his face when he saw Kelly sitting in the pilot's seat would remain forever emblazoned in her mind. Kirk, on the other hand, seemed completely at ease with the situation, explaining in a casual tone that he was giving a tour of the plane to one of the best WASP pilots in the wing in the hope of converting her from a proponent of fighters to one of bombers.

Kelly's eyes narrowed and her voice took on a decidedly frosty quality as she turned to the flight engineer and said, "It's all right, Lieutenant, I've seen all that I want to, so we'll just head along and give your ship back to you."

"That's not necessary, ma'am. Feel free to stay a little longer. I'll be out of your hair in a minute."

Kirk, taking the hint, gave him a pat on the shoulder. "Thanks anyway, but as the lady said, I think we've seen enough."

Squatting down on the edge of the open hatchway, he grabbed either side and swung down through it, dropping onto the runway beneath. Then he turned around and he started to reach up for Kelly, but she had already grasped the edge of the fuselage and managed to swing down without his help. As soon as her feet touched the apron, she pushed away from him and started walking quickly across the tarmac toward the edge of the field.

"Hey! Where're you going?" Kirk hollered to her.

Kelly kept on walking, refusing to respond to his call. When Kirk finally caught up to her, he took her by the arm and tried to swing her around to face him. She yanked her arm away and continued to walk. But he caught up to her in a few quick strides and took hold of her with both hands, and he held her tightly so she couldn't break away.

"Let me go, dammit!" she snapped, struggling to break out of his grip, "I don't have anything to discuss with you!"

"You will stand still and listen to me, Kelly, or I'll put you on report for being insubordinate!" he said, the snap of authority in his voice bringing her up short as it jolted her consciousness with the same impact as her first dive of the summer into Maine's coastal waters.

She stopped struggling and looked up at him. "You wouldn't do that to me."

"Damn right I would!" he said. "Just try me. You may be something special back in Seattle, Kelly, but here you're a WASP pilot. By your own choice, I might point out, and you will obey orders and do as you're told. Not only that, but you assured me there would be no complaining if you were given an assignment you didn't like. Remember?"

Kelly just looked at Kirk and remained quiet. A few minutes later she was calm, and Kirk let go of her. Putting his hands on his hips, he backed up a step or two and studied her for a moment before saying anything. "All right," he said. "I admit I had a reason for inviting you down here tonight." He took a deep breath before going on, "And, yes, it's true, I want you to give serious consideration to switching from fighters to bombers."

"Kirk," she said, trying to walk a narrow line between arousing his ire again and sounding too conciliatory, "I've been planning to fly fighters ever since I first reported to Avenger Field. Even before that. It's always been my dream to fly first-line fighters like the Mustang and the Thunderbolt. That's where the action is. Who the hell wants to drive one of those oversized buses, even if it is the latest technological marvel."

Kirk tried another approach. "I hear what you're saying, Kelly, but listen carefully. Something big is on the horizon, something that could possibly shorten the war in the Pacific. I can't say any more about it, because the whole operation is really hush-hush. But you may be able to help out if you're willing to go through B-17 transition at Lockbourne Field in Ohio."

"Does this mean I won't have the opportunity to ferry pursuit planes?" She couldn't imagine giving up that dream.

"No," he explained patiently. "It doesn't mean that because it will probably take a while to get you a slot in the program. When do you graduate anyway?"

"August 5th. Why? Are you going to be here?"

"I doubt it, but General Arnold hopes to be."

"How is he doing?" she asked.

"Not so good. He's already had three heart attacks. The strain on the general is unbelievable. It can't be much less than what Roosevelt is experiencing. This war will probably kill both of them."

Kelly started to say something but stopped as the B-17 engineer drove by in a jeep, throwing Kirk a casual salute as he headed across the tarmac toward the operations building. She glanced down at her hands, then up at Kirk who was watching her with an indecipherable expression on his face.

"Why me?" she asked. "Why can't one of the other **WASPS** do it? There are other **WASPS** who are just as capable as I am."

"Let's just say I have a hunch that you're the best person for the assignment."

✫ ✫ ✫

VI

August 5, 1944

Graduation day at Avenger Field dawned hot and dry with the promise of being unbearable by the time the graduates of class 44-W-6 walked across the platform to receive their silver wings. This was one of the first two classes to have new dress uniforms to wear for graduation. Unfortunately, though, the belted jacket and A-line skirt although a becoming shade of blue, were made of wool, and summer weight uniforms would not be available for some time.

The barracks had been in a state of bedlam ever since reveille, with several dozen WASPs vying for the use of half a dozen small bathrooms and showers.

"What's the matter, Kell?" Elaine asked, glancing up after giving her shoes a final swipe with the shoe brush.

"What's the matter is why do we have to wear the darn jacket today? We'd look perfectly presentable in the white blouse, black tie, skirt, and beret."

"The uniform isn't really complete without the jacket," said Elaine

"If the brass had to stand around in the heat in their dress uniforms, they might be inclined to show a little compassion for us underlings," she groused.

"But they do, as each flight passes in review."

"How long before we have to fall out for inspection anyway?" asked Kelly.

Elaine glanced at her watch. "An hour and a half. I think we got ready before we had to."

"Better that than having to fight for space in the bathroom. That's what would have happened if we'd waited another 45 minutes or so to get ready. Besides, I have an idea how we can spend that extra time," said Kelly.

"What do you suggest?"

"How about making one last visit down to our glorious dayroom for a Coke? Just for old times' sake."

"Why not? It wouldn't be right to leave our palatial quarters without enjoying the Taj Mahal of our recreational facilities for one final time."

Moments later, as the two friends reached the landing at the bottom of the stairs, they nearly collided with the Cadet Officer of the Day who burst through the doorway, a frantic look on her face.

"What's up, Lorraine?"

"I was just coming to get you, Kelly. You're to report to Colonel McGinnis over at Wing Headquarters at 1000 hours."

"Now what did I do?"

Elaine, with hands on hips, turned to face Kelly. "I'll never understand why you automatically assume that any news is bad."

Kelly gave Elaine a sour look. "You have to admit, Ellie, my track record at Sweetwater hasn't exactly been stellar."

Which was both true and not true. Although Kelly had her share of run-ins with the flight instructors, there was little doubt in anyone's mind that she was one of the best natural pilots to pass through the WASP program.

"I know you've had problems with your instructors, but who hasn't?" said Elaine. And I'm more than a little mystified about this list of transgressions you've mentioned several times. What transgressions are you talking about anyway?"

"There was the time I buzzed the tower and the Commanding Officer just happened to be up there giving some congressman a tour of the facilities."

"Okay," Elaine grinned. "So that got you a reprimand and a few demerits. It's happened many times before, and I doubt whether the practice will ever be successfully squelched. What else did you do?"

"How about the time I accidentally set the plane down in the grain field?"

"Oh, yeah. I forgot about that."

"Well, that was one time when Colonel Singleton's criticisms were well deserved. But of course I wasn't going to admit it."

"So you attempted to explain it and he didn't buy it."

"Right. And I've got to say I wouldn't have either. In fact, if I had been the instructor pilot, my student would have gotten a royal chewing out."

"So what else is there?" Elaine persisted.

"There's the time I accidentally bailed out of the PT-19 after practicing some spin recoveries and I became the second female member of the Caterpillar Club."

"But that was because your seatbelt buckle was defective. It wouldn't be fair for anyone to lay the blame for the loss of the aircraft at your feet."

"They claimed that the problem was it hadn't been properly latched, so I got the blame. Unfortunately, the belt was destroyed in the crash, so there was no way I could prove that. And Kirk Singleton rode me about it for the next few weeks."

"Why would he do that?" Asked Elaine. "Are you sure there isn't more to the story than you're telling me?"

Kelly looked sheepishly at Elaine. "Well, maybe he got annoyed because I said if the damned plane meant that much to him, I'd call my father and he'd buy a replacement for the one that crashed."

"You can't be serious, Kell. Tell me you didn't say that to Colonel Singleton?"

"I did. In fact, I said since they only cost ten grand apiece, my father would buy him two of them and how could he turn down a deal like that?"

"Kell, as bright as you are, sometimes I think you've got more brass than brains."

"I know. I know. He just got to me, that's all. Anyway, it's almost ten so I'd better be making my way over to headquarters."

"Do yourself a favor. Please don't make any more smart-ass comments."

"I promise I won't. I'll be on my best behavior. But I'm wondering about this summons to Wing Headquarters less than an hour before graduation unless they've discovered some minor requirement that I've failed to meet. I bet they're going to tell me I can't graduate."

"Oh, come on. What are the chances of something like that happening?" Elaine said, trying to reassure her friend.

"I don't know. Pretty remote, I suppose. So get me a Coke and wait for me in the dayroom. Whatever this is, I hope it won't take very long!"

As she walked across the quadrangle minutes later and headed toward the long, low concrete building that housed the wing administrative offices, Kelly continued to search her mind for possible reasons for this last-minute summons. She had checked her logbook just the other day, confirming that she had the requisite number of hours of solo, multi-engine, cross-country, and night flying experience to more than meet the minimum requirements for graduation. Her performance in ground school as well as her flying evaluations had placed her among the top 5 percent of the graduating class. The only topic she had ever had any trouble with was the damned radio class. If there was one thing that nearly defeated her, it was getting her Morse code reading skills up to the minimum passing level. Fortunately, she had finally managed to do that after getting extra help from the instructor in the evening. Shrugging, she walked up the stairs and stepped through the doorway into the outer office where the First Sergeant's desk was located.

"Hi, Sergeant Thornton!"

"Hi, Kelly." The First Sergeant smiled at her as he shook his head from side to side, an awed look on his face.

"Darned if you don't get more beautiful each day that goes by," he said.

"Thanks, Sarge. This has always been the best place to come for my daily booster shot."

"As if you really needed it!"

"I've yet to meet a woman who doesn't appreciate a compliment," she said. "What's up, anyway?" Kelly tried to calm her nerves by deliberately taking a couple of slow deep breaths while surreptitiously wiping her damp hands on the side of her skirt.

"It's a command performance, Kelly," Thornton said, grinning at her secretively. "The big man wants to talk to you!" He tilted his head toward the door to the inner office. "Just knock and go in."

Kelly eyed him suspiciously for a moment before turning toward the door. After knocking twice, she reached for the door handle, thinking: *the big man?* She had never heard Colonel McGinnis called that before. Strange. Admittedly, she did feel somewhat relieved by the First Sergeant's manner. If there had been something wrong, she felt sure he would've acted differently.

Years afterward, she would remember the two shocks she experienced that morning. The first one occurred as she stepped into the room and was greeted, not by Colonel McGinnis, but by a tall, stocky officer whose face was almost as widely known as the President's. He was one of only eight men in the United States armed services to wear the distinctive five-star circle on his epaulets. General Henry H. "Hap" Arnold, the Commanding General of the Army Air Forces, stuck out his hand and, in a gruff but oddly warm voice, said, "Hi, Kelly. Your father asked me to look in on you since I was going to be here for the graduation ceremonies." He paused for a minute before continuing. "And I have to admit, Colonel Singleton's rave notices about your beauty weren't in the least exaggerated!"

Her eyes as big as saucers, Kelly started to salute him, but then quickly stuck out her hand and grasped his.

"General Arnold! Ohmygosh! It's a good thing that I didn't know it was you that requested my presence at Wing Headquarters, or I probably would have had heart failure right on the spot!"

With a wide smile, General Arnold asked Kelly to take a seat. And turning to Colonel McGinnis, who had been standing behind his desk shifting from one foot to the other, Arnold said, "That will be all for now, Colonel McGinnis. I'll buzz you when I'm through using your office."

"Yes, sir," said McGinnis.

Kelly sat down on a straight-back chair and nervously crossed and re-crossed one leg over the other while clasping her hands on her lap, trying to find a position that was comfortable. Arnold had perched himself nonchalantly on the edge of Colonel McGinnis's desk, but when he saw Kelly's unease, he suggested they might be more comfortable on the large leather couch over by the window. After sitting down, he put one arm over the back of the couch, turned toward Kelly and asked, "So how does it feel to be all through with the program?"

"Great! But it's hard to believe we've been here that long. It seems like it was only yesterday that I first reported to Avenger Field. The weeks have really flown by—no pun intended."

"I understand you're heading for Pursuit School first but that Colonel Singleton has been pushing you to go to B-17 transition at Lockbourne Field in the near future."

"Yes, sir."

"I also understand that it wasn't something you were interested in doing but that Colonel Singleton applied a little gentle arm twisting to get you to change your mind."

Kelly couldn't help smiling. "Let's just say Colonel Singleton has a number of ways for getting people to do his bidding."

Arnold gave her one of his broadest grins. "Well, it's obvious that you're Bob Rossiter's daughter in at least one respect, you certainly have a knack for choosing the most diplomatic phrase."

"I'm afraid that Colonel Singleton has been on the receiving end of some of my least politic remarks as well, General Arnold."

"Yes," he said, chuckling softly to himself. "So I've heard."

Oh great, she thought, wondering how much Kirk had revealed to General Arnold about their confrontations.

"There are a number of reasons why we need some of the WASP pilots to be qualified in four-engine aircraft, Kelly, including towing targets at high altitude for gunnery practice by anti-aircraft gunners."

"Yes, sir."

Although Kirk had hinted at a much more important reason than towing targets, Kelly assumed it had been said in confidence, so it was probably not something she should mention to General Arnold.

"I brought someone with me who I thought you might like to spend some time with, Kelly."

"You did, sir?" Kelly said, trying to guess who it might be. Jackie Cochran? Possibly. Although she had her initial interview with Jackie after applying to the WASP program, their conversation was necessarily a brief one as there were another dozen women waiting to be interviewed that day.

Arnold opened a door off McGinnis's office that led to a secure storage area. He motioned with his hand for someone to come out.

Kelly's hands flew to her mouth in an unconscious gesture of astonishment as her brother Jack walked out of the storeroom into the office.

"Hey, sis—surprise, huh!"

"Jack!" she exclaimed, as she ran across the room and leaped into his arms.

"The real McCoy, Kell. But you look like you've just seen a ghost!"

"Well, what did you expect me to do, yawn and calmly say 'Hey big bro-it's nice of you to drop in and say hello?'"

Kelly abruptly realized she had forgotten all about Arnold's presence in the room. She stepped back from Jack's embrace and looked over at General Arnold with the intention of apologizing to him.

But Arnold was all smiles and told them they had a good hour to catch up on things before the graduation ceremony was slated to begin. He further suggested to Kelly that she take Jack over to the dayroom and introduce him to her bay mates.

"Yes, sir. And thank you for this wonderful graduation present," she added, as she came to attention and saluted him.

"It's been my pleasure, Kelly. Lieutenant Rossiter, you'll sit with me on the reviewing stand."

"It will be an honor, sir!"

"So why are you home?" she asked Jack on the way over to the dayroom.

"They brought a few aces back from each of the theatres to participate in some bond rallies."

"Did Dad know you were coming?"

"No, they planned to keep it secret until we actually got back to the States."

"When did you arrive?"

"Last night. General Arnold and Admiral King met us at the airfield. Arnold flew me here in his own B-25 this morning. I called Dad before we left San Francisco though."

"What was his response?"

"About what you'd expect. He grumbled because I hadn't given him any advance notice that I was coming back."

"How many cities are you going to visit?"

"As of this morning, a half dozen have already been scheduled, but they hope to have a few more lined up over the next couple of weeks."

"Is Seattle one of them?"

"You bet!"

"So what city is first?"

"LA. We'll work our way up the coast. After LA, we'll go to San Francisco, then Portland, Tacoma, and Seattle. After that it'll be Salt Lake City and Denver. At some point, I'll fly to Washington to meet Roosevelt. McCampbell will meet me there after working the major East Coast cities."

"Who will be with you on the West Coast ?"

"Bob Johnson, one of the highest scoring aces in the European theater."

"And how many times over are you an ace now?"

"Three times," Jack stated calmly. "I've shot down seventeen Japs so far."

"Bravo, big brother," Kelly said, as she led him up the steps into the barracks.

"And to top it off, I get to pin the wings on my sister today, unless, of course, you'd prefer General Arnold to do it."

"Considering the fact that wings signify formal recognition of my flying competence, it seems entirely appropriate that the person I've spent the most time competing against in the air do the honors," Kelly said, as she led him into the dayroom.

✯ ✯ ✯

VII

August 24th 1100 (three hours after the dogfight with Magnuson)

Kelly was still sitting in the ready room with Celeste and Doris waiting for the summons to Colonel Bentley's office.

"So here we are. Sweetwater survivors," Kelly said.

"Doris and I may be survivors, but you're a Sweetwater star, Kelly!" said Celeste.

Doris chimed in. "Celeste is right. After the show you put on this morning, every Sweetwater grad is going to look on you as their heroine."

"I don't feel like much of a heroine. As far as I'm concerned, the true heroines are women like Elaine Goodrich, Evelyn Sharp, and Cornelia Fort. Talk about sacrificing for your country. They made the biggest sacrifice of all."

"Can't argue with you about that, Kelly. But you're our *living* heroine!" Celeste said.

Just then, Tech Sergeant Pulvanis stuck his head in the open doorway.

"Hey, Kell, Colonel Singleton wants to see you ASAP over in the Operations Office."

"See you two around," Kelly said over her shoulder as she rose to leave.

Kirk was waiting for her at the counter and asked Kelly to come with him into Colonel Bentley's office.

Bentley returned her salute and motioned for Kelly to have a seat.

"Kelly, first I'd like to offer my apologies as an unofficial spokesman for the male pilots in our organization, all of whom have developed a lot of respect for you gals and your flying expertise. Unfortunately, the pilots coming back from the combat zone view you women as competitors for a limited number of flying slots. Even if that turns out to be the case, it certainly doesn't justify a personal attack like you were subjected to last night."

"Thank you, Colonel."

"Secondly, I want to compliment you on the piloting skill you demonstrated this morning. It won't take long for that story to get around. It puts the men on notice. 'Don't make any more disparaging comments about the women pilots. If you do, you might live to regret it!'"

Colonel Bentley took a sip of his coffee and made a wry face.

"Ever since the First Sergeant got transferred to a new assignment, I haven't had a decent cup of coffee. Kelly, I've been thinking about giving you a couple of days off from any ferrying assignments. Besides, Colonel Singleton would like you to fly over to Wendover Field in Utah with him. There's someone stationed there that he wants you to meet."

Kelly glanced curiously at Kirk, but he offered no explanation and simply asked how long it would take her to get ready to leave.

"How long will we be gone?" she asked.

"You might be there for several days."

"Just me?"

"Yeah. Just you."

"Why?"

"You'll find out when you get there."

"It all sounds pretty mysterious and kind of ominous."

"It's nothing to be worried about, Kell."

"All right. If you say so. I can probably be ready in less than an hour."

"You don't need to rush. It's almost 1130 now. Why don't you pack and then grab a quick lunch, and I'll pick you up at your quarters around 1400."

☆ ☆ ☆

On the flight over to Wendover Field, Kirk asked Kelly if she wanted to take over the controls for a while.

"Sure. How many WASPs will be able to say they flew General Arnold's personal B-25?"

"You mean, how many pilots of either gender will be able to say that."

"How long is this flight going to take?"

"Two maybe two and a half hours."

"What do we do when we get there?"

"Meet with the CO first. Tomorrow we're going to up to Minidoka so you can pay a visit to your high school classmate."

"That's fantastic, Kirk! But how are we going to get there?"

"We'll drive. It's only about 200 miles from Wendover. We'll leave first thing in the morning."

"Do you think we'll have any problem getting into the camp?"

"Not with this pass signed by General Marshall," Kirk said, removing a small laminated document about the size of a driver's license from his wallet. "It could get us into any military installation in the country with the possible exception of Fort Knox. But we can live with that restriction."

"Yeah, I don't have any interest in going there unless they're handing out free samples," Kelly added.

"I'd better call the tower at Wendover and tell them our ETA and let them know we'll be arriving in General Arnold's plane. They'll want to know who the hell is invading their airspace."

After contacting Wendover, Kirk asked Kelly what kind of clearance she had.

"Secret. Ever since I started assisting my father with his government projects. Why do you ask? Am I supposed to have a secret clearance in order to fly this plane?"

Kirk chuckled. "No, that's not why I asked you. You'll find out, all in good time."

"Who is this person you want me to meet?" she asked.

"An old friend of mine."

"Another Army Air Force type?"

"Yep. Lieutenant Colonel Paul Tibbets"

"Why do you want me to meet him?

"Because the two of you are a lot alike."

"How so?"

"Well, in addition to being one heck of a pilot, Colonel Tibbets is also someone who doesn't hesitate to disregard the rules if they happen to get in his way."

"When did I ever disregard the rules?"

"How about the time you landed the PT-19 right in the middle of that farmer's grain field?"

"I didn't mean to land there. I told you the reason that happened. I lost my concentration."

"The problem began when you ignored the rules, Kelly."

"So I broke a few rules. I got myself out of the jam, didn't I?"

"Yeah, that time you did. You were lucky, that's all. If you had done any damage to the grain crop, the government probably would have had to reimburse the farmer. And that, most likely, would have been the end of your flying career."

"Okay. You've made your point. Can we get off this topic? I've heard it all before."

Kirk acquiesced to her request as long as she promised him she'd fly by the rules from then on.

"There must be a more important reason you want me to meet this guy," said Kelly

"There is. I think you might be able to help him out."

"How am I going to be able to help him out?"

"I'll let him tell you."

"Why won't you tell me?"

"Because I don't want to step on anyone's toes."

"Okay. I won't pester you with any more questions."

Kelly abruptly changed the subject.

"I'm going to let you land this crate," she said. "I don't want to get as much as a small scratch on General Arnold's personal aircraft."

"Come on, Kell. What happened to your confidence? Can this be the same woman who demolished the male ego in one fell swoop this morning?"

"Yeah, but the only thing I was dealing with this morning was one over-confident first lieutenant who was probably nursing a hangover, not some high powered general with almost as many stars on his shoulders as the original American flag."

"All right. If you're really nervous about taking it in, I'll do the honors."

"It's all yours, Kirk."

As they taxied to a parking spot in front of the Operations Building a half an hour later, Kelly commented on the size of their welcoming party.

Kirk nodded. "I doubt there's a single person on this base who wouldn't recognize General Arnold's B-25. But there's going to be some surprise expressions on their faces when they see a woman in the co-pilot's seat. That tall guy in the front of the group, by the way, is Paul Tibbets."

Several minutes later, they were on the tarmac being welcomed by Colonel Tibbets.

"Long time no see," Tibbets said to Kirk, throwing him a casual salute that Kirk returned in the same off-handed manner.

"Welcome to Wendover, Miss Rossiter. Colonel Singleton has told me a lot about you. Plus he called this morning to give me a detailed description of your dogfight with the big-mouth first lieutenant."

Kelly wondered if she should shake his hand or salute him. But Tibbets provided an answer when he stuck out his hand.

"Kirk, I'm going to leave you in the very capable hands of my deputy CO, Major Tom Clifton, for a tour of the operation and a briefing on how things are going. I'll catch up with you after I've had a chance to talk with Miss Rossiter."

"Roger, Paul. See you later."

"Miss Rossiter, do you mind if I call you by your first name?" Tibbets asked as they walked into the Operations Building.

"No, sir. Please do."

A few minutes later, he ushered her into his office and told her to take a seat in front of his desk.

As Tibbets sat down opposite Kelly, he asked her if she'd like a drink, either hot or cold.

"Yes, sir. A cold drink would be appreciated."

"I could use one myself," he said as he reached over and buzzed for the Noncommissioned Officer (NCO) in the outer office.

A few minutes later, a tech sergeant brought in two glasses of iced tea.

"Colonel Singleton says he's been pressuring you to go through B-17 transition, but he temporarily relented and let you go through pursuit transition so you could ferry fighters for the Sixth Ferrying Group in Long Beach. Do I have the story right, Kelly?"

"Yes, sir. That's correct."

"Is he still pushing you to go through B-17 transition?"

"Yes. I'm supposed to start in a couple of weeks."

"Any idea why he feels so strongly about it?"

"I have a hunch it has something to do with you, sir. All he said was something to the effect that my piloting skill in handling the B-17 might prove to be extremely valuable at some point in the future. I had no idea what he was driving at. But when he said he wanted me to meet you, I figured you'd be able to shed some light on the mystery."

"Possibly. I think I know what Colonel Singleton had in mind," said Tibbets. "But the first thing I want to say is that you don't need to go through B-17 transition in order to help me."

"I don't?"

"No."

"Why not?"

"Two reasons. First, there's no time. Second, you've already demonstrated superior flying skills. I need your help, Kelly, and I need it as soon as possible."

"How can I help?"

"You might be able to directly influence the war effort by eliminating one of my most vexing operational problems."

"Me?"

"Yes, you! But first I have a question for you. I've been told you don't tend to crumble under pressure, or panic when the heat is on. Is that true?"

Kelly nodded. "Not to boast, but I do think that's true."

"Good, because you'll need that quality if you take on the challenge I'm going to offer you."

Kelly leaned forward in her chair and waited for Tibbets to elaborate.

"The B-29 is the latest and most powerful bomber we have available for long-range missions. Unfortunately, it went right from the drawing board into full-scale production without the time needed to pinpoint any bugs and get them corrected. The main problem is that the engine nacelles fit the engine too closely, which doesn't allow enough air to cool the engine properly. And the cowl flaps can't be opened for maximum airflow because they create too much drag on take-off for the amount of available runway. This leads to a high incidence of engine fires during take-off and even before that when the aircraft is being taxied out in preparation for take-off. So, not surprisingly, the pilots are putting up a lot of resistance when they're asked to fly it. I need to convince them that this bird is safe to fly. And you're going to show them it is. In other words, you're going to be my ace in the hole."

"Why do you think I can convince them? Why should I be any more successful in avoiding an engine fire than they've been?"

"Because I've got an idea how to minimize your exposure to the problem. Basically, what I'm going to have you do is use a different start-up procedure. You'll do your cockpit check first, then start the engines, taxi out, and take-off without any engine run-up prior to take-off. We're going to shame these big tough he-men by showing them a woman can tame the monster."

"All right, sir. I'm game."

"Excellent. Colonel Singleton thought you would be. I understand he plans to take you up to Minidoka to visit an old friend tomorrow."

"Yes, sir."

"We'll talk more when you get back from there. I'd like to hear more about your background too."

✯ ✯ ✯

Kirk and Kelly left for Minidoka early the following morning. The drive to the camp was without incident, but the visit with Ami Takahashi was emotionally draining for Kelly. Ami and her mother were both glad to have visitors from the outside world. But Ami's mom had always been an exceptionally beautiful woman who never seemed to age. Now she appeared old and haggard and beaten down. And Ami was far too thin. When Kelly hugged her, all she felt were bones.

Living conditions at the internment camp were horrendous. The quarters were Spartan to say the least. No running water. Paper thin walls between the rooms. The bathrooms were a five minute walk away. The rooms were frigid in the winter but hot enough in the summer to bake a chicken. And when the wind blew, which was often, a fine layer of dust covered everything. Kelly and Kirk felt a mixture of guilt and relief when the visiting time was over.

Beginning their return trip to Wendover Kelly glanced over at Kirk as the camp receded from view behind them. "It's hard to believe we can treat our fellow citizens so badly just because they happen to look different from the typical American citizen."

"Nothing surprises me, Kell. Look at how they're treating the Negroes. They're being forced to serve in segregated units just like the Nisei. Or look even closer to home at your own situation, simply because you happen to be the wrong gender."

Kelly nodded thoughtfully. "You're right, I've tasted that firsthand. It seems that prejudice in one form or another has roots deep in the heart of mankind and it doesn't take much to bring it to the surface."

"Is that a quote from some famous author?"

"Not that I know of. By the way, I intend to honor Ami's request and check on their house when I get a chance to visit Seattle."

"We can definitely do that."

"We?"

"Uh-huh. I'm going along with you to Seattle."

"Why?"

"Several reasons."

"When are we going?"

"We'll leave next Friday."

"I thought Colonel Tibbets was going to start breaking me in on the B-29."

"He was, but it turns out he's not going to be able to do it."

"Why not?"

"Paul has to fly back to Washington on Sunday to meet with General Arnold, and there's no telling when he'll get back here."

"Did you know that when we left for Minidoka this morning?"

"I did."

"So who's going to check me out on the B-29 then?"

"A couple of the Boeing engineering test pilots. Paul talked to them about his theory of dispensing with the engine run-up right before take-off. And they agreed it was probably the best way to avoid engine fires until modifications are made to solve the cooling problem. So they'll handle your training."

"Okay."

"We'll head back to Long Beach after an early dinner tonight."

"How are we going to get to Seattle?"

"We're going to drive. Arnold gave me a week's leave."

"Why did he do that?"

"Because I haven't had any leave in over a year. I told him that I wanted to spend some time with you before my next big assignment."

"Any particular reason you want to have the pleasure of my company?" she asked in a playful tone.

"There might be, but you'll have to wait and see."

"So you're going to keep me hanging?"

"For a short while, yes."

✫ ✫ ✫

August 26th

Once back at Long Beach, Kelly was given an assignment to ferry a P-51 to the East Coast. Since a new engine was being broken in, she was told to keep her air speed down on the first day, but even at that lower speed, the Mustang slurped up fuel at the rate of 60 gallons per hour.

There were three fuel tanks: one in the fuselage and one in each of the wings. The correct procedure was to burn off the fuel in the fuselage tank first and then alternate between the two wing tanks. If that wasn't done, the plane would be thrown seriously out of balance and become extremely difficult to control.

Kelly's problems began a couple of hours into the flight. When she switched over to the left wing tank, the engine coughed a few times and shut down. There she was sitting in mid-air, trapped in a 9000-pound coffin with nowhere to go but straight down. She held her breath and uttered a short prayer as she flipped the switch over to the right wing tank. The engine hiccupped a few times and then came back to life. At that moment, she started breathing again. A quick check of the terrain beneath the Mustang convinced her that bailing out was not an option. She hoped she would be able to make it to Kirtland Field in Albuquerque.

Although there was no further problem with the engine, as the fuel burned off from the right wing tank, the plane became more unbalanced.

The only way to counter that was to apply increasing pressure on the left rudder pedal to maintain directional control.

When Kirtland Field appeared on the horizon, she contacted the tower and got clearance for an emergency landing. By the time she completed her approach, the list had reached the danger point. Even with the left rudder pedal jammed to the floor, it was extremely difficult to keep the aircraft aligned with the runway. She willed the Mustang down to a three-point landing, and after taxiing to a parking spot, she saw that the right wing tank was virtually empty. After sliding the canopy back, she sat in the cockpit until her left leg stopped shaking. A couple of the ground crew helped her climb out of the cockpit and provided support until she regained enough strength in her leg to walk unassisted.

By noon the next day, the fuel transfer problem had been corrected and Kelly continued on her way, however, she fell short of her goal to reach Newark during daylight. Darkness arrived when she was about to pass near Langley Field in Hampton, Virginia.

Kelly called the Langley tower more than once and requested landing instructions. By the time she finally got a response it wasn't exactly what she was looking for. The airman on duty was very curt and ordered the woman who was calling in to stop cluttering up the airwaves with her transmissions because they were trying to contact the P-51 that was circling the field.

Kelly told them in no uncertain terms that the lady they were complaining about was the pilot who was trying to land the Mustang.

Following that announcement, Kelly turned onto final approach and made one of the smoothest landings of her career. The tower personnel were so impressed that they apologized profusely and complimented her on her plane handling.

By the time she taxied the Mustang to a parking spot, word had gotten around that a P-51 had just landed. That drew a good size crowd of pilots who would have given much to get their hands on the Mustang. When Kelly slid back the canopy and stood up, one of the pilots grumbled, "I'll be damned; it's a broad!"

"That's no broad. It's a filly," said a pilot standing next to him. "And a real beauty!" another one added. Kelly stood on the wing and let a spontaneous round of applause wash over her. After a couple of minutes, several pilots reached up for her, and with Kelly on one of the pilot's shoulders, they escorted her to Operations, where she checked in, and then to the officers club.

August 28th

Shortly before noon the next day, Kelly made it to Newark. As she walked into the Ops office, Cheryl North, a classmate from Avenger Field, was on her way out. Cheryl had just received orders to fly a C-47 back to Romulus Field in Michigan. When she offered Kelly a hop, Kelly decided to take her up on it, even though it wasn't the most direct route back west. On her way out of Operations, Kelly ran into Lieutenant Magnuson who greeted her like an old friend.

"I still owe you an apology for my behavior that night and my compliments on your success in our Mustang duel."

"Thanks for both the apology and the compliment," she said, shaking his outstretched hand. "I wish you the best of luck during the remainder of your tour and good hunting too," she added, giving him a friendly pat on the shoulder.

A few minutes later, a frantic Operations officer caught up with Kelly and asked her if she would be willing to ferry a P-51 cross country to Sacramento. She agreed without hesitation, partly because it was a more direct route back to Long Beach and also because the Ops officer was desperate to get the aircraft to its West Coast destination.

With external wing tanks, Kelly covered 1600 miles the first day, making it all the way to Peterson Field in Colorado Springs.

When checking in with the operations officer, she ran into Todd Neville, a high school classmate from Seattle who was now a fighter pilot on his way to an embarkation point on the East Coast. Todd invited Kelly to join him for an early dinner at the Officers' Club. She accepted and they agreed to meet there at 1800.

After showering and pressing her uniform as best as she could, Kelly got dressed and hitched a ride over to the O Club.

Todd was waiting for her at the entrance. All the smaller tables were taken, but a few seats were available at a large table at the far end of the room. When they claimed two seats, a couple of officers at the table nodded at Todd and then cast an admiring look at Kelly.

Once they were seated, Todd asked Kelly, "How do you like this ferrying business?"

"It's okay but it can get rather crazy at times."

"How many different aircraft have you flown?"

"Well, let's see. There's the P-47, P-51, P-38, and the B-25 so far," she said, ticking them off on her fingers.

"Were you formally checked out in each of them?"

"No, not officially. I checked myself out in the Mustang."

"How did you do that?"

"I sat in the cockpit and read through the tech orders."

"And that's it?"

"No. I practiced a few take-offs and landings, too."

Todd shook his head in disbelief. "I'd like to know how many of the WASP pilots have checked themselves out like you did."

"I have no idea, Todd but I do know that it's not uncommon. If there aren't any experienced pilots around to formally check us out, what else can we do? We're expected to ferry every plane in the inventory, you know."

"Hell of a way to run an operation. That's all I can say."

Kelly shrugged. "All I know is that our accident rate is lower than the men's."

At that moment, a colonel walked over and seated himself at their table. After glaring at Kelly, he beckoned to the maître d' and said something while motioning in Kelly's direction. A moment later, she was told that she would have to move elsewhere.

She stood up and, after shooting the colonel a scorching look, tossed her napkin down on the table, grabbed her purse, and marched angrily to the front entrance. As she crossed the room, the colonel complained in a loud voice that it was bad enough that women were being allowed to fly military aircraft but that he was not about to let them eat at his table, too.

Todd and the maître d' both caught up with her at the door. The maître d' apologized profusely and pleaded with Kelly to sit at his private table and have her meal on the house. But Kelly refused to stay.

"It's clear that I'm not welcome here. Todd, don't let this stop you from having your dinner."

Todd shook his head. "I'm not going to eat without you. I could go off base to a local diner, pick up something for both of us, and bring it back to your room. How about it?"

"Thanks, but I don't feel like eating. I'm too angry."

"Kelly, it's been a long day of flying and you need to eat. I insist that you let me bring you something."

"Okay. You win. I really do appreciate your support, Todd."
"It's the least I can do for an old classmate and a fellow pilot."

✯ ✯ ✯

August 29th

Kelly left Colorado Springs at 0800 the next day and made it to Sacramento before noon. Shortly after arriving, she caught a hop down to Long Beach in a B-25. That brought her back to base two days before she and Kirk were scheduled to leave for Seattle.

✯ ✯ ✯

VIII

September 1st

They left Long Beach early on Friday morning as planned. As Kirk drove the car, he glanced down lovingly at Kelly who was lying on the front seat with her head resting on his lap and her feet partially out the open car window. Comfortably dressed in a denim skirt and a sleeveless white cotton blouse, she had a serene, peaceful look on her face.

Things were going well. During a phone conversation the previous week, General Arnold had approved Kirk's request to drive rather than fly to Seattle.

✯ ✯ ✯

"How long has it been since you've had any leave, Colonel Singleton?" asked General Arnold.

"Over a year, sir."

"Well, you're overdue then. How much time do you want?"

"A week, sir. It'll give me some time with Kelly. We need some time to discuss a number of things."

"I hope you don't mind if I ask but when are you two going to get married?"

"Well, I haven't exactly asked her yet. But that's one of the things I want to talk to her about."

"You're in love with her, I presume."

"Yes, sir, I am."

"And she with you?"

"Yes, sir. I'm quite sure she is. And if she says yes, I have a hunch she'll want to do it sooner rather than later. And I sort of feel the same way, particularly since I don't know how long you're going to leave me on my current assignment."

"Funny you should mention that, Colonel Singleton. I was planning on informing you about your next assignment some time during the next couple of weeks."

"You were?"

"Are you aware that LeMay has already gone to the China-Burma-India theatre (CBI) to take over the helm of the 20th Bomber Command?"

"Yes, sir. I knew that was to be effective this month."

"Well, I want you to go to the CBI during October and then on to the Marianas as my personal representative to check on our B-29 operations. Now I know how much you would like an operational assignment. But you can make a more important contribution to the war effort in this capacity. I need you, Colonel Singleton, because I have a lot of faith in your ability to assess how things are going and prepare a full and accurate report on what's going on over there."

"Thank you, sir. I appreciate your confidence in me."

"But you should also know that I have no intention of sending a lieutenant colonel on such a mission so I've already forwarded a promotion list to Marshall to go to the Senate for approval as soon as they reconvene in the fall. Your name is on that list for promotion to brigadier general."

"That's fantastic, sir! I don't know what to say or how to thank you."

"There's no need to. You've earned it. Both you and Kuter. If Marshall had his way, your names would have gone forward a year ago. But I couldn't have done it then without having a mutiny on my hands among the rest of my staff."

"I understand, sir. When will all this be effective?"

"I'm not exactly sure when the Senate will act upon it, but your promotion will be retroactive to September first."

"Thank you, sir. I guess Kelly and I will just have to squeeze in our wedding sometime next month."

"I hope it's not going to complicate things too much for the two of you."

Kirk paused for a minute. He was more than a little taken aback at Arnold's comment since his boss had not previously exhibited any reservations about throwing a monkey wrench into his subordinates' personal plans if he thought military necessity dictated it.

Then he answered Arnold, "I don't think so, Sir. It will probably be a small wedding, since neither of us have many living relatives we'd feel obligated to invite. And, of course, Kelly's three brothers are still overseas. While I'm on the subject of our wedding," he said, pausing for a minute, before continuing in a somewhat tentative tone, "I've been thinking for quite a while now about asking you to be my best man. How do you feel about that, General?"

"I'd be delighted! It would be an honor."

"That's excellent, sir. Kelly will be thrilled, too."

"Well, I'm going to let you go, Colonel, while I head off to one of those interminable meetings that are a part of the baggage that goes along with this position. That's something you don't need to worry about—not yet, anyway."

"Yes, sir, and thank you, for everything!"

"You're welcome, for everything. Now, relax and have an enjoyable few days with Kelly. Do give her my best and be sure and tell her how pleased I am that she took on this special assignment. And check in with me at some point before you leave for Alamogordo, New Mexico."

"Roger, sir. Goodbye."

✯ ✯ ✯

Kirk glanced down at Kelly. "How long have you been awake, you little squirt," he said as he playfully tousled her hair with his fingers.

"You know, no one's ever called me that before, but I guess you're big enough and special enough to get away with it," she said, grinning up at him as she pulled her feet back inside the car window, sat upright, and slid over next to him. "In answer to your question, I've been lying here for the last few minutes thinking about everything we've been through."

"How about looking ahead instead of back for a few minutes?"

"Sure. What's on your mind?"

"Okay, here goes. I'm putting all my cards on the table."

"What's that supposed to mean?"

"Just this. I'm in love with you, Kell. Will you marry me?"

"I don't know."

"What do you mean, you don't know? Is there someone else in the picture I don't know about?"

"Kirk, I have the same number of hours in my day as everyone else. When would I have managed to see someone else? If I'm not on the road delivering planes, then I'm back at Long Beach trying to catch up on my paperwork and my sleep."

"Okay, so what's the problem?" he asked.

"I'm just not sure that I want to be a camp follower, moving from base to base every few years, raising our kids as service brats with no real roots."

"There are lots of kids who do all right under those circumstances."

"I suppose."

"Come on, Kell, it'll be a good life—and one that should offer quite a bit of material comfort now that I'm being promoted."

"You mean they're making you a full colonel?"

"No, not exactly."

"Then what?"

Kelly stopped abruptly when she realized the implications of his statement.

"You can't mean that you're being promoted to general," she said.

"Yep. That's exactly what I mean. The old man's giving me my first star, or to be more precise, the United States Senate is."

"Honey, I'm so proud of you!" she said, twisting his head sideways and planting a big kiss on his lips.

"Hey! Hey! Be careful or neither one of us will live long enough to enjoy it," he said, turning the steering wheel sharply to the left to avoid swerving off the road.

"Stop at the next overlook," she ordered, her mood changing in an instant from serious to partly sensual, partly silly.

"Why?" he asked.

"Because I always wanted to make love in broad daylight while parked at some romantic spot overlooking the ocean," she said as she reached under her skirt and pulled her panties off and twisted around on the seat and leaned back against the dashboard and began to unbutton his shirt.

"Suppose someone else comes along and decides to pull over to see the view?"

"Lucky them!" she said, teasing him as she reached down and started to unzip his pants. "If they get bored looking at the ocean, they can watch the action here!"

"Wait a minute, Kell. Let me get the car parked before you undress me!"

Sticking out her tongue at him, she said nothing while continuing to tug at his shirt in an effort to get it off his shoulders. As soon as he stopped the car, she straddled him, and after pulling his shirt the rest of the way off his shoulders, she tossed it in the backseat along with her panties. Lifting her head up moments later, interrupting a passionate kiss, she asked, "Can't you push this damn seat back any further?"

About twenty minutes later, another car pulled off the road and parked about 50 feet away from them, but after a few minutes the driver started up the car and moved it down to the end of the overlook.

After their blissful interlude, Kirk said, "We'd better get on the road again." As he pushed the starter button and the engine came to life, he continued, "I want to get to Monterey by late afternoon. It's a great day to drive along Route 1 through Big Sur."

As they pulled back onto the highway, Kelly leaned out the window, bra-less with her shirt only half buttoned, and began waving at the people in the car that had moved closer to the overlook. As she did so, she looked over at Kirk and said, tongue in cheek, "Honey, do you think we disappointed them? Is that why he moved the car away from us? Is it possible that our performance wasn't up to its usual high standards?"

"You really are something else, Kell," Kirk said, chuckling, as he pulled her down beside him, mussing her hair with his free hand. "General Arnold was right--the mold was broken after you made your debut on earth!"

Leaning back against the seat, Kelly pulled her legs up and wrapped her arms around them. "Is that really what he said about me?"

"In so many words!"

"Is that good or bad?"

"Knowing General Arnold, I'm sure it was meant to be a compliment. In fact, to show you how favorably he views us, he's agreed to be the best man at our wedding!"

"Kirk, that is so fantastic! I can hardly believe it, the commanding general of the whole Army Air Force standing up for you at our wedding!"

"So then, you will marry me," he said, grinning down at her.

"Well, yes, now that you'll be a general. But I would have had to think twice before I consented to marry a lowly lieutenant colonel."

"Honey, you're so full of–you know what."

"At least my eyes aren't brown, so it hasn't gotten that high yet," she added, pushing playfully against his shoulder.

"Okay. Here's the downside of my promotion: I'll be getting a new assignment in October which means we'll need to squeeze the wedding in next month."

"Don't tell me," she said, her tone abruptly changing to reflect a mixture of frustration and anxiety, "that General Arnold's going to take you away from me."

"Sorry, honey, but it'll probably only be for a few weeks."

"Do you really have to go?" she said, wrapping her arms around his neck and resting her head on his shoulder. "Can't you somehow get out of it?"

He glanced down at her with an amused look on his face. "Sure, Kell. Just like the way you wiggled out of this B-29 assignment!"

"But that's different!"

"Tell me how it's different," he said, his tone clearly indicating he knew she was grasping for straws.

"I don't know," she said, petulantly. "It just is."

"Honey . . . !"

"Okay. Okay," she said, a faint smile of concession crossing her face, "I'm off base. I admit it. I just want you all to myself, all the time–and I don't want anything to ever happen to you," she said, her tone suddenly becoming quiet and pensive. "If I ever lost you, there would be absolutely no point in living anymore."

"Nothing's going to happen to me. And if something did, it wouldn't be the end of your life. You've touched so many lives in your first two decades. And I'm sure that's only the beginning. You have a lot to give and, therefore, a lot to live for. So I don't ever want to hear another comment like that."

"All right. But where is General Arnold sending you?"

"First to the CBI, then to Saipan to check on B-29 operations. By the way," he said glancing down at her, "don't you think it's time to put your bra back on, or at least button your shirt all the way up?"

"Why? No one can see anything."

"Not while we're moving but I'll have to stop for gas pretty soon."

"Warn me when we're getting close to that point and I'll humor you by putting some of this clothing back on," she said, pouting in mock disappointment at the prospect of having to get dressed again. "How far are you going to drive today?"

"A good 300 miles by the time we get to Monterey."

"How far is it to Seattle?" she asked.

"It's about eight hundred miles from Monterey."

"How long will it take us to get there?"

"I'm planning on five days."

"Can we spend some time in San Francisco?"

"Half a day; that's about all. For this trip, anyway. Do me a favor, please. Get my briefcase out of the backseat and pull out the map of the California coast."

"Okay. I have it," she said. There's also a map of San Francisco along with maps of the Oregon and Washington coasts.

"Yeah, I scrounged them from the motor pool."

"You sure do have a lot of stuff in here. What's this anyway? It looks like some type of knife."

"It is. It's called a switchblade. Here's why," he said pressing the button to release the spring coil and deploy the blade.

"That looks like a pretty lethal weapon. Where did you get it?"

"Actually, I won it in a bet over the outcome of an Army-Navy football game."

"Who were you betting against?"

"An Annapolis graduate who comes from my hometown."

Kirk pushed the blade back into the handle with the flat of his palm. As he handed it back to Kelly, she asked if she could try it.

"Sure," he said. "Hold it out like this."

She did so with some trepidation.

After she reseated the blade back into the handle, she handed it back to him and asked him what it was used for.

Kirk's only response was to look over at her with a quizzical expression on his face.

"Forget I asked," Kelly said. "I guess it was kind of a stupid question."

✫ ✫ ✫

IX

September 5th

It took three days to get through California, but only slightly more than one to drive through Oregon. They arrived in Seattle around noon on the fifth day, and after a quick lunch they decided to check out Ami Takahashi's house.

Kelly remembered it as a nondescript two-story house near the waterfront.

"What a mess, huh?" Kelly said, nodding at the trash scattered around the front yard. "Mr. Takahashi would have a fit if he saw the place looking like this."

"The magnolia trees look like they've seen better days," Kirk surmised.

"It makes you wonder what the inside of the house looks like."

"We'll find out in a few minutes if the door is unlocked or if we can find another way to get in," Kirk said.

He opened the car door and stood next to the fender waiting for Kelly to come around to his side.

"Look," she said, pointing to the front door. The hasp was swung back away from the staple, and the padlock hung open on the hasp.

"It looks like someone is trying to protect the interior of the house," said Kirk

"I think they were a little late in doing it," she answered after pushing the door open and peeking inside.

Kirk looked over her shoulder. The odor of food that had gone bad hung in the air, along with other unpleasant odors. Kelly tried breathing through her nose after she realized that the idea of taking the air directly into her lungs was an even more revolting prospect.

"I'm going to check the upstairs bedrooms to see what condition they're in," she said, using a handkerchief as a face mask to cover her mouth and nose.

"I'd better go along with you just in case. The open padlock tells me someone is here or close by. And they might not take too kindly to us snooping around," said Kirk.

"Well, whoever it is doesn't belong here either."

"He or she may not feel that way, so I'm going up there with you," he insisted.

She nodded as she took her first tentative steps up the staircase with Kirk right next to her.

They were only a few steps from the second floor when Kirk paused briefly. He put his finger to his mouth, indicating she should be quiet and then pointed overhead to the stairs that led to the attic. Kelly nodded. She had heard it also. Whenever they took a step, there seemed to be an echo of it immediately afterward, from the direction of the attic staircase.

The muscles in her throat constricted, and her pulse raced. They took a half-step upward, then stopped simultaneously by mutual unspoken agreement to see if it really was just an echo or if there was someone or something else in the house. The creaking sound continued for several seconds after they paused in mid-step. Someone was there! And whoever it was would reach the second floor just about the same time they did.

When they arrived at the second floor landing, Kelly turned to the right, pushed the first door open and, followed closely by Kirk, stepped into Ami's bedroom. Ami's dresser was gone along with her headboard and wooden bed frame. The mattress, badly soiled and smelling of urine and human excrement, lay in the middle of the floor. Someone had used lipstick and written the crudest graffiti on her walls. The curtains on the window were in tatters. After a few minutes, Kelly had seen enough. She wanted to get out of this foul-smelling place and into the fresh air. But it wasn't going to happen right away. As she turned to go, the door was flung wide open and she was confronted by a wild-eyed man clenching a small baseball bat in his right hand.

"You people are trespassing on my property," he snapped. "And that doesn't make me very happy. What are you doing in my house?"

"This isn't your house. It belongs to the Takahashi's."

"Now you listen to me, missy. I bought this from the lawyer who owned it. He said that the title was clear and he was free to sell it, which is what he did because he was moving to the East Coast."

"Who are you anyway?" asked Kirk.

"My name's Fallon, not that it's any of your business."

"The Takahashi's left their house in the hands of a lawyer who was supposed to rent it while they were gone and deposit the rent checks in a bank account set up for them," Kelly said.

"What are you, lady? Some kind of Jap lover? The Japs are the enemy—remember? They should all be deported back to Tojo-land. Good riddance to the whole bunch of 'em. That's what I say."

"Then why aren't you out helping to fight them, Fallon?" Kirk asked.

"I know why," Kelly said, chiming in before he could say anything. "None of the services would take him because he smells so bad."

The sneer on Fallon's face was instantly transformed into a look of pure hatred.

"Okay, lady," he snarled. "I've had about enough of your comments. If you want to play rough, then that's what we'll do."

He raised the bat overhead and swung at Kelly's head. But Kirk moved in quickly, grabbing Fallon's right hand with his left while driving his right fist into Fallon's solar plexus. As Fallon doubled over, Kirk spun him around, pushed him down on the floor, and knelt on him with his knee pressing into the small of Fallon's back.

Kirk grabbed a handful of Fallon's greasy hair with his left hand and, with his right hand extracted the switchblade from his pocket and handed it to Kelly. She released the blade and pressed it against Fallon's throat. Fallon's head was turned sideways so he could see the expression on Kelly's face.

"Wha—what are you going to do?" he stammered.

Kelly slowly applied more pressure to the knife blade. "Does this give you a clue, creep?"

The expression on Fallon's face was one of raw fear. "For God's sake, mister, get this crazy woman away from me before the blade slips."

"I wouldn't kill him in here, Kelly; it would be too messy."

Kelly nodded. "If we do it outside in the backyard, we can wash away the blood and bury the body in the garden. No one will ever know. Besides, someone that smells as bad as this guy can't possibly have any friends."

Kirk continued to play along with Kelly. "Maybe we should hose him down first.

It doesn't seem right to send him to the great beyond in this condition. I've got a bottle of full strength bleach in the trunk of the car. Want me to go get it?"

"Let me go, and I'll promise to stay away from here," Fallon blurted out in a panicky tone.

Kelly held the edge of the knife against his throat.

"Please don't hurt me. I'll give up any claim to this house."

"Let's get something straight, Fallon," Kelly said. "You don't have any claim to the house to give up. That lawyer had no legal right to sell you something that wasn't his."

"You mean, I'm out all that money?"

"It kind of looks that way doesn't it? Okay, let's get down to business," said Kelly. "Maybe I won't kill you, at least not this time. I have a lot of powerful friends in Seattle. If word gets back to me that you've been seen skulking around this property, we'll come back, track you down and . . ." She he lightly drew the blade sideways across his throat.

A minute later, Kirk rose to his feet as Kelly removed the knife blade from the threatening position under Fallon's neck. The man stood up shakily to his feet, glanced quickly at Kirk, then shifted his gaze to Kelly.

"All right, Fallon. You're free to go," she said. "But first give me the key to the padlock." Pointing the knife blade at him, she continued, "and remember my warning."

As Fallon handed the key to her, she said, "Just in case you have another key, we'll be back later today to put a new padlock on the door."

By the time they descended to the first floor, Fallon was gone.

Once they were outside, Kirk reached out for Kelly. After taking in a deep breath of fresh air, she turned around to face him. He put his hand under her chin and tilted her head back so he could hold her gaze.

"You're one tough lady, Kelly."

"Hmm. It's easy to do, Kirk, when you're around to back me up."

"Good thing you weren't alone when you stopped here," he pointed out.

Kelly nodded. "Yeah. It could have ended badly."

"Okay, let's go see if we can find Boeing's guest quarters and check in. Then we'll head over to their flight test section."

✫ ✫ ✫

"Honey?"

"Hmm?"

"What's a putt-putt?"

"An APU," he said, without looking up from the paper he was reading.

It was the evening of their second day in Seattle. Kelly and Kirk had enjoyed a lingering dinner in the executive dining room of Boeing's corporate headquarters for the second night in a row. After a leisurely walk along the elaborately landscaped walkways that connected the dining room to the VIP quarters, they returned to their room with the intention of turning in early as both of them had experienced two particularly demanding days. Kelly felt like she couldn't absorb one more piece of information about the B-29.

For two days, she had been inundated with data pertaining to the plane's performance characteristics and operational procedures. And Kirk had spent the majority of that time bouncing back and forth like a ping-pong ball between Boeing and The Rossiter Company trying to resolve a conflict between the two companies that could delay the installation of an advanced radar unit in the B-29. By nine-thirty, they were stretched out on the bed in various states of undress. Kelly had slipped on a shorty nightgown and was lying stomach down on the bed, head propped up on the palms of her hands, with the B-29 checklists for each crew position spread out before her on the pillow. Kirk, dressed only in his boxer shorts, was lying on his back, reading the latest edition of the *Seattle Examiner*.

Twisting her head sideways, she gave him one of those looks that spoke volumes. "That wasn't exactly the type of answer I was looking for. Could you be a little more specific?"

"Aircraft pilot understudy," he said, holding the paper up in front of him so she wouldn't notice how hard a time he was having with keeping a straight face.

"Aircraft pilot understudy . . . ," she repeated slowly, frowning down at the checklist. "But that doesn't make any sense, honey." Then, as she heard him start to chuckle behind the newspaper, she grabbed it out of his hands, threw it across the room, and rolled over on top of him. "A lot of help you are. I don't know what I'm going to do with you."

Wrapping his arms around her, he rolled back over and ended up on top of her: "I have an idea about what you can do with me," he said, grinning suggestively.

"We already did that once tonight. In fact, if memory serves me correctly, you also enjoyed something along similar lines this morning when we first woke up," she said.

"Oh," he pouted, pretending to play the role of an aggrieved husband. "So, was I the only one who enjoyed it?"

Sticking her tongue out at him, she said, "Seriously, Kirk, I'm worried about my ability to digest all this information and then turn around and apply it successfully less than 48 hours from now."

"Kell," he said, as he rolled off her and onto his back, arms behind his head, "one of Tibbets's main points is to prove to his crews that any pilot of average competence can learn to safely fly the Superfort.

"Yeah, as long as you don't push the engines too hard before take-off. But if you don't baby them right after engine start, you could end up with a serious engine fire. And that's not an uncommon occurrence. Right?"

"Right. That's why Tibbets decided to have you come up here and get trained by the experts—so you'll feel comfortable flying the bird before you start trying to change the attitude of the male pilots who've been assigned to fly it. The other thing you want to do is give the radar operators a chance to demonstrate the improved efficiency of the new radar unit to the navigators. Which means you're going to be pushing an officer to be open to being instructed by an enlisted man. The fact that this new radar will make the task of long range navigating in bad weather a lot easier and safer should be a strong selling point."

Kelly looked over at him with a slight frown on her face, her brow furrowed in thought. "I like challenges, but with this one I may be biting off more than I can chew."

"I don't know what else I can say to convince you that it's going to work out all right."

"Okay. I promise I'll try hard to let this thing go," she said, exhaling a long slow sigh. But you still haven't told me what an APU is."

"It's an auxiliary power unit."

"And what, pray tell, does it do?" she asked.

"Provides the electrical power needed to start the engines, among other things."

"Okay. Now what can you tell me about the autopilot?"

"It's a black box on the console between the pilot and copilot," he said. There are sensors in various locations in the aircraft—like in the elevators, ailerons and rudder. Once the aircraft is manually trimmed to fly straight and level—hands off controls—you turn on the autopilot, and it takes over the job of keeping it trimmed."

"I'm not going to use that; I'd rather fly the bird myself," she said.

"You'll soon get your fill of flying the B-29, Kell. Rather than placing too much of a load on the autopilot by letting it make all the corrections on an out-of-trim aircraft, the pilot routinely turns it off and re-trims the aircraft manually."

"Okay. I get the picture."

Kelly pushed the checklists aside and rolled over on her back. "I think I'll pay a brief visit to the plant tomorrow," she said. "It's time to tell Dad about our wedding plans. You didn't mention anything to him, did you?'

"Not me. That's your responsibility."

"I can hardly wait. At least he likes you. That's more than I can say for everyone else I ever dated."

"The protective father, huh?"

"More like the controlling father. A classic example, unfortunately."

"I'm glad I never had to deal with anything like that. But I guess parents are more likely to do that with a daughter than a son. By the time I got to the dating age, my parents were so caught up in their own deteriorating relationship they weren't paying much attention to what I was doing or who I was hanging out with."

"Were you ever seriously involved with a girl?"

"Sure. There was this girl Ginny Childress. She was widely considered to be the one of the best looking girls in the high school and she happened to be my next-door neighbor. Just about every guy in the school had the hots for her at one time or another."

"Including you, I suppose."

"Not at first. We squabbled constantly from kindergarten up until we got into junior high school. I don't exactly know how it happened, but we stopped fighting and began to get along. In fact, we became the best of friends. It wasn't until our sophomore year in high school that I began to view her in a different light. You know, like romantically. On our first real date, I took her to the Sophomore Spring Fling. We started going steady in our junior year. And, by the following summer, we were going at it hot and heavy. Especially when she invited me to spend some time at her family's summer cottage on the Maryland shore."

"What happened to your relationship?"

"It ended shortly after she left for college."

"That's not at all unusual."

"I know. Besides, she was at Tulane in New Orleans and I was at the Military Academy in West Point. We wrote back and forth for a while, but that tapered off and finally stopped. The plebe year at the academy is very demanding anyway, so there wasn't much time for romance."

"Did you see her at Christmas?"

"No, I never saw her again. In fact, I have no idea where she is or what became of her. Shortly after she left for college, her family moved out of the neighborhood, and that would have been the fall of '27."

"Who was the last one to write?"

"She was, but the tone of her writing sounded like the equivalent of a Dear John letter. At least, that's the way I saw it. Getting back to our wedding," Kirk said, "although we have the best man lined up, I assume there's still the matter of choosing a maid of honor. Do you have any ideas about who it might be?"

"Ami Takahashi and I talked about this back in high school and we made a pact to serve as each other's maid of honor. With Ami out of the picture—at least for my first wedding—."

"Your first wedding!"

"You heard me right. You marry for love the first time and for financial security the next time! You've heard that line before, haven't you?"

"Yes, but I didn't expect to hear it from you."

"Come on, Kirk! You ought to know by now when I'm teasing and when I'm serious."

"I guess."

"I think I'll ask Angeline Alexander. She's my first cousin on my mother's side. We were very close when we were younger."

"That's an unusual first name."

"She was given the same name as Chief Seattle's eldest daughter."

"Is she part Suquamish like you?"

"Yes. Only more so. Her father's a full-blooded Suquamish. Angie's a real beauty and would really enhance the wedding party."

"The wedding party doesn't need any enhancement. Not when the bride is so beautiful!" Kirk said, lifting Kelly's hand to his lips.

Rolling over on her side, she curled up against his shoulder.

"It would please my father, too," she continued. "He really likes Angie, but never did like Ami."

"Why not?"

"He always thought she was arrogant and somewhat of a show-off."

"Was she?" Kirk seemed surprised.

"Not at all. She just happened to be exceptionally bright and wasn't shy about voicing her opinions. On top of that, she was the class valedictorian, and she's Japanese."

"Your father doesn't like the Japanese but has no problem with the native Indians?"

"Yeah. I know it's kind of odd. His prejudice toward the Japanese goes back well before Pearl Harbor."

"Why is that?"

"He had a few bad dealings with them. Actually, I think it could be traced to some cultural misunderstandings by both parties. But he places all the blame on them. And now he believes every one of them is evil."

"How did your mother feel about Ami?"

"She loved her, and Ami felt the same way about Mom. In fact, I think Ami felt the loss of my mother almost as deeply as I did. That's how close they were."

Kirk shook his head and crossed his arms over his chest. "It's a real messed up world we live in, Kell."

"In some ways," she said. "But we have a lot of things to be thankful for, like our love for one another." Kelly placed a feather-soft kiss on his cheek.

"Can't argue with you there, Baby."

Although physically on the verge of exhaustion, Kelly's mind was still running at full speed, reviewing all the information she had been exposed to in the past 48 hours. Consciously willing her thoughts into another channel, they drifted back a couple of hours and settled on their lovemaking of earlier that evening.

What struck Kelly more forcibly than anything was how incredibly considerate Kirk was for a man of such strength and power. Unlike previous lovers, he was concerned about meeting her needs first. In fact, from the very first time they had made love, he made it clear in words and actions that their lovemaking was to be a shared, mutually satisfying experience with an emphasis on the word *mutual*. And the obvious pleasure he took in gradually bringing her to the peak of fulfillment ensured that each experience would be deeply satisfying. Time and again, she replayed in her mind's eye each step of their lovemaking. In fact, if she closed her eyes and shut out her surroundings, she could actually recreate the heart-stopping touch of his hands and lips on her body.

As she lay on the bed, drifting along on a current of sensual memories, a vagrant concern gradually took form in her mind. It had popped into her mind on previous occasions, but she had always dismissed it as inane. But now she was willing to admit that it had been a source of mild anxiety ever since they had first made love. Acting on impulse, she abruptly spoke out.

"Honey, do you think my breasts are too small?"

Kirk opened one eye and looked down at her. "What?"

"You heard me. Do you think my breasts are too small?"

"What could possibly have prompted you to ask me that?"

She hedged a little. "I don't know, I just wondered. That's all."

"Well, stop wondering about silly things like that, and go to sleep. You've got a busy day tomorrow," he said, as he rolled over on his side and faced the wall.

Kelly was inclined to agree with him, but was also a little annoyed at the way he had summarily dismissed her and her concern. "But you haven't answered my question yet."

"I think they're just right," he said, his voice slightly muffled since he hadn't bothered to lift his head off the pillow.

By this point, she was even more reluctant to let him off the hook. "How do I know that you're not lying to me?"

That got to him. He slowly rolled over, propped himself up on both elbows, and fixed her with his most frustrated look. "What in hell has gotten into you anyway?"

"Nothing. I just want to know the truth. That's all."

"Kell, have I ever hinted in any way–either by words or actions–that I think your breasts are too small? Have I ever shied away from kissing or touching them or indicated in some way that they turned me off because they're too small?"

Kelly glanced up at the ceiling and grinned self-consciously. "No, you haven't.""Well, then what's to worry about?" He shifted from one side to the other, and as he did so, couldn't resist adding, "I thought it was only guys who carried on like that, worrying about whether they were less well-endowed than the next guy."

"Sorry. I guess I'm acting kind of silly about the whole thing."

Kirk shook his head slowly from side to side. "Stop worrying and go to sleep! Tomorrow's a long day, and we keep getting closer and closer to it."

"But I'm not that tired. No, that's not true. I'm very tired but I can't seem to slow my mind down. What do you do when you can't get to sleep, count sheep?"

"No. I like to picture this long line of big-busted women passing by in review–and none of them have anything on from the waist up."

"You what!" Kelly blurted out, sitting straight up in bed.

By the time she began pummeling him over the head with her pillow, Kirk was laughing so hard that he was unable to put up even token resistance. As he put up his hands to fend her off, he lost his balance and rolled off the bed onto the floor, pulling her along with him. After a few minutes, the playful wrestling took a sensual turn and, before she realized what was happening, they were caught up in another frenzy of lovemaking. Aside from the sexual fulfillment, the best thing about the whole experience from Kelly's standpoint was that it turned out to be the perfect answer for her insomnia; within minutes of disengaging herself from the tangled sheets on the floor, she was back in the bed, sound asleep.

* * *

X

September 8th

Some things had definitely changed at The Rossiter Company. Kelly was concentrating on keeping a tight rein on her temper while explaining to the new gate guard why she shouldn't need a pass to enter the plant. It wasn't simply the fact that he didn't recognize her. That was understandable since he was new to the company. But he continued to be suspicious of her even after she had shown him her driver's license. Furthermore, he was carrying a side arm, and she had the distinct impression that he was not wearing it simply for show like the guards who had previously manned the gates.

"Look, Johnson," she said, after glancing quickly at his name tag. "If you don't believe that I'm who I claim to be, just call the President's office and let me speak to him."

"Oh sure, Miss, like I'm really going to bother the President," the guard replied. Although the words themselves reflected no change in his hard-line attitude, Kelly thought she detected a trace of doubt mixed in with the sarcasm.

She was silent for a minute. "Is Bob Paxton still the Chief of Security," she asked, hoping that would be the case.

"No. He retired a few months ago."

Kelly could feel her anger rising but she had vowed to herself and to Kirk to try to keep a lid on her temper. Suddenly, she thought: *why not just walk through the gate and see what happens?* Surely, he wouldn't attempt to stop her with his pistol. Or would he? She studied him carefully. He was young, relatively nervous, and obviously unsure of himself. But did that nervous quality mean he was unlikely to act or did it mean he might act precipitously? Fortunately, it wasn't necessary to put him to the test because, the elderly gate guard who had known her since she was a little girl suddenly showed up.

"Hi, Miss Rossiter! It's great to see you again. You've been missed around here!"

"Thanks, Charlie," Kelly said, beaming him a broad smile. "It seems I've been gone forever, although it's only been about six months."

"And you really look sharp in your uniform, too!" he added. Then glancing from her to the other guard, he said, "What seems to be the problem. Is there anything wrong?"

Kelly glanced over at Johnson who looked as though he had just taken an unexpected blow to the solar plexus.

"No, Charlie, there's nothing really wrong," she said. "I was just having a little trouble convincing Mr. Johnson that I wasn't some spy trying to infiltrate the plant, and he was just doing the job he's paid to do."

Kelly threw them both a casual salute as she turned and started down the long walkway that paralleled the production lines and led directly to the offices of the manufacturing and production staff.

Most of the executive offices were located in a separate part of the plant, including that of the chief executive officer, but her father had insisted on having another office next to the production lines, so he could personally monitor the production effort. That was where he spent most of his time. His other office was used mainly for meetings with visiting dignitaries and high ranking military personnel.

Kelly stopped in front of her father's office in the production area and paused momentarily to steel herself, before raising her hand and rapping sharply on his door.

A gruff voice from within snapped, "Come in."

She opened the door and walked in. Her father, who was munching a sandwich as he scanned a sheaf of production reports, blurted out before looking up to see who it was, "I'm extremely busy right now, so this better be im—Kelly! What a surprise! What are you doing here, honey?" He laid his sandwich on the desk and walked around the desk to greet her.

"Hi, Dad," she said, responding in lukewarm fashion to his hug.

Stepping back and eyeing her critically, he said, "You've lost weight since you've been gone." It was a statement, not a question.

"About seven pounds," she admitted.

"Well, you can't afford to lose any more, so I'm glad you're finished with the program," he said. "You haven't answered my question. What are you doing up here?"

"Learning to fly the B-29. Then I have to report to the heavy bomber base in Alamogordo, New Mexico, to show the male pilots the best way to keep the engines from overheating during take-off, among other things."

"A B-29! I'm not too keen on you flying those beasts! That plane has a lot of bugs that haven't been worked out. Especially those damn engines. I tell you, Kelly, if the powers to be had listened to me and gone with Pratt and Whitney instead of Wright for the engines, they wouldn't be having these problems."

Kelly glanced down at her hands for a moment so her father wouldn't see the look of anger that had flashed across her face. *He hasn't changed*, she thought, *and he never will.* That was one thing she had learned early in life. People don't change. A miser doesn't suddenly transform into a spendthrift; a pessimist doesn't become an optimist overnight; nor does a self-centered man undergo a dramatic reformation that turns him into a selfless one.

"Look, Dad, I didn't come here to argue with you. And I don't have the slightest interest in listening to you tell me why they chose the wrong engine for the B-29."

Her father walked back behind the desk and sat down. He leaned forward in his chair and rested his forearms on the top of the desk. "Well, what *did* you come here to tell me then?"

Kelly took a deep breath and let it out slowly. "I'm marrying Kirk Singleton in three weeks. I came to personally inform you that it's being rushed because Kirk will be getting an overseas assignment in October."

"I was wondering when you were going to tell me. Seems like everyone else has already heard the news," he grumbled. "But I like Singleton. He strikes me as a real solid individual. And I know that Hap Arnold thinks the world of him, so he must be good. I'll say this, too. He's a heck of a sight more impressive than either Keith Whitaker or Chris Manley."

"Do you realize this is the first guy you've approved of since my junior year in college?"

"That's because I have stricter standards than you do, Kelly. Or maybe I'm just more experienced at taking the measure of a person."

."Even if you are, and I'm not necessarily granting that to be the case, do you still think it was within your rights as a father to do whatever you could to discourage those men who displayed any interest in me from pursuing that interest?"

"If you're referring to that divorced professor that you got involved with, I seem to recall that he ended up dropping you!"

"Keith Whitaker didn't drop me; it was a mutual decision. Unfortunately, he got a position on the East Coast along with a promotion, so there was no feasible way to continue our relationship."

"You already knew at that point how I felt about him."

"As far as I was concerned, age was one of his best features. He was much more mature than most of the guys I dated. And as far as Christopher Manley goes, what business did you have putting him in a position where he had to choose between me and his career at the company?"

"You can't complain about that, Kelly. I ended up doing you a favor. He wasn't good enough for you. He proved that when it took him only a few days to decide in favor of his career."

Kelly put her hands on her hips and stared down at him. "Actually, it was only a single day, but that's beside the point," she said, as she started pacing back and forth in front of his desk. "It was totally unfair of you to put him in a position in which he had to choose between me and the company. I might have made the same decision if I had been in his place. The point is, it wasn't your decision to make, and that's what you did when you gave him that ultimatum. I don't know why you can't see that!"

"All I was trying to do was protect you from getting hurt."

Kelly stopped next to the side table and stared absentmindedly at the scale model of the B-29 that the Boeing Company routinely presented to each of its major subcontractors. She ran her fingers idly along the length of the wing before making eye contact with her father. The flash of anger that had swept over her at his words was gone. There would be no giving in to her temper. For that, she was grateful.

"I can take care of myself. Thank you. I'll tell you this, Dad," she said as she picked up her flight cap and walked toward the door. "When I came here today I wasn't sure whether or not I was going to ask you to walk me down the aisle. If you had been at all critical of my decision, I would have asked Uncle Bill to give me away. But I've decided to let you do it, if you want to, that is."

"Well, of course I want to, Kelly. What's the date of the wedding?"

"September 30th."

"That soon!"

"It has to be. Kirk's going overseas in October."

"Where's it going to be held?"

"At our church in Port Orchard."

"What about the reception?"

"I'm planning on having it catered and it'll be held at our house. The number of guests is going to be kept to about forty. That includes Kirk's family and friends."

"Forty people? Kelly, I can think of at least seventy people who should be invited. And that doesn't take into account the people from Colonel Singleton's side."

"Forget it, Dad. No business associates. No distant relatives. Only close relatives and a few good friends."

"That's not the way your mother would have wanted it, Kelly."

"Maybe not. But that's the way it's going to be, it's my wedding. And I intend to make sure it doesn't turn into some kind of spectacle. Goodbye, Dad, I've got to get going. But I'll be in touch. And I'll be home in time to give the house a good cleaning," she said, as she reached for the doorknob.

Just before stepping through the doorway, Kelly glanced back at her father. He was leaning forward with his elbows on his desk, his forehead resting in the palms of his hands.

✼ ✼ ✼

Both calls came in as Kelly was stepping into the shower the next morning. She heard the phone ringing and a moment later Kirk's voice as he spoke to the caller.

Just as she got out of the shower and was reaching for the towel, Kirk stuck his head in the door and announced that Paul Tibbets had called to ask them if they would rescue a B-29 that had made an emergency landing at Long Beach and if they'd fly it over to Alamogordo. Following that, a call from General Arnold, instructing Kirk to return to Washington ASAP to handle some urgent business. Kirk told Kelly he would be leaving for the airfield within a half hour. Kelly, still dripping wet, grabbed for her terrycloth robe and followed Kirk out into the living room where he was hurriedly stuffing his clothes into a flight bag.

"Wha...what do you mean you have to go back to Washington? Do you mean to tell me you're leaving me to handle this flight all by myself?"

Kirk glanced up at her with a preoccupied look on his face. "Sorry, beautiful, but that's exactly what I'm telling you. The old man wants me in Washington ASAP, and I have no choice but to get on the road and in the air as quickly as possible."

Despite herself, along with a sharp increase in her anxiety level, Kelly felt a surge of anger rise within her. "So you're deserting me at the moment I need you most and when I counted on you for support?"

"Come on, Kell," he said, "I'm not deserting you." Tossing the clothes he was packing down on the chair, he turned and stood facing her, hands on his hips. The frustration was evident in his tone. "I don't have any choice in the matter. When the old man calls, I have to respond. That's my job. You know that."

"All I know is you're leaving me to face the B-29 crews at Alamogordo by myself! And realistically, what's the likelihood of my being taken seriously by this group of male prima donnas once I get there?" Kelly said, as she began pacing back and forth from one end of the room to the other. "I can just see myself. 'Hi! I'm Kelly Rossiter. I'm going to teach you all that you need to know about how to safely fly the B-29. How many hours of flying time do I have? Why, I've got almost a dozen hours in the left seat. And just how much do I know about the operating systems of this new bomber? How dare you ask me such a question? I'll have you know I spent almost two full days in training sessions getting briefed on all aspects of the operating procedures; what more do you want? And you say you're concerned about all the little bugs that still need to be worked out of the plane? Come on, guys, so there's a slight tendency of the engines to overheat and catch fire from time to time. That's no big deal. All you have to do is keep the cowl flaps at full open. Of course, it's probably not the best of ideas to do that right after take-off when the aircraft is trying to gain altitude and needs all the lift it can get. But then again that is when the engines typically tend to overheat. However, I don't think you should lose any sleep over it. You see, you can always abort the mission or, if you don't think you can make it back to the base, feel free to set the bird down in the water. Test results have shown that the B-29 floats like a duck! In fact, the Navy is thinking of commissioning some of the earlier models as floating gunnery targets . . . .'"

Kirk folded his arms across his chest and regarded her with an expression reflecting an equal mixture of amusement and annoyance. "Are you through now?"

"No! I'm not through yet. And another thing while I'm on this roll. I'm sick and tired of you being at the beck and call of the government 24 hours a day. It's bad enough that I'm losing you to some overseas assignment in October. Why in hell can't General Arnold leave you alone for the few short weeks we have left before the wedding?" She stopped pacing, but the agitation was still clearly evident in her tone and gestures. "Why can't he find someone else to handle this assignment? Why does it always have to be you?"

"We've been through all this before, Kell. What's important is that it doesn't matter whether or not you're with me. You don't need me! You're fully capable of carrying out this assignment on your own. Besides, I'm quite sure that Paul Tibbets plans on being at Alamogordo to greet you and pave the way for your acceptance by the flight crews."

"Yeah. Just like he was there to train me on the B-29," she said.

"That wasn't his fault."

"I know," she said. "It was General Arnold's fault. And who's to say that he might not call him to Washington again?"

Kirk walked slowly across the room and turned to face her. "Come on, Kell, stop pouting. I shouldn't need to remind you that things aren't always going to go the way you want them to. Especially during wartime. You don't need me or anyone else to hold your hand when you're facing a challenging task. You have all the resources needed to handle it, whatever it is!"

Reaching for both of his hands, she looked up at him with a worried expression on her face. "I don't mean to sound like a complete wimp, but you were always there for me until now!"

"I wasn't there when you took on Magnuson in the dogfight."

"Yes, you were. You saw me off, and you welcomed me back. And you were there on the ground rooting for me. That's why I was able to do so well."

Kirk grasped her gently by the shoulders. "Listen, that's a nice thing to say, and I'm really glad that my presence means that much to you. But the fact of the matter is you were the one who managed to hang onto Magnuson's tail in spite of his efforts to shake you off. There was no one else in that cockpit but you. Regardless of what you say or what you think, it was your victory and yours alone."

He paused momentarily, then continued, "You know, it really bothers me that you have so little faith in yourself. I wish you could learn to see yourself as other people do. On more than one occasion you've proved that when the pressure is on, you can do it! So you'll do it again! Now, I've got to get going," he said as he turned away to continue packing his flight bag. "But before I do, I need to call and see if I can arrange a hop for you down to Long Beach."

Kelly nodded. "What happened to the pilots of the B-29?"

"They refused to fly it any further, claiming it wasn't airworthy. Rather than argue with them, Tibbets decided that bringing it over to Alamogordo would be a perfect opportunity for you to do your first demonstration flight."

"But what if it *isn't* airworthy?"

"Paul assured me that his best team of mechanics have gone over it with a fine toothcomb."

"Then why didn't he order the pilots to fly it?"

"Because they were a couple of colonels who outranked him."

✭ ✭ ✭

XI

Kelly grimaced as she stood on the flight line at Long Beach the next day and stared absent-mindedly at the sleek lines of the long, silver cylinder that sat silently in front of her. For a moment, she had a strange feeling it was a giant aluminum bug that was eyeing her with its next meal in mind. The worst part of that odd thought was that it might actually come to pass. *The damn thing might just eat me alive before this day is over!* she thought.

Another thing that worried Kelly was the most recent weather forecast. She was faced with the unenviable task of taking the B-29 off under the worst possible conditions for generating the necessary lift. The forecaster had predicted the temperature would reach the low nineties by noon. With that much heat, she knew the take-off roll would be stretched out to the point of needing the entire length of the runway to get off the ground. In fact, as she waited for the copilot to gather the crew together for the pre-flight briefing, she could feel beads of sweat on her forehead even though it was not yet eleven in the morning.

Kelly looked up as Daniels, the copilot, walked around the nose of the aircraft and headed over to where she was standing. She had to admit Kirk was on target when he suggested the crew was going to be intimidated by her. Daniels was obviously in awe of her, and the rest of the crew all appeared to be walking on eggshells whenever she approached them or asked them a question. Except for Petersen. It was a pleasant surprise for both of them when she discovered he was the flight engineer on the B-17 that made an emergency landing at Avenger Field several months earlier.

Daniels was young, medium height, and quite slender. From a physical standpoint, he resembled Maynard Magnuson. However the resemblance ended there. Daniels proved to be as pleasant and non-confrontational as Magnuson had been unpleasant and confrontational.

Saluting Kelly, he said, "The crew is ready for the briefing, Miss Rossiter."

"The salute is unnecessary, Daniels, and please just call me Kelly."

"Yes ma'am, or Kelly, that is."

"Okay. Let's go," she said, as she followed him back around the nose of the aircraft to the spot where the crew was waiting. It was with an equal mixture of mild anxiety and tempered exhilaration that she approached the moment of truth, pausing to survey the men individually before speaking to them as a group.

They ranged in age from a few years her senior down to the tail gunner who didn't look a day over sixteen although she knew he had to be a minimum of eighteen. Their rank ranged from the silver bars of a captain—those belonged to Petersen—to the double stripes of a corporal—on the baby-faced tail gunner. She was amused that, aside from Daniels and Petersen, not one other crew member would meet her gaze. They were either looking down self-consciously at the ground or staring into space a few feet above her head.

Kelly handed the clipboard to Daniels, pushed the pencil into one of the pockets on the sleeve of her flight suit, and prepared to speak her first words as an aircraft commander. The peculiar significance of the moment was not lost on her. Undoubtedly, this was the first time in the history of the modern-day armed forces that a group of military personnel from any service had been placed under the command of a civilian, especially a female civilian.

"All right, here's the situation. We're stuck with an unusually hot day for the Long Beach area. In addition, we've got a low-lying cloud bank up to around 2500 feet. This could pose a problem because we're going to have to head out over the ocean for a while to get above 10,000 feet before we turn back and head east over the mountains.

"Here's the drill, so listen carefully.

"It will probably take most of the runway to get airborne. Once we're off the ground, I'm going to nose the aircraft down and stay as low to the water as I can until we pick up the needed airspeed. Now, we're still likely to be pretty low to the water by the time we get out over the open ocean, and we will be flying over a busy shipping lane, so we need to be especially alert for any ships moving through the area at the same time we are. I've been told to be on the lookout for a carrier and a battleship as well as couple of heavy cruisers. Now, although we have nothing but admiration for our naval colleagues, I don't think that any of us are especially interested in establishing an intimate association with them at this particular time." Kelly paused, hoping that her attempt at humor would defuse some of the anxiety she saw stamped on their faces, and then continued. "Nor do I have any interest in being credited with the first attempt to land a B-29 on an aircraft carrier!

"What I need from you are two things: first, the two scanners will need to monitor the engines very closely from start-up through take-off, particularly when we're struggling to pick up airspeed at the lower altitudes. The engines tend to overheat and a hot day like today will increase the potential. Also, I'd like a couple of extra people up front to keep an eye out for those ships that are supposedly in the area. That reminds me; which one of you is the tail gunner?" She glanced down the line of crew members.

"I am, sir, I mean, ma'am, or whatever you are," he blurted out, glancing around nervously at the other crew members.

Kelly placed her hands on her hips and looked down at the ground so the young airman wouldn't see the smile on her face. When she looked back up, she said, with a trace of amusement in her voice, "You can call me Kelly, Corporal. What's your name?"

"Wainwright, ma'am, I mean, Kelly."

She raised an eyebrow. "Are you by any chance related to General Jonathan Wainwright?"

"Umm, I think he's a distant relative, ma'am."

Kelly nodded thoughtfully. "All right, Corporal Wainwright, this is what I want you to do for me. Your services are going to be much more valuable to me if you're up front in the bombardier's position with a pair of binoculars. From the moment we break ground, I want your eyes glued to the horizon, and the second that you see anything there, or think you see anything, I want you to yell out loud and clear. Got that?"

"Yes, ma'am."

"All right. Are there any questions before we get started?"

After glancing quickly up and down the line, the tail gunner cleared his throat and spoke again, his voice breaking a little, "I have one, ma'am, or Kelly."

"Yes?" Kelly said, looking at him questioningly.

"Is it true that you're going over to this base in New Mexico because the men there are afraid to fly the B-29?"

Kelly pursed her lips momentarily, not quite sure how she should respond to that question. "Let's just say I have a little more confidence in this bird than they do."

Wainwright licked his lips nervously, glancing down the line at the Copilot who was looking at him with a slight frown on his face. "Scuttlebutt has it that you beat up a fighter pilot at an Officer's Club in New Mexico because you didn't like what he was saying. Is that really true?"

The question hung in the morning air as Kelly's gaze slid slowly past Daniels' deepening frown, Petersen's wry grin, and the look of consternation on the faces of several of the crew members. Her eyes came to rest on Wainwright. She jammed her hands down into the pockets of her flight suit and walked slowly over to where he was standing. Stopping directly in front of him, she studied him for a long minute. Wainwright stiffened, as if he was worried she might decide to take a swing at him. And there seemed to be a palpable increase in tension among the rest of the crew.

"Actually, Corporal, I didn't exactly hit him. I tried to strangle him," she said, her tone as casual as if she were discussing what she was going to have for dinner that evening, "because he talked too much."

As Kelly's words came forth she realized she was savoring the feeling of total power that she momentarily held over Wainwright and the rest of the crew.

Wainwright's eyes widened and his prominent Adam's apple jumped up and down a couple of times. Clearly, even though it was not true, the Corporal sensed a veiled threat behind her words. Swallowing hard, he finally managed to say, "You mean, like I've been doing?"

Kelly stared at him for another minute and then relented, smiled and gave him a friendly pat on the arm. "No, not at all," she said. "In fact, Corporal Wainwright, the only way you could get me that annoyed is if you fail to warn us about a ship crossing our path."

"Yes, ma'am," he said, his face sheathed in a grin as he simultaneously let out a loud sigh of relief. "You can count on me!"

Kelly turned to the rest of the crew, a half-smile still on her face, and asked, "Are there any more questions? Mission-related ones, that is."

There was an immediate relaxation of tension as the crew members looked at each other and grinned.

"No further questions? All right then," she said, as she started walking toward the open hatchway leading to the crew compartment. "Let's get this show on the road!"

As Kelly sat down and strapped herself into the left-hand seat, she was conscious of the enormous responsibility sitting squarely on her shoulders. Not only was she responsible for the lives of her nine-man, but Kirk and Colonel Tibbets had both pointed out that she had the opportunity to bring great credit to the entire **WASP** program while making a significant contribution to the shortening of the war.

Letting out a long, low sigh, she glanced over at Daniels and indicated that the two of them should continue working their way through the pilot's checklist. As he read each item on the list, she carried out the required actions while reading back the appropriate response to indicate that it could be checked off as completed.

"Landing gear transfer switch?"

"Normal."

"Overcontrol?"

"Engaged."

"Battery switch?"

"On."

"Putt-Putt?"

"Started," she replied, suppressing a chuckle at the thought of what her simple question to Kirk had triggered two nights earlier.

"Hydraulic pressure, main."

"Okay."

"Hydraulic pressure, emergency."

"Okay."

"Flight controls?"

"Checked."

"Propellers?"

"High RPM," she said, leaning forward and switching them from the low to the high position.

"Turbos?"

"Off."

Kelly flicked on the intercom switch and spoke to the flight engineer. "How soon will you be finished with your pre-flight checklist, Petersen?"

"Can you give me about 5 more minutes, Kelly?"

"You've got it," she said. After flicking off the crew intercom switch, she looked over at Daniels, waiting for him to ask the inevitable question.

"Do we have a go/no-go point today?"

"Yes. If we're not up to 120 knots at the 5000-foot marker, then I'm going to have to stand on the brakes and hope to hell I can stop this crate before we go off the end of the runway."

Daniels nodded but said nothing.

Kelly continued. "I assume you can guess what my main concern will be during the take-off phase."

"You're hoping that the engines don't overheat or worse yet, catch on fire!"

"That's it," she said.

"So what do we do to head off that problem?"

"Well, we won't do the usual engine run-up before we take off. And as soon as we leave the ground, the flight engineer will pull the cowl flaps in from full open, which is 15 degrees, to half open or a quarter open. That's standard operating procedure. But after that we'll have to see. If we have to close them all the way, we will, but I'd like to avoid that if possible. You don't look very confident, Daniels. What's bothering you?"

"I was just thinking about the possibility of having to plunk it down in the drink."

"The B-29 has a reputation as a real fine floater, Daniels. In fact, the record belongs to one that was ditched in the Indian Ocean. It stayed afloat so long that they had to sink the darn thing with naval gunfire because it became a hazard to shipping."

"You're kidding!"

"No, I'm not."

"Well, I sure hope we don't have to test the seaworthiness of this bird."

"Don't worry. I don't plan to."

Petersen turned around in his seat and spoke across the intervening space. "Kelly, the checklist is completed. Are you ready for engine start?"

"Negative. Not until we finish the pre-flight checklist."

Kelly looked over at Daniels as he continued reading the last few items on the "before taxiing" checklist.

"Gyros?"

"Uncaged."

"Instruments?"

"Checked."

"Bomb bay doors?"

"Closed."

"Chocks?"

"Out left."

"Out right. Parking brakes?"

"Off."

"Okay, Petersen. We're all set up here, but let me make sure the scanners are ready." Kelly flicked the crew intercom back on. "Left scanner, do you read me?"

"Roger."

"Right scanner?"

"Roger. Ready on this side also."

Kelly slid the side window open, and putting her hand out, held it in an upright position while rotating her fingers in a circular motion. The ground crewman who was standing by as fire guard moved back a few steps and held the nozzle of the fire extinguisher in the ready position.

"All right, Petersen, crank 'em up."

"Roger. Starting number three."

Kelly was still bemused by the fact that she couldn't even see the wing of the B-29 unless she leaned out the side window and looked back toward the rear of the aircraft. The sensation was somewhat akin to sitting in the front of a long aluminum tube, with the instruments in front of her the only clue that she was sitting in the cockpit of an airplane. The other thing that took some getting used to was the position of the seats in relation to the centerline of the runway. Since the cockpit of the B-29 was quite wide, both the pilot's and copilot's seats were off to the side so that each pilot was lined up with either the left or right side of the runway.

Once the engines were all started and running smoothly according to the instrument readings, Petersen got back on the intercom. "Everything looks all right at this point, Kelly. Ready to taxi whenever you are."

"Roger. Remind me again of the military power rating for these engines."

"Max RPM is 2600, Kelly."

Should have remembered, she mumbled to herself.

"Stand by to taxi." There was a pause, then Kelly looked over at Daniels. "All set?"

He nodded. "All set." She pushed forward on the throttle grip. Simply taxiing the B-29 called for a delicate touch because she had to utilize the brakes in combination with the application of differential power to the engines. As she coaxed the aircraft out from the hardstand and began taxiing toward the end of the runway, Kelly hoped her moves would be seamless enough so that no one would suspect what a small amount of taxiing time she actually had with the aircraft. While they were taxiing, she had the crew go through their final pre-takeoff checks and .

Kelly flicked on the intercom and asked Petersen if he had completed his "before take-off" checklist.

"That's affirmative, Kelly. All items on the checklist are complete."

"Right after lift-off, I want you to be prepared to close the cowl flaps all the way, not just halfway, if I sense it's causing too much drag."

"Roger. Per standard operating procedures, I'll pull them in from 15 to 7&1/2 degrees as soon as we lift off, but I understand that I should be prepared to close them all the way on your orders. I hope that won't be necessary."

At the end of the runway, Kelly set the brakes. Turning to Daniels, she quickly went through the last of the "before takeoff checklist items.

"Windows and hatches?"

"Closed."

"Auto pilot?"

"Off."

"Emergency brakes?"

"Checked."

"Nose wheel?"

"Straight."

"Wing flaps?"

"Set at 25. And remember, Daniels, we want to raise them to 15 right after liftoff. That's one thing that will help reduce our drag."

"Roger. Trim tabs?"

"Hand set to zero."

"OK. That's it."

"Roger. Let's go."

She gradually pushed the throttle forward until the needles on the engine instruments were quivering on the redline. Since the cabin of the B-29 was built for pressurization, it was a lot quieter than the cockpit of the B-17, but Kelly could feel the vibration through her hands and feet as the four engines strained toward their maximum power output. After a moment's hesitation, she released the brakes and the plane began moving, so slowly at first, she wondered if they would ever get off the ground. Gradually, inexorably, however, the giant aircraft gained speed.

Kelly glanced over at Daniels out of the corner of her eye. She noticed he was nervously tapping his fingers on the tops of his knees. And she suddenly realized that she wasn't at all nervous. *It is true*, she thought. *The anticipation is worse than the reality*. Or maybe Kirk had put his finger on it. Maybe there were inner resources she could draw upon of which she hadn't previously been aware. On the other hand, it could be the result of an unconscious decision to concentrate on more immediate and manageable concerns in order to postpone facing the unseen and unquantifiable dangers that might await them behind the layer of haze.

Her thoughts returned to the engines. Eighty-eight hundred horsepower at her fingertips. Suddenly, without any forewarning, Kelly was caught up in one of those inexplicable, bizarrely poetic shifts of which the human mind is capable. She found herself picturing eighty-eight hundred horses straining at the bit, waiting to drag one hundred and ten thousand pounds of dead weight down the runway and into the air. But how could you possibly tether thousands of horses to a single plane? And even if that were possible, and even if they somehow managed to pull it down the runway, they'd never get it off the ground unless, of course, they were flying horses. Flying horses! Kelly shook her head to clear her mind of such strange musings.

"Kelly?"

"Yes, Daniels?"

"Do you think we can make it off the ground with only around 6,000 feet of available runway?"

"We'll make it. We have no choice!" she said.

Daniels looked over at her and solemnly admitted that his confidence level wasn't quite as high as hers.

Kelly grinned. "That's all right," she said. "You know, I admire your honesty."

As the runway markers began sliding by, Kelly kept an anxious eye on the airspeed indicator. The Boeing pilots had said to hold the plane down on the ground until it reached at least 130 miles per hour, even if it feels like it wants to get airborne before that. Apparently, the B-29 had a tendency to lift off and then settle down again several times before it left the ground for good. As they passed the four thousand foot marker, the airspeed indicator crept slowly past the 100 mile-an-hour mark.

"Pilot to scanners, what's your visual on the engines so far?"

"Left scanner to pilot. Everything looks okay so far."

"Right scanner to pilot. Same report from this side."

This bird was eating up even more of the runway than the B-17, Kelly thought. *In spite of the fact that the engines of the B-29 developed more than twice the horsepower of those on the older bomber.*

"Five thousand feet," the copilot intoned, deliberately pitching his voice in as neutral a tone as possible.

Kelly glanced at the airspeed indicator. It was hovering between 118 and 120 miles per hour. *Not the suggested 120, but is it close enough? What to do?* She had only seconds to decide. This was the point of no return. She either had to abort or commit to going all the way. Even as she was weighing those two options, another several hundred feet of runway slid under the wing of the plane. And every second that she delayed her decision, an additional 170 feet of runway passed beneath the wheels. There was no more time to think. It was already too late to abort! She was committed whether she liked it or not—she had to go!

At fifty-five hundred feet, the airspeed was barely 125.

Shortly afterward, it reached 130. Kelly pulled back gently on the yoke and could feel the plane lift off slightly before it settled back down onto the runway.

"Six thousand feet coming up!" This time there was no mistaking the note of urgency in Daniel's voice.

The airspeed was hovering around 135. This is it. Now or never. Kelly pulled back tentatively but firmly on the control column and the B-29 lifted off, settled down briefly, then rose again, this time to stay. *Just in time*, Kelly thought, as the end of the runway flashed by.

"Gear up," Kelly ordered.

"Gear coming up," said Daniels.

Within a few minutes after Daniels acknowledged her order to raise the landing gear, a series of crises occurred in rapid-fire order that would have been enough to daunt even the most experienced pilots. As Kelly later admitted to Kirk, it helped that they followed one on the heels of the other, because there was no time to let her guard down, no time for the horror of each close call to sink in and paralyze the thinking process.

✯ ✯ ✯

XII

As Kelly nosed the B-29 down to pick up the needed airspeed, three things occurred almost simultaneously: the fire warning light for number three engine flashed on, the right scanner yelled into the intercom that flames were shooting out of the right inboard engine, and Petersen, who had already closed the cowl flaps down to 7 1/2, requested permission to open them back up again to try to extinguish the fire.

Kelly glanced at the airspeed indicator. It was barely reading 160. She knew it wasn't enough airspeed to begin the climb to safe altitude. They needed at least another 30 miles an hour. Panic momentarily clawed at her heart, and her breathing became rapid and shallow. Her mind raced. She concentrated all of her mental energy on regaining control of her mind and body, and staying focused on the absolute essentials.

"Petersen, close the cowl flaps all the way."

"But, that's only going to..."

"Close the damn things now. That's an order!"

"Yes, sir, I mean, ma'am!"

Kelly remembered being told that there was a reasonably good chance of blowing out the fire if the engine were kept running at full power. But there was no time to explain that to Petersen now. She hoped the results would bear out the rightness of her decision. If not, well, it probably wouldn't matter, because none of them would be around to second-guess her.

"Wainwright!"

"Yes, ma'am. I'm looking as hard as I can!"

"Good. Don't you dare even blink or I'll get extremely annoyed at you!"

"Yes, ma'am!"

"Right scanner to pilot. Fire appears to be out on number three engine. It's still smoking, but, repeat, there are no more flames!"

"Roger. I read you." At about the same time, the fire warning light on the instrument panel blinked a couple of times and then went out. Kelly breathed a sigh of relief.

She glanced at the altimeter. They had only slightly more than one hundred feet of distance between the plane and the water! The morning fog still blanketed the open ocean. Hidden somewhere behind those mists in the Pacific was a small task force. But where were they in relation to the flight path of the B-29? That was the crucial question! Although Kelly's attention could not have been diverted for more than a couple of seconds, it was sufficient time to raise the specter of an abrupt and violent ending to their flight. In fact, it was Daniels's sharp intake of breath coupled with Wainwright's short cry of terror that brought her gaze back up to the mind-numbing image that had materialized out of the mists directly in their path.

"Daniels, we need the extra power we get from the military power setting on the manifold pressure."

"Roger, Kelly! Turning the manifold pressure knob to 9."

As one part of her mind attempted to come to grips with the sheer size of a heavy cruiser at close range, another part calculated the degree of bank that a B-29 could handle without going into a fatal plunge to the ocean floor. Another fear, of course, was the possibility of catching a wing tip in the waves when banking the plane at such a low altitude.

Fortunately, the cruiser was steaming perpendicular to their flight path and the bulk of the ship had already passed across their line of flight. Kelly banked the plane steeply to the left, watching out of the corner of her eye as the turn and bank indicator stopped well short of the 40-degree mark. It was just enough to enable them to clear the fantail of the ship.

Bringing the aircraft back to level, she began systematically searching the near horizon in an effort to pierce the mists. In less than a minute, her eyes began to ache from the strain of staring with such intensity. After a couple of minutes, she spotted a large ship off to their right. It was much larger than the cruiser, so Kelly thought it must be the battleship that the radio message had referred to. Since it was well to the right of their flight path and rapidly moving away from them, there was no need to deal with that. But one cruiser and the aircraft carrier were still unaccounted for. *Damn! If only this fog would lift.*

"Over there, Kelly," Daniels said, pointing to the left. *That must be the other cruiser,* she thought. Although they were on converging paths, the B-29 would be well past the point of intersection by the time the cruiser reached that spot. Nevertheless, Kelly banked the plane slightly to the right, changing their direction so they would be on diverging paths.

Glancing down at the airspeed indicator, Kelly saw that they had passed 185 and were approaching 190. Good. That meant she could begin the climb to cruising altitude. Easing back on the yoke, she banked the B-29 slightly to the left, beginning a gradual climbing turn that would bring them eventually to their cruising altitude and place them on the right compass heading.

"Look at the size of that monster!" Daniels blurted out. If the cruisers had been large, the aircraft carrier, which had steamed out of the mist less than a mile in front of them and was rapidly filling up the entire viewing area of the plexiglass windshield, was nothing less than enormous. And there seemed to be no way to avoid it! Banking to the left or to the right would not bring them clear of either the forward or aft sections of the huge ship. The only remaining choice was to skim right over the top of it!

The airspeed was reading around 192 when Kelly, pulled back steadily on the control column, resisting the urge to initiate too steep a climb, which would cause them to lose crucial airspeed. As the distance between the bomber and the ship decreased at the rate of over two hundred and eighty feet per second, Kelly was the first one in the cockpit to sense they were going to clear the deck of the carrier. But that tentative conclusion was not comforting, since there remained two possibilities for imminent disaster: either they would not be able to avoid the carrier's superstructure or there could be a plane in the process of being launched as they passed over the flight deck of the ship.

Even before those two disastrous possibilities could begin to be weighed in her mind, the danger had passed. Kelly's one clear impression, as the aircraft skimmed over the deck of the carrier, was of looking up and catching a quick glimpse of the frozen expressions of fear etched on the faces of the crew members who were on duty in the superstructure.

Kelly leaned forward and looked down at Wainwright in the bombardier's position. He was slumped back in the seat with his eyes closed, and although his mouth was moving, there were no words coming forth. When she glanced over at Daniels, he simply shook his head slowly from side to side and gave her a weak grin. It had all happened so fast that even Petersen, whose seat faced the rear of the plane, was probably unaware of how close a call they just had.

Several minutes later, they passed through fifteen hundred feet with the airspeed indicator registering just under 200 miles an hour. Kelly turned to Daniels and asked if he would like to take over the controls. "Or perhaps you'd like a little time to calm your shattered nerves," she added, smiling over at him.

He grinned back at her. "No, I'm fine. I'll take over if you like. I think you deserve a break."

Kelly lifted her hands off the yoke to signify that she was relinquishing control of the ship to him. She looked down, but the mists obscured the face of the ocean. Up ahead, the sky was cloudless, ranging in color from an azure blue to deep cobalt. At the moment, the skies were uncluttered, empty of any other human object save for them. They were all alone. It was with a feeling of relief that she let out a low sigh and then, turning towards Daniels, said, "Remember, we're cleared to nineteen thousand feet. Once you get to our cruising altitude, what are you going to do?"

"Set the plane for cruise conditions."

"Which involves what?"

He glanced over at her, a frown of concentration appearing on his face. "Well," he said, hesitating momentarily, "cutting back on the throttle, that is, changing the power settings, switching the propellers to low RPM, reducing the manifold pressure and uh . . . I guess that's it."

She nodded. "Do you know how to engage the autopilot?"

"Sure," he said. "But I have no intention of letting some mechanical contraption fly this bird. I want all of the flying time I can get in it."

Kelly smiled at the thought of how closely his reaction paralleled her own when Kirk had suggested that she might want to utilize the device after several hours in the air.

She leaned back in her seat and closed her eyes when Daniels cleared his throat as if he was about to say something.

Kelly opened one eye and looked over at him.

"I just want to say that . . . well, I can't imagine there are many pilots out there, male or female, who would have handled the whole situation as well as you did. I'd be honored to fly as your copilot anywhere, under any conditions, combat included."

"Thanks, Daniels. That's a real nice compliment. Probably the nicest I've ever received. And by the way," she added, "you're a pretty cool customer yourself."

He shook his head. "I'm not in your league, Kelly."

Leaning back, she closed her eyes again and let her thoughts drift. After what she'd just been through, she was now convinced she could handle anything. The training assignment with Tibbets's operation no longer loomed as a dark cloud on her personal horizon. But once past that, what then? With the war rapidly winding down, what new opportunities would be available to her? What could she reasonably expect to happen in her life over the next three to five years?

She knew she wanted to have children with Kirk. Two boys and two girls would be nice. The deep love she and Kirk had for one another and the wonderful relationship they had established, would be an example to everyone of what is possible when two people totally commit to one another. The downside, of course, was that Kirk would often be away, flying around the world from one assignment to another. Kelly hoped she would be able to accompany him on some of those tours, but even if she couldn't, it would be all right. She was proud of him and knew that as important as his career was, it him, would never be as important as she was to him.

Kelly realized that there was her own future to be considered as well. The big question was whether there would be something available in the aviation field by the time she was ready to pick up the threads of her career again. She remembered Kirk's speech at Avenger Field when she sat enthralled as he spoke with such eloquence and power. But he had warned the assembled WASP that the gains of the war years might not be realized in the immediate post-war period. It was highly probable that there would be a backlash and some of the progress made during this time would be reversed once the war was over. He was also convinced that it would be a temporary setback and he stressed the importance of thinking positively and holding on to their vision during that period. And he had promised Kelly that he would support her in keeping that vision alive until it became a reality.

Two other people were urging her on as well. Although her mother and Elaine were no longer physically with her, they were no less real to her. In fact, there were numerous occasions when she felt their presence in her daily life. Two lives that ended before either one could begin to tap their true potential. So, in addition to living for herself and Kirk, she was determined to live for her mother and Elaine. Her achievements would be their achievements and in realizing her dreams, she would be able to, in some sense, realize theirs as well.

She opened her eyes briefly and glanced around. Daniels had a contented look on his face, and he was whistling softly as he continued to coax the bomber up to cruising altitude. Glancing over her shoulder, she saw that Petersen was already lost in his endless round of calculations. Probably figuring the rate of fuel consumption for each 1,000 feet of altitude and every increment of airspeed. A good man. There was no such thing as a flight engineer who was too meticulous. Wainwright had finally managed to pull himself together, slip quietly past Kelly, and work his way back through the long tunnel to the tail gunner's position. Kelly had to smile at his youthful naïveté.

She looked out at the distant horizon. After a moment, she smiled, closed her eyes again, and leaned back against the seat. For the first time since that night when her mother's earthly life had come to a close, Kelly felt at peace with herself.

☆ ☆ ☆

The navigator had estimated it would take approximately two and a half hours to reach the Very Heavy Bomber base at Alamogordo, New Mexico. The rest of the flight went without a hitch, and they arrived at Alamogordo within several minutes of the navigator's original estimated time of arrival (ETA).

After contacting the tower and receiving clearance to land, Kelly, at Daniel's request, brought the huge bird down for a flawless landing.

As she taxied up to the Operations Building, she noted a large crowd awaiting their arrival. Once she parked the aircraft, set the brakes, and shut down the engines, Kelly spotted Colonel Tibbets standing in the front of the crowd with a big smile on his face.

As soon as she set foot on the tarmac, Tibbets was there to greet her. "Nice landing, Kelly. Sorry I had to leave you in a lurch the week before last."

"It worked out fine, sir."

"Yes, so I heard. The report is that you took to the B-29 like a duck to water."

"I'm not sure I would go so far as to say that, Colonel, but the Boeing people were great teachers."

"And you obviously proved to be a first-class student, Kelly. What I'd like to know is whether you can be ready to make your first demo flight tomorrow. Or do you need a day's rest?"

"Tomorrow will be fine, sir."

"Excellent! Will it make you nervous if I fly one of the first demo missions with you this week?"

She had anticipated such a request and she assured Colonel Tibbets he was welcome to accompany her on any of the demonstration flights. As it turned out it, the Colonel became too busy to fly with her over the next few days and instead asked his executive officer, Major Kowalski, to fly one of the missions as Kelly's copilot.

☆ ☆ ☆

XIII

Major Kowalski joined Kelly as copilot on her third demonstration flight at Alamogordo. She was carrying a full crew including a pilot and copilot who took up positions behind her and Kowalski. By that time, Kelly was comfortable enough in her role as instructor pilot to keep up a running commentary on how to handle the aircraft at each point during engine start-up and take-off. On this flight as on each of the first two, they flew due north to Santa Fe, which sat at the southern end of the Sangre de Cristo Mountains. Heavy cloud cover to the north would give the navigator and radar operator an opportunity to work together guiding the aircraft safely through the cloud-covered mountains. Major Kowalski was at the controls when they overflew Santa Fe at 19,000 feet and continued in a northerly direction for another 20 minutes. But on a hunch Kelly suggested they turn around and start back to Alamogordo. Shortly after that a serious carburetor fire broke out in the number three engine. There was always the danger that the magnesium induction system might catch fire and spread to the wing spar which could lead to catastrophic wing failure. Kelly thought it prudent to have the crew bail out now before the fire burned through the wing root. She got on the intercom and briefly summarized the situation, admitting that bailing out over mountainous terrain was far from ideal.

Kowalski suggested that Kelly go ahead and jump and he'd keep the plane flying straight and level as long as he could. Kelly nixed that idea and said as the aircraft commander, she was responsible for everyone on board and that he was to bail out promptly without any further delay.

Kowalski made it out in time. But shortly after he exited the B-29, it exploded in a huge fireball. The compressed air hit his body with colossal force before he had a chance to even think about pulling his rip cord. Fortunately, he wasn't struck by any pieces from the disintegrating aircraft.

After Kowalski yanked the rip cord and watched his parachute canopy deploy overhead, he crossed his hands in front of him and pulled the risers in opposite directions to swing himself around in an attempt to make a quick count of the number of parachutes in the air. He counted twelve, including his own.

Kowalski wasn't certain, but thought there had been thirteen people on board, which meant one person didn't make it out. *Damn!* he thought. *I should have forced Kelly to bail out even if it meant picking her up and throwing her down the hatch past the nose wheel.* He figured there would be hell to pay now, as his boss had told him that Kelly was Singleton's girlfriend and Kowalski should watch over her

✯ ✯ ✯

"Sergeant Ramsey."

"Yes, sir?"

"Would you see if you can locate Colonel Singleton? He's not in his office, and I need to see him ASAP."

"Will do, General Arnold."

Ramsey encountered Kirk returning from the Pentagon café with his first cup of coffee of the morning.

"The Chief wants to see you pronto, Colonel Singleton."

"Any idea what's on his mind, Ramsey?"

"No, sir. Although he did seem preoccupied. In fact, he forgot about a bet we made the other day on the outcome of the Yankee-Red Sox series."

"Who won the bet?"

"He did, sir, and it's not like him to put off settling the bet."

"Especially when he wins—right?"

"Yes, sir. That's about the size of it."

"Hmm. Something must be bothering him."

"That's the way I've got it figured, too."

A few minutes later, Kirk was knocking on General Arnold's door.

"Come on in, Kirk. Have a seat."

Although not without precedent, it was unusual for Arnold to call him by his first name.

As soon as he sat down, Arnold proceeded to tell him about the news from Alamogordo.

Kirk suddenly found it difficult to breath. Afraid that he would pass out in front of Arnold, he gripped the arms of the chair so tightly that his fingers ached. His natural English reserve in combination with a dozen years of exposure to military discipline normally enabled him to keep his emotions under control. But this revelation had the same visceral impact as the news about his father's sudden death a few years earlier.

"All of the crew have been accounted for except Kelly. I can't tell you how badly I feel. She was a very special human being— as you know better than anyone else. Anyway, I assumed you might want to fly out there and take part in the search."

"Yes, sir. I'd like your permission to do so."

"You've got it, Colonel, and there's a fully fueled P-51 waiting for you at Bolling Field."

"Thank you, sir. Will there be anything else?"

"No. You can go ahead and pack whatever you need and then one of my drivers will take you to Bolling as soon as you're ready. Just be sure to keep me informed about things."

"Yes, sir," he said as he rose to his feet and saluted Arnold.

It took Kirk a little over six hours to get to New Mexico. He made a few low passes over the mountains north of Santa Fe before continuing on to Kirtland Field in Albuquerque.

On the ground, he got a briefing from Captain Bealer, the pilot who had flown an L-5 light observation plane up into the mountains on a preliminary search of the area. Bealer wasn't very encouraging and Kirk's hopes hadn't been high to begin with. Bealer doubed that Kelly could have survived the destruction of the aircraft the wreckage was scattered over several square miles of mountainous terrain. And although most of the locations were accessible to a search team trying to reach the site on foot, no significant pieces of the aircraft could be detected from the air.

By the time Singleton finished talking to Bealer, the mountains lay in the shadow of the late afternoon sun. Kirk ate an early dinner in the Officers Mess and retired to his room shortly afterward to be alone with his thoughts and memories.

He arose early the next morning and was airborne just after sunrise. Kirk flew a search pattern in the area between Taos and Santa Fe, landed around noon to get some lunch and refuel, and then took off again and spent the afternoon dropping down to check some areas that remained in the shadows through the morning hours.

The search team had reached one of the first sites with a significant amount of aircraft wreckage but when Kirk dropped down and flew a low pass over their heads, and waggled his wings at them, a couple of the team members looked up, shook their heads, and gave him a thumbs-down.

On his way back toward Santa Fe, he looked out the cockpit and glanced down at the mountainside. For a moment, he thought he saw the sun glinting off something shiny, but when he circled back it was no longer visible. *Maybe it was nothing*, he thought, *or maybe the sun had to be at that exact point in the sky to reflect off it.* But on the way back, Kirk couldn't get it out of his mind. When he got to Albuquerque, he looked up Captain Bealer and asked him if he would take Kirk along as an observer the next day in order to check out the shiny spot. Bealer was agreeable, but even if he had thought it a waste of time, he would still do whatever Singleton requested because his commander had told him to stay and do whatever Colonel Singleton asked him to do.

In the afternoon, they arrived at the location as best as Kirk could remember. Bealer made a low pass as Kirk surveyed the mountainside with a pair of binoculars. One advantage of using the L-5 was that it could fly lower and slower than the Mustang.

"I see it!" Kirk said. "So I wasn't imagining it. Can you drop down a little lower, Captain Bealer, and come at it from a different angle?"

Bealer complied with Kirk's request.

"Well, I'll be damned!" Kirk exclaimed. "There's someone dangling from a parachute that's caught on a tree branch."

"It must be Miss Rossiter, Sir. There are no other reports of planes going down in this area. And I think the search crew is not very far away. We'll establish radio contact and get them headed in this direction."

"Good idea, Bealer. But I have another thought. We passed over a fairly flat strip of land a couple of miles south of here. It should be long enough for you to land and take off. I'd like to get to Miss Rossiter as quickly as possible."

"All right, Sir. We can give it a try. But there's no way you're going to be able to cut her down by yourself."

"I know, but I'll feel better just being there with her."

"I do have a small medical kit on board and a couple of blankets. I'll leave those things with you. Of course, there's a medic with the search team. Lucky thing it's been unusually warm these last few days and there hasn't been any rain, so she's probably not suffering from exposure. But she's bound to be dehydrated."

"Plus we don't know the extent of her injuries. Or if she's even alive," Kirk added in a low voice.

"Well sir, she was in good enough shape to yank the rip cord and deploy the parachute. I take that as a good sign."

"I hope some of your optimism rubs off on me, Captain Bealer."

Bealer brought the L-5 down safely on the open area as planned. "My estimate is that the search team should make it to the site in about 45 minutes, Colonel."

"Okay, I'll be waiting for them."

"Yes, sir. And I'll be back with an L-5 that's got a full tank of gas. And is modified to carry a litter." With those last words, Bealer turned the plane around and took off.

When Kirk arrived at the tree where Kelly was dangling, he saw there was a gash on the right side of her forehead and a line of dried blood that ran down the side of her face. Her eyes were closed but he knew she was alive by the rise and fall of her chest as she breathed. He also discovered that by stretching, he could reach up and take hold of her foot.

Kelly opened her left eye. Recognizing him, she tried to speak, but no words would come forth. Then she raised her hand to her mouth, motioning as if she was taking a drink.

"There's a rescue team not far away, so we'll have you down in short order, Kell. And then you can have something to drink. Nod if you understand what I just said." Kelly nodded, and Kirk continued. "Do you think you have any serious injuries?" She shook her head but then shrugged and pointed to the injury on her forehead. "I see that," he said.

"It looks like you hit your head on a tree branch on the way down. But it doesn't look serious from here.

Kirk heard the search team working their way through the underbrush, and about 15 minutes later they came into sight. Two of the men put climbing spurs on their boots and rigged a rope so they could get up above Kelly, cut the shroud lines, and lower her into the arms of the men waiting below. As soon as she was lowered to the ground, they wrapped her in a blanket and gave her water.

"Small sips, Kell. That's the only way you can handle it," Kirk said. "But you can have as much as you want over the next several hours. Isn't that the procedure ,Corporal?" Kirk asked the medic.

"Yes, sir. That's correct."

The medic examined and cleaned the wound on her forehead, satisfied that it was not serious. Kelly was then taken down to the landing area in a light-weight aluminum litter. When Bealer returned about an hour later, Kelly was transferred to the litter in the plane and the medic accompanied her to the hospital at Kirtland Field. Bealer picked up Kirk on the second trip and flew him back to the hospital to see Kelly.

"How do you feel?"

"Tired and sore, but at least I'm clean. They actually brushed my teeth."

"How about your make-up, Kell? Didn't you miss that? Especially your lipstick?"

Kelly managed a weak grin. "Well, I knew that there was something wrong when I was shunned by all the creatures of the forest. A couple of birds landed on a nearby branch, but they didn't stay long. Probably because I smelled so bad."

"Ummmm. Hopefully not as bad as Fallon."

That elicited another grin. "I wonder whatever became of him?"

Kirk shrugged. "We'll probably never know. By the way, it was smart of you to remember to pull the small mirror out and let it dangle from your flight suit. That's how I spotted you."

"I'm glad I was able to reach it and really fortunate you saw it."

"The doctor told me you'll be out of here in about three days. And Colonel Tibbets will be flying in to visit you tomorrow morning."

"I hope he doesn't blame me for destroying his bomber, Kirk."

"Blame you! What he's likely to do is put you in for a medal because your quick actions most likely saved the lives of the crew.

"Anyway, it's getting late. I think I'd better be going. You're having a hard time keeping your eyes open."

"You mean it's that noticeable?"

"You are kidding, aren't you?"

"Yeah. I am."

Kirk ran his hand lovingly through her hair as he bent over to kiss her. "I love you, Kell. Now go back to sleep and I'll see you in the morning."

"Goodnight, you wonderful man!"

At 1000 the following day, Kirk returned to the hospital with Paul Tibbets in tow.

"Morning, Kelly. It's great to see you on the road to becoming well."

"Thank you, sir. I hope you're not going to tell me I can't fly any more demo missions."

"If you're still up for it, Kelly, when you're fully recovered, you can pick up where you left off."

✯ ✯ ✯

XIV

The second week of September, the commander of Alamogordo Field held a special meeting on Saturday, September 16th for all base personnel. The only place that could accommodate that number of people was one of the large hangars. By 1100 that day, hundreds of people had filed into the hangar. A few early arrivals claimed one of the limited number of folding chairs. At the front of the hangar, a temporary platform had been erected.

Kelly, fully recovered, was seated with Kirk up on the platform in the front row of chairs.

"What's the purpose of this big meeting?" she asked. "Does it have anything to do with me?"

Kirk glanced over at her and raised an eyebrow. "Why do you think you're sitting up here on the platform, Kell?"

A few minutes later, Colonel Thompson, the base commander, entered through a side door and called everyone in the hangar to attention. Then he accompanied a three-star general up onto the platform and stood next to him at the podium. A small entourage of officers followed behind them, and after mounting the platform, stood at attention in front of the chairs.

Colonel Thompson stepped up to the microphone and introduced Lieutenant General Barney Giles, Hap Arnold's Chief of Staff and deputy commanding General of the Army Air Forces.

Giles stepped to the podium and told the people to be seated.

"Ladies and gentlemen and honored guests," he said, turning and looking directly at Kelly, then glancing at someone seated at the opposite end of the platform, "it is with special pleasure that I come before you this morning."

Kelly leaned back in her seat and was startled to see Jackie Cochran sitting at the far end of the row. Where did she come from? Kelly hadn't seen her come into the hangar.

"Miss Rossiter, would you come up here and stand beside me, please," General Giles said. "You also, Mrs. Cochran."

Kelly quickly glanced over at Kirk, and stood and walked up to the podium. She smiled at Jackie, saluted the general, and stood at attention next to him.

"It is my great pleasure today," intoned General Giles, "to recognize Miss Rossiter's superior airmanship in managing to keep a B-29 that was experiencing a catastrophic engine fire, flying straight and level long enough for the entire crew to safely evacuate the aircraft. Because this pilot made a decision to try and save her crew at great risk to her own life, the United States government and the United States Army Air Forces take great pride in bestowing the Distinguished Flying Cross upon Kelly Rossiter."

At that point, General Giles took the medal pinned it on the lapel of Kelly's jacket. Then he shook her hand, and moments later, Jackie Cochran gave her a big hug. A burst of cheering erupted and grew into a two minute standing ovation. When the cheering finally subsided, General Giles spent the next several minutes praising the WASPs for their contributions to the war effort and thanking Jackie Cochran for the magnificent job she did in building a successful program. Then he asked Jackie if she'd like to say a few words. Never one to pass up an opportunity to sing the praises of her WASP pilots, Jackie stepped up to the microphone and praised Kelly for a job well done.

A small reception followed in Colonel Thompson's office. Kelly had an opportunity to chat briefly with the general. Shortly afterward, Jackie took her aside and told her that the press had raised such a stink about the whole episode that Congress was now up in arms about women flying dangerous missions.

Kelly wondered if Congress could put an end to her training men to fly the B-29. Jackie thought it was possible but said it was up to Kelly's immediate superiors to inform her of any decision.

A short while later, Kelly cornered Colonel Tibbets who had arrived too late to witness the presentation.

"You said I would be allowed to start flying the demo missions again as soon as I was fully recovered. Is that still the case, Colonel Tibbets?"

"It looks pretty doubtful, Kelly. But we haven't stopped yet. So I'll continue to use you for that type of mission until I'm told to stop."

When Kelly was alone with Kirk after the reception, she asked him what he thought.

"What I think is that it won't be long before you're back to your first love: ferrying fighters."

"But I do like flying the B-29s, Kirk."

"Yes, but what you especially like is showing off your flying skills to a bunch of men. And being able to order them around."

Kelly gave him a big grin. "I won't deny that."

"Tomorrow's the 17th of September . . . Isn't there something of a personal nature that has an even higher priority?"

"You mean, like getting the house in order for our wedding reception?"

"That's exactly what I mean. And I've already arranged a hop back to Seattle for you."

"You have?"

"Uh-huh."

"With anyone I know?"

"Yeah. With the prospective groom!"

✵ ✵ ✵

XV

October 2th 1944

Two days after Kelly and Kirk's marriage

Wartime life in San Francisco was, for the most part, comparable to that in other large American cities. There was the constant ebb and flow of military personnel coming and going–generally either on their way to or back from the Pacific Theatre. Housing–both temporary and permanent–was scarce and, when available, went for a premium.

Being a port city, freighters, troop ships, transports–row upon row of them–lined the waterfront. Night and day, around the clock, the wharves were beehives of activity as the West coast longshoremen strove to match the efficiency of their east coast counterparts. As soon as one ship was loaded and sent on its way another one claimed the empty berth.

The city had long since ceased to worry about the possibility of being shelled by a Japanese sub. The shelling of the oil field several miles north of Santa Barbara had occurred during the first year of the war when Japan was still on the offensive.

One thing that most visitors to the city had not been prepared for was the famous—or perhaps the word should be infamous—San Francisco fog.

Carl Sandburg's affectionate description of fog arriving and departing on little cat feet didn't do justice to a San Francisco fog that rolled in and smothered the city in an oppressive mist-laden cloak that could occasionally last for days.

✫ ✫ ✫

"When is this supposed to break anyway?" Kelly asked, glancing out their hotel window at the curtain of gray fog which obscured everything farther than fifty feet away. "Seems like forever since we last saw the sun."

"It's only been two days, Kell. Besides we've made good use of the time!"

"I won't deny that," Kelly said, flashing him a seductive smile. "In fact, considering how many young couples we saw downstairs at dinner last night, I think the whole building must have been vibrating later in the evening."

"Yep. With all the bedtime gymnastics, it's a wonder the hotel didn't collapse like the Tacoma Narrows Bridge did four years ago."

"Based on the number of guys in uniform and snatches of conversation overheard I assume they're about to ship out and are spending their last few days stateside with their wives or girlfriends," she added.

"Yeah, and what's heartbreaking about the whole scene is that a lot of these guys won't be coming back so it is literally their last time together."

"With the war in Europe winding down they must be heading for the Pacific Theatre," Kelly said.

"Probably. And unless the bombing campaign eventually brings Japan to their knees and convinces them that it's time to sue for peace we're going to have to invade the Japanese mainland."

"What's that going to mean in terms of casualties?"

"No one knows for certain. But we've seen how they fight to the last man in the island campaigns. And with the Japanese dedication to their homeland and to the emperor it will surely mean the resistance is going to be many magnitudes greater. The general feeling is that casualties on both sides could be well over a million."

"The insanity of war—especially modern warfare," Kelly said, shaking her head. "I think it was Bertrand Russell who said war doesn't determine who is right, war just determines who is left."

Kirk nodded. "Looking at it in one light, that's true. But on the other hand, there can be no question that the Nazis and the Japanese military are the bad guys. They fully deserve everything that's being handed them. And the world will be a better place when they're gone."

"It's actually getting lighter outside and the visibility is definitely improving. Only a few minutes ago, I couldn't see a thing," Kelly said, changing the subject as she pressed her face against the small window that faced the harbor. "Can we take a walk?"

"Sure. How about a walk to the top of Nob Hill then a stroll through Chinatown where we can have lunch.

"Okay."

Following that I'd like to walk up to the top of Turtle Hill."

"Turtle Hill?"

"Yep. There's a park on top of the hill—Grandview. And when it's clear it lives up to its name. There are fantastic views of the city, the ocean, and if you look hard, the Golden Gate Bridge. Hopefully by the time we get there the fog will be gone. After that we'll catch a cable car down to the ocean, wander around there for a while, and then have dinner."

"Did you have a specific place in mind?"

"Yes. Cliff House. It's one of San Francisco's oldest and most historic restaurants."

✣ ✣ ✣

Following lunch they climbed to the top of Turtle Hill and sat down on a bench to catch their breath and enjoy the view. There were only tatters of fog left and, as they watched, those were swept away by an off shore breeze.

Kelly was the first to speak. "Just what I needed after being stuck in our room for the past few days," she said, holding up her arms in a paean of praise for the return of sunlight and the magnificent vistas which were now visible in each direction.

"Yep. Not only that but it helps to sweep away the gloomy thoughts about the world situation," Kirk added.

"Kirk?"

"Yeah?"

"I'd like to continue to go by my maiden name for the next few months because that's what I'm known by in the service. Is that all right with you?"

"I suppose so. As long as it's just for the remainder of your time as a WASP pilot."

"I promise. You know, honey, this has been a wonderful weekend but I would like to do something special after the war. Like go somewhere that's really exotic and romantic—for a real honeymoon."

"Sure, after the war is over we'll do it up right and go to Hawaii or someplace like that."

"So, what most impressed you about our wedding ceremony?" Kelly asked.

"Why, how beautiful you looked, of course!"

"But I gather you were also duly impressed with my bridesmaid," Kelly said, poking him gently in the ribs.

"Angeline's attractive all right. But your mix of Irish and Indian blood along with those blue-green eyes of yours set you apart from any other woman I've met."

"You're prejudiced, honey."

"Maybe. But I recognize exceptional beauty when I come face to face with it. And that's exactly what happened when I visited the Rossiter Company for the first time one day last spring. And, by the way, you never have told me what your initial reaction to my appearance was when you first met me."

Kelly smiled nervously. "I'm not sure you want to hear what my first impression was."

"You mean it was that bad?"

"No. Not really. But to be perfectly frank—or maybe blunt is the word—I have to admit, I didn't think you were particularly handsome."

"Well, I'm not. That's for sure."

"But you are ruggedly good-looking."

"You mean like Gary Cooper?"

Kelly nodded. "More or less. I hope I haven't insulted you."

"Nope. You know, Kell," Kirk continued, "I used to watch an old farmer—a neighbor of my Uncle Joe's—sculpt small wooden figurines of famous people using only a jackknife and different grades of sandpaper. The initial result was pretty rough, although recognizable. But by the time he got finished, the final product bore a genuine likeness to the person. In fact, I have one of his sculptures of my favorite American—George Washington."

Kelly looked at him quizzically. "I have a distinct feeling that you're heading somewhere with this story other than simply telling me a tale about an old farmer's hobby," she interjected.

"Yeah, I am. One of my girlfriends once said that I looked like one of Charlie's rough sculptures. She theorized that God must have gotten bored when he made me or maybe He just ran out of time and had to go on to someone else."

"Wow! Talk about an ego-bruising comment," Kelly said, but then acknowledged to herself that his girlfriend's assessment was not that different from what Kelly's initial reaction had been.

"I only have two regrets about our wedding, Kirk."

"What are they?"

"I wish my mother and Elaine could have been there to be a part of it. You know, mom started a Hope chest for me when I was only thirteen. I thought it was silly at first but then after she died I couldn't bear to look at it because it made me sad to think of how much she loved me and how much I lost with her passing."

Kirk slipped his arm around her shoulders, leaned over, and kissed the top of her head.

"And then on top of that you lose your closest friend in a freak accident that never should have happened," he added. "But there's always, Ami, Kell. When the war is over you two can pick up that special friendship where you left off."

"I hope so. But maybe after all that Ami's been through she'll be so bitter she won't want anything to do with me."

"What's the likelihood of that happening, Kell? Remember how warmly she greeted you when we visited her at Minidoka?"

"Yes."

After a minute or so of silence, Kelly asked, "After this weekend getaway—what then?"

"It's on to Washington for me and back home to Seattle for you. You'll need to pack for an extended stay at your next assignment."

"My next assignment?"

"Uh huh. If you're up for it, that is."

"I thought the WASP program was going to be shut down."

"It is," Kirk acknowledged, "but there's still work to be done over the next few months."

"So when is the program scheduled to end?"

"The week before Christmas."

"Some Christmas present."

"Yeah. But the news isn't all bad."

"How so?"

"That new assignment I mentioned a few minutes ago . . ."

"Yes. What about it?"

"I pulled some strings and, as a special wedding present, arranged for you to spend the next few months with the Fighter Flight Test Division (FFTD) at Wright Field in Dayton."

"No kidding!"

"Nope. I'm serious."

"But why Wright Field?"

"Partly because of your encounter with compressibility in your dogfight with Magnuson. There's a lot of research being carried out on the topic right now. But mainly because there's a constant stream of brass coming and going from Wright Field. And they need to be shuttled back and forth between there and Washington as well as various other bases. So there's an ongoing need for someone to help out Amanda Wilton with the administrative flights that have to be made."

"Who's Amanda Wilton?"

"Another WASP who's been assigned there for the past several months."

"Her name doesn't ring a bell. She must be from one of the early classes."

"Yep. And according to what I hear she's done a great job. So you might say she's paved the way for you."

"I can't believe they're shutting down the program. With the war still going on, it seems like the WASPs could continue to play an important role in support of it. Couldn't General Arnold have done anything to save the program?"

"He tried. In fact, he testified before the House Committee on Military Affairs. But in addition to the lobbying effort by returning combat pilots there were a lot of complaints from male civilian pilots who couldn't meet the entry requirements into the Army Air Force and as a result became eligible for the draft. And mainly negative articles by the media only added fuel to the fire."

"Men!" Kelly sputtered. "I swear. Male pilots are so damned insecure—especially when it comes to a woman challenging them in what they see as their own private domain."

Kirk shrugged. "What did you expect? To be greeted with open arms and told they welcomed the competition?"

Kelly shook her head. "I suppose not. I guess there was bound to be some backlash to the whole idea of women flying military aircraft. By the way, does Amanda do any test flying?"

"I'm not sure. She might. But don't get any ideas, Kell."

"Why not?"

"Because I'm totally opposed to the idea of you doing any test flying."

"But you were the one who encouraged me to take the B-29 assignment."

"Yeah. And after you were reported missing I was mentally kicking myself for pushing you to take the assignment."

"Look, Kirk, you're beginning to sound like my father. And that's one thing I don't need from you. I don't need anyone to protect me. Just love me and respect my wishes. That's all I want!"

"Kell, you can fly as much as you want, but test flying is a whole different ballgame. It's far too dangerous. Most test pilots know that their chances of living to a ripe old age are pretty slim.

Kelly shook her head. "There must be some test flights that are more routine in nature and not inherently dangerous. You know, like testing a new piece of avionics equipment."

Kirk frowned. "All test flights have some element of danger associated with them. There's no such thing as a routine test flight, Kell. So get used to it; that's the way it's going to be."

Kelly bit her tongue, deciding it was pointless to argue anymore. There would be opportunities later on to address the topic again. Besides, the whole idea of getting into an argument on their honeymoon was absolutely ridiculous.

Kirk stood up and stretched. "Let's walk back down the hill and catch a cable car that will take us down to the ocean. Once we get there we can walk down to Cliff House."

"All right," she said slipping her hand into his.

✯ ✯ ✯

XVI

October 9th, Wright Field

Kelly was standing at attention in front of Lieutenant Colonel Harvey Harmon's desk. Harmon was the head of the Fighter Flight Test Division at Wright Field, Dayton, Ohio and was known to hold women pilots in low regard—particularly those who flew military aircraft.

"Let me be perfectly clear, Rossiter. I already have one WASP on my staff and I don't want or need a second one. Furthermore, I'm not particularly impressed by the story going around the service about how you supposedly out- flew a fighter ace from the European Theater of Operations, although everyone else apparently is. And the fact that you happen to be a protégé of General Arnold doesn't cut any ice with me either. Do I make myself clear?"

"Perfectly."

Harmon pursed his lips and studied her for a minute or so before speaking again. That was the first and only time he met Kelly's gaze.

"Good. You may stand at ease."

"Thank you, sir," was what she said. What she thought was *it's about time*.

"Anyway," he continued, "since you're here and I'm apparently stuck with you for the next few months you can help out Simpson on the Operations desk. Wilton will give you a briefing on the duties she performed before being given some flying assignments."

"What about my encounter with compressibility while diving in a P-51? From what I'd been told, FFTD would be interested in hearing about the details of my experience," Kelly said.

"There are a number of test pilots in our group who have encountered compressibility under actual combat conditions," was Harmon's response. "And a few of them have duplicated the experience in a controlled test dive here at Wright Field. So I don't think there's anything you can tell us that we don't already know. However, since Wilton does do some test flying now and then, you will be expected to help out by handling a few administrative flights. But first you need to become familiar with the responsibilities of the Ops Office. That will be all, Rossiter," Harmon said, as he turned away from her and started flipping through a stack of file folders on a small side table.

"Yes sir," Kelly said, saluting Harmon's back before exiting his office while mentally giving him the finger.

Shortly afterwards, Kelly met Captain Charles "Chuck" Simpson, the Operations officer (informally known as the Ops officer). Although his greeting was not overly enthusiastic, it was at least gracious. Simpson sketched the major responsibilities of the Operations office while awaiting the arrival of Amanda Wilton who would give Kelly a detailed briefing on what her specific duties would be.

Less than ten minutes after meeting Simpson, a tall attractive blonde strode briskly into the Ops office, walked across the room, held out her hand and said, "Kelly Rossiter, I presume. My name's Amanda Wilton. Welcome to FFTD."

"Thanks, "Kelly replied, while shaking her outstretched hand. "I'm pleased to be here."

I think, she said to herself.

"I'll take you over to the ready room sand introduce you to the pilots. They're all curious to meet you.

Curious to meet me, Kelly thought, rolling the words around in her mind. "Why?" She asked.

"Your reputation has preceded you."

"Is that good or bad?" Kelly asked.

"Depends on how you handle yourself when you first meet them," Amanda said. "If I were in your shoes, I wouldn't rattle on about my flying adventures. Wait for them to ask about your experiences."

Kelly was annoyed that she had already been labeled a braggart by her fellow WASP. Maybe it was because Amanda liked being the only woman among the test pilots and resented Kelly's presence there.

"Look, Amanda," Kelly said, "I didn't come here with the idea of trying to displace you. So do me a favor. Don't judge me until you've had an opportunity to get to know me. Okay?"

"Sorry, I didn't mean to sound so critical. It's just that your achievements are well known throughout the Army Air Force. Well known and appreciated for the most part, I might add. Having been fighter pilots themselves, the test pilots all have a pretty good idea of the kind of flying skills it takes to out-fly one of their own. Besides, the fact that you—a civilian—or at least a non-military type, were awarded the DFC (Distinguished Flying Cross) for your B-29 flight also carries a lot of weight with the flyboys. Especially the bomber pilots."

"Colonel Harmon certainly wasn't very impressed," Kelly said. "In fact, he was downright indignant that I had been foisted on him against his will."

"Don't worry about him. He won't bother you. It's just that he's all caught up in his own importance," said Amanda.

"I'm more than a little familiar with that type. I lived with someone like that for most of my life," Kelly said. "At least until I signed on with the WASP program last year."

"One other thing. Colonel Harmon doesn't allow any smoking in the Operations office and he especially disapproves of women smoking anywhere in public so you'd better plan on sneaking off to another part of the building if you get desperate for a cigarette."

As they approached the ready room where the pilots waited to be called for duty, a major of medium height with prematurely gray hair was on his way out of the room.

"Kelly, this is Major Feranno, Assistant Chief of the FFTD," Amanda said.

"Nice to meet you, Kelly. We've heard a lot about you," Feranno added, dryly, as he extended his hand.

Kelly nodded and managed a tight-lipped smile.

There were around a dozen pilots in the ready room. Their greetings for the most part were cool but not unfriendly. Except for one of them. Peter Hellman, who happened to be one of the most highly regarded of the test pilots, looked disgruntled at her abrupt appearance in the ready room. He apparently viewed women pilots in the same light as Colonel Harmon.

Two of the test pilots, Jack Lathrop and Rob Latimer, actually greeted Kelly warmly. Lathrop and Latimer were known as the "L and L boys", partly because they looked like they could be brothers and partly because they often worked on the same test assignments. It turned out that both of them had flown with Maynard Magnuson in the European Theatre. Not only did they acknowledge that Magnuson was a superior pilot—which made Kelly's accomplishment all the more impressive—but they also admitted that he could be difficult to take after having had a little too much to drink. So they could easily picture him saying something which would get under someone's skin.

Kelly shrugged. "Water under the bridge."

After the introductions were completed Lathrop motioned for Kelly to take a seat on the couch between him and Latimer. Hellman, who was sitting opposite her, scowled but said nothing.

Unlike Colonel Harmon, all the pilots but Hellman showed genuine interest in her encounter with compressibility in the P-51. Before describing her experience, Kelly first asked for an explanation of what precisely compressibility was.

Lathrop gave her a brief but readily understandable explanation.

"When an aircraft is flying relatively slowly, the air flows smoothly over the wings and fuselage. But when the aircraft approaches the speed of sound, as it does in a dive, the air in front of it is compressed. It splits apart instead of maintaining a smooth flow along the surface of the wings. This produces a dramatic loss of lift and a matching increase in drag. As a result, the controls stiffen and become unresponsive. And depending on your air speed and altitude when you begin your dive recovery you may or may not have room to level off before you crash."

Kelly nodded. "I guess I was lucky. I was following Magnuson as he went into a steep dive in an effort to shake me off his tail," she explained.

"What altitude were you at when you started the dive?"

"Twenty-five thousand feet."

"What happened next?"

"The stick began to jump around just like the fight manual said it would. At that point I chickened out and started to ease back on the throttle in order to reduce my speed and begin my pull-out"

"You didn't chicken out, Kelly," Latimer interjected, "you just showed yourself to be a careful flier. And careful fliers live longer."

"Rob is right, Kelly," Lathrop said. "You did the smart thing. You got yourself out of a potentially dangerous predicament while you still had control of the aircraft. Of course," he added, "it helps that you were flying the Mustang with its laminar flow wing."

"Laminar flow wing?" Kelly said, with a quizzical expression on her face.

"Yep. The wing on the P-51 was especially designed to postpone the development of the shock wave which causes the loss of lift. What was your air speed at the point that you began to throttle back?"

"Around 475."

"And your altitude when you began to pull out of the dive?"

"Thirteen thousand feet. By the time I got down to seven thousand feet I had fully recovered from the dive."

"Magnuson must have begun his recovery about the same time or he wouldn't be alive to talk about it," one of the other pilots offered.

"He did," Kelly acknowledged. "I didn't get a chance to talk with him after we landed, but," she continued, "I did run into him at Newark a couple of months later."

"Rob and I saw him about the same time. And he was quite vocal in his admiration for you," Lathrop said. "In fact, he admitted that you really put him through the ringer and proved to be the better pilot, Kelly."

Kelly raised her eyebrows and uttered a low whistle of surprise. "I thought his oversized ego would prevent him from ever making an admission like that," she said.

"He really didn't have much choice, Kelly. The story circulated around the Army Air Force pretty quickly. So, Maynard couldn't very well deny it or dismiss it as an exaggeration of what actually happened."

"Anyway," Latimer said, picking up the conversation from Lathrop," Colonel Harmon is leaving for England in a few days. It's supposed to be a temporary assignment, but he'll probably be gone for a few months. In the meantime, Major Feranno is the acting Chief of FFTD. You'll find him a lot more sympathetic to your desire to keep on flying. But your primary responsibility once you learn the ropes around here will be to help Simpson run the Operations office."

"Okay. But what's the possibility of doing a test flight or two?"

"Nonexistent, if I have anything to say about it," Hellman grumbled. Although spoken under the breath, his words were audible to anyone sitting near him, including Kelly, at whom they were obviously aimed.

"You'll have to discuss that with Feranno, Kelly," Latimer answered, trying to soften the harshness of Hellman's comment.

✯ ✯ ✯

XVII

The next morning, back in Operations, Amanda informed Kelly that her primary responsibilities would be to meet with the maintenance officer each morning to determine which aircraft were ready to fly. And to make sure she received a signed document from this officer formally releasing them for flight.

"We also do an operations check and give the pilots a release form to hand to the linesman before engine start up."

"How about that chart?" Kelly asked, pointing to the status board that kept track of the various tests that were underway. "Is that another responsibility of ours—or rather mine?"

"Yes. It has to be updated on a daily basis. One other thing that I do," Amanda added, "is to help Simpson keep track of how long each of the pilots has been gone. If they're not back at the time we expected them, then we do a quick calculation of the amount of fuel they had on board to determine if they're seriously overdue."

Several days later, after Colonel Harmon had left for England, Major Feranno called Kelly into his office. "I understand you'd like to do a little test flying."

"Yes, sir. I would. But I don't want to be seen as horning in on Amanda's territory."

"No need to worry about that, Kelly. It's not as though anyone has an exclusive claim on the test flying business. There's always room for another pilot. There are three main requirements to be a successful test pilot," he said, placing his forearms on the desk while leaning forward and studying her intently. "First, you need to have superior flying skills—which you obviously do. Second, you need to be able to maintain your cool under pressure. Again, you've more than proved you meet that qualification. And third, you have to be able to follow directions very precisely. Since you flew for Paul Tibbets, I assume you know all about following instructions exactly."

"Yes, sir. You can be sure of that."

"There's another asset you bring to the board, Kelly. Your engineering degree."

"Yes, sir. I thought that might count for something."

"What was your field of study?"

"Mechanical engineering, Major Feranno. With an emphasis on power plant development. But I also took a few courses in the aeronautical curriculum."

"Excellent. That leaves us with just one little problem, Kelly."

"What's that, sir?" Kelly said, frowning slightly.

"There's a one star general who doesn't want you to do any test flying."

Kelly was incensed but kept her thoughts to herself. "You're not obligated to do what he asks, are you, Major Feranno?"

"Technically, no. But if he wanted to push the matter he could bring pressure to bear through someone above me in the chain of command."

"I assume you're referring to my husband, General Singleton. He knows how strongly I feel about doing my part in the war effort, sir. Especially since three of my four brothers are flying combat missions every day. Two in the Pacific theatre and one in the European Theatre."

"All right, Kelly. I'll see what I can do but first I need you to make a couple of administrative flights for me. You are checked out in the C-47 aren't you?"

"Yes, sir."

"Good. I need you to deliver a two star back to Bolling Field in DC. After you've arrived there give me a call. I may have another assignment for you before you return to Wright."

"Understood, sir. What time should I be ready to depart for Bolling?"

"Around noon will be fine. The name of the two star you'll be transporting to Newark is Hardison. Milton A. Hardison."

"What's the A stand for?"

"Try 'annoying'."

"Are you suggesting that this might be a less than pleasant flight, Major Feranno?"

"Let's just say that General Hardison has an inflated idea of his own flying prowess, Kelly."

"What if he wants to take over the controls for a while? Should I let him?"

"Yes. You don't have much choice in the matter anyway. Besides, it's not that he's a bad pilot. It's just that he does have a tendency to be a little reckless on occasion. Just remember, you're the A/C (aircraft commander), Kelly. If he makes any off-the-wall suggestions, you have the right to reject them—politely, of course. But you're the boss, and he knows that so don't let him push you around."

"Yes, sir."

"All right, Kelly. That will be all for now. Remember: check in with me as soon as you get to Bolling."

"Will do, Major Feranno."

✼ ✼ ✼

XVIII

By noon, Kelly was at the aircraft conducting her walk around inspection while mulling over her prospects for getting any test flight assignments.

Shortly before noon General Hardison arrived at the plane, returned her salute and asked if they were ready to go. Kelly said they would be in the air within fifteen minutes.

After they'd been at cruising altitude for around an hour, Hardison asked to take over the controls. Kelly relinquished them reluctantly because it had given her something to do. The general was more non communicative than anyone with whom she'd ever flown. Perhaps he was simply uncomfortable with a woman in the cockpit. Especially one half his age. And one to whom he had to defer with regard to decisions concerning the flight of the aircraft.

About a half hour after he took over the piloting responsibilities, Hardison spoke for only the second time since they'd gotten airborne.

"What's our ETA, Rossiter?"

"1515, sir. Although it could take longer if the weather officer's prediction is accurate about encountering a line of thunderstorms as we approach Washington."

"We should be able to slip through that without too much trouble. I have a meeting at 1600, and I don't want to be late for that."

"Yes, sir," was Kelly's response, but her thoughts were of a different order. She wasn't about to take any chances with a thunderstorm. They were home to just about every aviation hazard one could conceive of, including torrential rain, lightning, hail, even ice. Plus, there was often severe turbulence in the form of powerful vertical downdrafts and updrafts of air.

As they approached the Allegheny range in West Virginia, Kelly could see an ominous looking squall line stretching across the horizon. Straight ahead of them the cumulonimbus clouds rose up like the sheer wall of a canyon. Flashes of lightning blossomed from within the depths of the cloud but faded away as quickly as they appeared.

When Kelly took back control of the aircraft from General Hardison, he grumbled to himself but didn't argue about her decision. A few minutes later she began a gradual bank to the left, flying parallel to the storm front while looking for a break in the squall line through which she could safely fly.

"What are you doing?" Hardison asked.

"Avoiding trouble," was Kelly's laconic response.

"What's the matter, Rossiter? Are you afraid of a little ol' thunderstorm?"

"Yes, sir. I am." *And you would be, too,* she thought, *if you had any common sense.*

"You're going to make me late for my meeting."

"Better to be late than a no-show because you were killed in a storm-related crash, General Hardison."

"Look, Rossiter, it's imperative that I be on time for this meeting."

"Sorry, General, but I'm the A/C and we'll do it my way."

"You'll have to answer for this, young lady."

So that was how he viewed me, Kelly thought.

She shrugged but said nothing. Several minutes later a break appeared in the cloud wall. Kelly decided to give it a go but not without some serious misgivings. First, she asked General Hardison to contact Bolling tower and request clearance to fourteen thousand feet.

"Why? We're already at ten thousand."

"Because if we get caught in a serious downdraft I want an ample cushion of safety," she replied.

Kelly had never before suffered from claustrophobia but as soon as the roiling cloud mass enveloped them she could feel her throat constricting and her breathing become more shallow. She was determined to keep her fear under control. Not only because it was imperative to be able to think clearly and act decisively in these conditions but also because she was darned if she'd let some chauvinistic general see any weakness in her. With that, she tried to disregard what was happening outside the cockpit and concentrate instead on her instruments.

The steady splatter of rain on the windshield was a precursor to a violent cannonade of water which Kelly had never before experienced. And hoped to never again. It was as if a dozen fire hydrants had been opened simultaneously and directed at the windshield from point blank range. She was amazed that the engines continued to perform after swallowing all that water.

The water did find a number of points of entry into the cockpit and it wasn't long before Kelly was soaked from top to bottom. But so was General Hardison which was at least a small source of satisfaction.

The most unnerving part of the experience thus far was the blinding flashes of lightning accompanied by ear-deafening explosions of thunder. An observer on the ground could not begin to imagine what Kelly and her companion were experiencing. No matter how loud the thunder claps seemed from ground level they were magnitudes worse from within the storm.

As it turned out, the storm gods were just beginning to draw from their warehouse of afflictions. The aircraft abruptly plummeted downward after being caught in a severe downdraft. If it hadn't been for the seatbelt, Kelly would have banged her head against the cockpit ceiling. The disorienting feeling of weightlessness which Kelly experienced during the downdraft didn't prevent her from watching in astonishment as the altimeter unwound at the rate of several thousand feet per minute. Her next move was to switch the propeller controls to low pitch and increase power to the engines. Unbelievably, this had no discernable effect on their situation. Their downward plunge was brought to a halt, however, by a sudden updraft which kicked in just seconds before they would have slammed into the Allegheny ridge that lay just beneath them. According to the instruments they were now being pushed upward at a faster rate than their descent. When the altimeter indicated they were passing ten thousand feet with no diminution in their rate of climb, Kelly, remembering some advice from an experienced airline pilot, yelled to Hardison to lower the landing gear, reinforcing her verbal order with a vehement hand gesture. Hardison, who had been nervously clenching and unclenching his fists, complied after a quick glance to see if she still appeared to be in command of her senses. The aircraft was now nose down in a steep dive or at least it should have been except for the fact that the instruments confirmed that they were still climbing.

Their ascent slowed down as they approached fourteen thousand feet at which point Kelly finally got the aircraft back under control. But with the artificial horizon now useless because it had been pushed beyond its limits and tumbled, Kelly had to rely on the turn indicator and airspeed indicator to keep the aircraft flying straight and level.

The last trial they were subjected to was the sudden onslaught of hail. Luckily, it was relatively brief but upon landing it was apparent that the hailstones, though not very large, had struck with enough force to cause significant dimpling on the nose of the C-47, the engine nacelles, and the leading edge of the wings. After the hail had ceased, the storm gods had either depleted their bag of tricks or had relented, deciding to take pity on those puny creatures who had dared to challenge them in their own arena.

The remainder of the flight was without incident for which Kelly was thankful since she didn't have the energy to do battle with nature again that day. They arrived only 15 minutes past their original ETA.

Within minutes after she brought the C-47 to a stop in front of the Operations building a staff car pulled up to the plane and a small contingent of field grade officers spilled out of the car to greet a soaked, and therefore very grumpy, General Hardison, as he climbed down the ladder onto the tarmac.

Kelly descended from the aircraft several minutes later and saluted General Hardison just as the staff car pulled away. He acknowledged her salute with only the slightest nod of his head. However, to give him the benefit of the doubt, there were so many officers crammed into the car there might not have been room for him to raise his hand and return her salute.

When Kelly stopped in the Ops Office to use the bathroom facilities she was told that the tower had lost contact with another C-47 which was about 20 minutes behind them. It was assumed that the aircraft had suffered catastrophic structural failure and crashed.

There but for the grace of God . . . she thought.

When she checked in with Major Feranno he told her to continue on to Logan Airport in Boston and pick up an Army Air Force colonel by the name of Matthews before returning to Wright Field.

But after hearing about her hair-raising and energy-draining flight through the thunderstorm, he strongly suggested she postpone her flight to Logan until the following morning.

Kelly's next step was to call Keith Whitaker and see if they could get together for a brief visit while she was in Boston. Admittedly, she viewed the prospect with mixed emotions. As soon as she placed the call the initial surge of excitement at the expectation of seeing Keith again was followed by a feeling of uneasiness. Since her relationship with him had lasted only a few months, it had still been in the infatuation stage when he left for the position on the east coast. Whether it would have deepened into something more lasting if Keith had continued to teach at the University of Washington was a question mark in her mind. However, since she was now Kelly Singleton that was a moot point.

✯ ✯ ✯

XIX

Logan Airport

As Kelly taxied up to the Logan terminal the following day she could see Keith Whitaker standing behind a gate that opened onto the tarmac. Keith was frowning as he shaded his eyes and tried to see into the cockpit. But the glare from the mid-day sun prevented him from seeing who was at the controls. Kelly doubted if he would recognize her anyway because she'd had her hair cut short since he last saw her and was wearing military issue aviator sunglasses.

By the time Kelly exited the aircraft and took a few steps towards the terminal Keith realized who it was and ran towards her with a big grin on his face.

She knew what he was about to do. It was still the same, that special feeling of exhilaration when Keith lifted her up and spun her around in the shared exuberance of the moment. It would be nice if Kirk could learn to be a little more spontaneous and a little less serious about things. *Whoa, Kelly. You'd better not go there.* Her moment of elation was followed by a feeling of guilt.

Comparing Kirk to Keith was totally unfair to both. Especially to Kirk, whose selfless devotion to Kelly was not something she could ever see Keith exhibiting.

"Kelly," Keith said, as he stepped back, shook his head, smiled and clucked his tongue in amazement. "I had no idea you were still flying with the WASPs."

"Yep. There are a few of us still flying."

"You know you're like a bottle of fine wine. You just keep improving with age."

"Come on, Keith, It's only been slightly over a year since you last saw me. What did you expect? That I'd look old and decrepit!"

He smiled, but there was a touch of sadness to his smile. "No, of course not. But I see that some things have changed," he said glancing down at the wedding band on her finger. "Who's the lucky man?"

"An Army Air Force officer."

"Pilot?"

Kelly nodded. "But he's a staff officer so he doesn't fly much anymore."

"Uh," Keith said, "are you flying back to Wright Field today?"

"No."

"Do you have plans for dinner tonight?"

"Actually, no. Although I am meeting a friend for coffee this afternoon. In fact she's meeting me at my hotel around 1400. That's two o'clock your time. So I'd better be going," Kelly said, as she started walking towards the entrance to the terminal.

"You don't need to translate military time into civilian time for me, Kelly," Keith said, as he increased his pace to keep up with her. "The twenty-four hour clock is a much easier and much more logical way to keep track of the passage of time unless, of course, you happen to be one of those uncounted millions who are bound by tradition and/or arithmetically impoverished," he added, with a self-satisfied grin.

"I see that the low opinion you hold of the hoi polloi hasn't changed to any degree."

"But of course not, my dear. It's important to keep things in their proper perspective even if there is a war going on, or maybe I should say especially since there is a war going on. So, tell me, where are you staying?"

"At the Parker House."

"How did you manage that? It's always been one of the most popular places to stay in Boston. And what with all the wartime traffic in and out of Boston it's almost impossible to get a room there."

"My boss back at Wright Field is third generation Italian from Boston's North side and knows most of the Parker House staff well. So he called ahead and asked them to squeeze me in."

"How do you feel about having some company for dinner?" Keith asked, as he stepped into the street to flag down a taxi for her. "Just for old time's sake," he added.

Kelly hesitated briefly before agreeing to meet him for dinner. Keith took Kelly's flight bag in hand while opening the taxi door for her.

Noticing her hesitation, he asked what was wrong. "Sounds like you're not so sure about it."

"No. I mean yes. I'm fine with it. Meet me in the hotel lounge around six." Kelly said.

"Six? Let's see; you mean 1800 hours, don't you?" Keith said with an amused grin.

Kelly's only response was to stick out her tongue at him.

✯ ✯ ✯

Parker House Lounge
1800 hours

"I ordered your favorite drink, Kelly," Keith said, placing a hurricane on the coffee table in front of her.

"Thanks. So tell what you've been up to."

"Same old stuff for the most part although I have done some consulting with naval intelligence."

"Something to do with code breaking?"

"Can't talk about what I do, Kelly . . ."

"You're not going to remind me that 'loose lips sink ships,' are you?"

"It's got nothing to do with you. Of course, I know that you're not going to go around blabbing about what I tell you but if someone overheard us they might not view it in the same light. So you'd better not be heard asking me questions about my work. Or you might find yourself under investigation by the security types."

"Are you serious?"

"Yes. Entirely. Now, change of subject. I'd like to hear more about this guy who managed to snag you for his wife—or were you the one who did the snagging?" he asked.

"I'd say it was more of a mutual snagging, Keith. Anyway, Kirk is a brigadier general on General Arnold's staff."

That revelation elicited a low whistle of respect from Whitaker. "How old is this guy anyway?"

"Thirty."

"Thirty! And he's already got his first star. That's pretty impressive! I think LeMay and Norstad were both in their mid-thirties when they were promoted to brigadier general."

Kelly nodded. "Arnold relies heavily on Kirk. Apparently, he plays the role of General Arnold's alter ego."

"Interesting. But that could prove to be an awkward position to be in at times."

"Yes. I can see where it has its downside," she said. "But since Arnold thinks very highly of Kirk and values his judgment on matters—military and otherwise—he's apparently spared a lot of the heat that other staff officers are subjected to."

"Okay. Now it's your turn. What have you been up to?" Whitaker asked.

"Helping out in Operations at Wright Field. And handling an occasional administrative flight."

"Have you had an opportunity to do any test flying?"

Kelly shook her head. "Not yet."

"Isn't the WASP program about to be shut down?"

"Yes. In fact, most of the WASPs have already been released from duty. The only reason I'm still flying is because Kirk pulled some strings to get me assigned to Wright for my last few months of active duty."

A tall slender man who had been relaxing in one of the overstuffed chairs a few feet away from where Keith and Kelly were sitting looked over at Kelly and said, "Excuse me, but aren't you Kelly Rossiter, the woman who went around to the B-29 bases and taught the pilots how to minimize the chances of an engine fire while getting the bird safely into the air?"

"Yes, but how did you recognize me?"

"Your picture was printed in papers all over the country when they ran the story about how you managed to keep a B-29 in the air until the crew got out safely. Now, I didn't mean to be nosy but I couldn't help overhearing your comment about wanting to do some test flying. But before I say anything more, let me introduce myself, my name is John Myers and I'm a test pilot for both Northrop and Lockheed."

Kelly leaned over to reach for his outstretched hand. "Nice to meet you, Mr. Myers. This is an old friend Keith Whitaker."

Keith threw Myers a casual salute by way of greeting since he wasn't close enough to shake his hand.

"We're about to have dinner Mr. Myers," Kelly said.

"Can we dispense with the formalities? I go by John and you? Is it all right if I call you Kelly?"

"Sure. And why don't you join us for dinner, John, if you have no other plans."

"Thanks for the invitation, Kelly, but you know the old saw about three being a crowd."

"Keith and I are simply friends, John. It's not as though you'd be interrupting a romantic tryst. *Not anymore, at least*, she thought. So I'm sure Keith won't mind. Will you Keith?"

Although John Myers may not have picked up on it, Keith knew from considerable exposure to the subtle nuances in Kelly's tone that there was only one acceptable answer to her query.

"No, of course not. We'd both like to hear more about your experiences as a test pilot."

"And I'd be curious to know how one manages to be a test pilot for two different companies," Kelly added.

Myers chuckled. "I'm a lawyer but flying is my first love so when an opportunity came along to join the legal staff at Lockheed I jumped at it. I already had a lot of flying experience under my belt—more than most of the pilots on their air staff, as it turned out. So instead of handling legal matters, my first assignments were to shuttle Lockheed management around the country to meetings and conferences. Then when they discovered firsthand the breadth of my piloting skills, I was asked to test fly their newest aircraft."

A few minutes later the headwaiter came over to inform them that their table was ready.

After they finished ordering their meals, John picked up the thread of the conversation from where he had left off in the lounge.

"When Jack Northrop heard about my piloting experience he contacted me and requested a meeting. Since I felt a strong loyalty to Lockheed, the first thing I did was to go and see Bob Gross, Chairman of the Lockheed Board. He actually encouraged me to meet with Northrop, saying they were good friends. So I did.

"The upshot of that meeting was an offer to become Northrop's chief engineering test pilot, which I accepted on the spot. When I reported back to Bob Gross, he congratulated me but said that he was not about to lose someone of my experience so I was kept on at Lockheed as a test pilot also. So there you have it. The whole story in a nutshell.

"As the chief engineering test pilot for Northrop, I'm in the market for someone who can handle the scheduling function and do some occasional flying for me as well. Is this something that might be of interest to you, Kelly?"

"Yes. Does this mean I might get to do some test flying, too?"

"Possibly. Certainly your handling of the B-29 crisis is strong evidence of how you would function under extreme pressure."

"One other experience you should be aware of, John. I had an encounter with compressibility in a high-speed dive in a Mustang."

"How did you handle that?"

"I got a jump on the situation because I began pulling out of the dive when I still had sufficient altitude and the controls were still responsive."

"That's the sign of a good pilot—test pilot or otherwise," Myers said. "One who recognizes the point at which prompt action is required if he—or she—is going to survive the flight."

After their meals arrived, John continued to regale Kelly, in particular, with anecdotes about his flying experiences with such highly experimental aircraft as a flying wing and a rocket aircraft as well as more conventional aircraft including the P-38 Lightning and P-61 Black Widow.

When they got to the dessert course all three opted for the Parker House specialty of Boston cream pie accompanied by a second cup of coffee. It was at this point that John told Kelly he was prepared to make her an offer of employment as soon as her WASP assignment came to an end.

Kelly thanked him and said she would be in touch.

A short time later Myers excused himself and Kelly and Keith went back out to the lounge.

"Whew!" Keith said, shaking his head in disbelief. "Now there's a guy who's not lacking in self-confidence."

"Your sarcasm is uncalled for, Keith. High self confidence is the hallmark of all test pilots. If the typical test pilot had any doubts his or hers ability to handle a difficult—or even dangerous—situation, most of them would have chosen a different career."

"Are you serious about a career in test piloting?" Keith asked.

"Sure."

"Since it is pretty dangerous work, Kelly, how does your husband feel about this whole idea?"

"He's opposed to it."

"So you plan to disregard his feelings?"

"Uh huh. I already told him that I intended to build a career in aviation and that he'd darned well better get used to the idea."

"Good thing you aren't my wife. I wouldn't tolerate you getting involved in that line of work."

"Now that I know how you feel, Keith, I can see that our relationship would have been doomed even if you had stayed on the West Coast. Not that it matters at this point anyway."

"How about inviting me up to your room for a nightcap, Kelly?"

"In light of the fact that I'm now a married woman I don't think that would be such a good idea." *In fact, it could be downright dangerous in addition to being totally inappropriate*, she thought.

"What does that mean? That you don't trust me, Kelly?"

"It's not just you, Keith."

His eyes widened in surprise. "Oh, I see."

"Besides, I'm really tired so I think it's time to call it an evening."

"Okay. I'll see you to your room."

"That isn't necessary."

"When are you flying back to Wright Field?"

"I plan on leaving Boston around nine tomorrow morning. So I'll grab a quick breakfast here around seven-thirty, then head over to Logan."

"Can I join you for breakfast, Kelly?"

She shook her head. "I'm supposed to have breakfast with a colonel who I'm going to be flying back to Wright Field."

They parted after a perfunctory hug and the exchange of a kiss on each other's cheek.

✷ ✷ ✷

XX

When Kelly walked into the dining room the following morning a youthful looking full colonel rose from a corner table and walked towards her with a look of surprise written across his face.

"Kelly Rossiter?"

"That's me. And you must be Colonel Matthews."

"Forget the rank, Kelly. Paul Matthews is what I prefer to be called."

"Yes, sir."

"You're a lot younger than I expected," he said, as he pulled out the chair for her to be seated.

"I could say the same thing about you, Colonel!"

"Touche! Anyway," Matthews continued, as he sat down across from her, "I've heard a lot about your flying adventures, Kelly. So, I guess I expected to see someone in their early to mid-thirties. And you don't look like you could be a day over twenty-one. But then I suppose you must be a few years older than that."

"Yes, sir. I'll turn twenty-five in a couple of weeks."

"I have to tell you, Kelly, what most impresses me about your record is your ability to handle both fighters and bombers and apparently excel at piloting both types."

"Well, sir, not to boast, but each of my flying instructors has pointed out that I'm an example of a natural pilot; that the plane is a virtual extension of me. And to tell the truth, I've always known intuitively how to get the aircraft to do what I want it to do. I don't ever have to say to myself 'okay what am I going to do next'. I just do it automatically."

"A valuable quality for a pilot to have," Matthews said. "Especially when faced with a situation that requires an instantaneous response. And I gather there has been more than one occasion when it's served you well."

"That's for certain, Colonel Matthews."

"Paul."

"I'm sorry, sir. I'm simply not going to be comfortable calling you by your first name. I'm not used to calling any high-ranking officers by their first names. Except for my husband, of course."

"Your husband?"

"Yes. My husband is a general officer. His name is Kirk Singleton."

"So Kirk got his first star! That's great news! I know Kirk quite well because we worked together in the plans section during the early years of the war trying to make an educated guess as to how many and what type of aircraft we'd need to conduct a successful air war, plus determine the numbers of different categories of pilots that would be required to fly those aircraft. When the rest of us in the group got carried away and began projecting numbers that were totally unrealistic, Kirk was the one who would rein us in and force us to take another look at the projections based upon the availability of limited resources and the demands being made upon them by the other services."

Kelly nodded. "That sounds like my husband all right. Ever the pragmatist. A corollary to that rule is that emotions can never be trusted because they'll inevitably lead one astray."

"I gather you're the exception to that rule, Kelly."

"I like to think so, Colonel Matthews."

There was a momentary lull in the conversation while they placed their breakfast order.

Her dining partner then asked, "Since you're going to be formal and call me Colonel Matthews should I refer to you as Mrs. Singleton?"

"No. Kelly is fine. Besides, if you were going to be formal then I would encourage you to use Rossiter. I'm going by my maiden name until my military service is over."

"Did Kirk agreed to that?"

"Yes. But then he didn't have much choice."

"Hmm," Matthews said, looking reflectively at Kelly. "I have to admit, Kelly, I thought Kirk might end up an old 'batch' because he always seemed completely impervious to the overtures of a woman. And I'm sure you won't be surprised to hear that there were quite a few women who would like to have dated him."

"Neither of your comments surprise me. But the Kirk that I've come to know is a man who definitely enjoys the company of the opposite sex."

"Especially beautiful examples of that gender, I see," Matthews added.

Kelly shrugged, not knowing what to say. She'd almost forgotten how to blush since the compliment was one she had received countless times before and knew to be true.

"Can you tell me what brings you to Wright Field, Colonel Matthews?"

"Sure. As the war winds down, Kelly, I've been made responsible for collecting as many examples of German aeronautical technology as I can get my hands on. So as our troops advance into Germany proper, my Air Technical Intelligence Teams are going to be following closely behind, scouring the liberated areas for those items which are still intact. Whatever we do get our hands on is going to be shipped back to the states to Wright Field for analysis and evaluation. That's the reason I'm flying out to Wright. To see what needs to be done to ready the base for the arrival of all these aircraft and associated equipment, plus the pilots and the necessary support staff. In addition, we'll probably have to provide housing for a cadre of German aircraft mechanics. That alone could prove to be a logistical nightmare!"

"I don't envy you your assignment, sir, but if German aeronautical technology is as advanced as we hear it is, then I can see the importance of getting our hands on as much of it as possible."

"What do you plan to do once the war is over?" Matthews asked.

"I've been promised a job with John Myers's team at Northrop, which I can claim as soon as my WASP assignment ends. In the meantime I'll continue to make these occasional shuttle runs. And the head of the Fighter

Flight Test Division at Wright Field did promise to give me a couple of test flights before I finish my assignment there."

"If any pilot can be referred to as a genius, Myers would be it," Matthews said. "This past summer he spent several weeks in the Pacific showing our pilots how to handle the Black Widow. According to the feedback from the P-61 pilots, Myers is a magician in the air but, unlike most magicians, he's one who is willing to share his secrets with his fellow pilots. In fact, Myers is so good that he's earned the nickname of Maestro from his peers, if one can say that he has any peers!"

"So I wouldn't be making a mistake by going to work for him."

"Nope. It's bound to be a fantastic experience!"

Matthews was silent for the next minute or so, tapping his lips with the tip of his forefinger. Kelly waited, wondering what was going through his mind.

He placed his forearms on the table, leaned forward and looked intently at Kelly. The expression on his face suggested that he had come to a decision about something.

"What aircraft have you flown?"

"The Thunderbolt, Mustang, Lightning, B-25, C-54 and the B-29, of course."

"I gather you haven't had an opportunity to fly the Bell P-59 yet?"

"No, sir. I haven't. But based on what I've heard about its performance, I don't think I'm missing out on much."

"I'll tell you what. When I get an Me-262 back to the states, I'll check you out in it.

"Really?"

Yes. I'll get you a temporary assignment as a civilian test pilot with NACA."

"You can do that?"

"Sure. I have friends at pretty high levels in the aviation world. And some of them are indebted to me so I can call in a few of the credits that have been sitting there waiting to be collected."

"Wow!" was all Kelly could think to say.

Matthews responded with a big grin. "And there's one other thing with which I may need some help. We're going to be shipping back examples of German piston engine aircraft like the BF-109, Focke-Wulf 190 (Shrike), and whatever else we can get our hands on. Once they're off-loaded from the ship, I'll need pilots to pick them up at Newark and fly them back to Wright Field. I'd like to be able to call upon you to help me out because I have no idea how many Army Air Force pilots will still be on active duty then."

"I'll be happy to help you out, Colonel Matthews. It would be an honor."

"Excellent. But it might be a good idea to get checked out in the P-59 before trying out the Messerschmitt."

A half an hour later they were traveling through the Sumner Tunnel on their way to Logan Airport and within an hour were winging their way back to Wright Field. They took turns flying the C-47 but kept the cockpit conversation to a minimum. Kelly was still on a high between John Myers' offer and Colonel Matthews's promise. Matthews, on the other hand, was preoccupied with concerns about the feasibility of carrying out the study of German aircraft technology at Wright Field.

When they taxied in from the end of the runway at Wright Field approximately four hours later Matthews pointed out an ominous looking fighter parked on the flight line between a Mustang and a Thunderbolt.

"That looks like one of the German fighter planes I've seen on aircraft recognition flash cards," Kelly said.

"Yep. That's the Shrike, Kelly. Probably the second best all-around fighter of the war, after the Mustang."

"How was it acquired?"

"From what I understand, after their breakout from St Lo, Patton's Third Army overran an advanced Luftwaffe base and got to the aircraft before the Germans could blow it up."

Moments later they arrived at the Operations building where a staff car was waiting to whisk Colonel Matthews to General Kirby's headquarters.

"Who is General Kirby?" Kelly asked.

"He's the head of the Air Service Technical Command (ASTC). That's the organization which controls the Wright Field Experimental Laboratories and has oversight responsibilities for the acquisition, storage and evaluation of all German aircraft and related aeronautical equipment."

When Kelly checked in with Operations, Captain Simpson told her that Major Feranno wanted to see her as soon as she arrived.

A few minutes later she was knocking on the door to Feranno's office.

"Come in, Kelly," he said, waving her in. "How was your room at the Parker House?"

"It was fine sir. Thanks for calling and booking it for me."

"My pleasure, Kelly. And how was your return flight? More pleasant than the outgoing one I hope."

"Yes, sir. The flight with General Hardison went just as you predicted," she said, with a smile.

"Sorry about that, Kelly."

"No need to be, sir. I learned a long time ago that it takes all kinds."

"The main reason I wanted to see you," he interjected, "was to tell you I had a test flight lined up for you."

"That's great, sir!"

"Well, it's not exactly the most challenging assignment but it is important. One of the Mustangs has been fitted with a new gun sight which needs to be tested. There's a small island up in Lake Erie which is used as a firing range. A target has been set up on its eastern edge. You can't miss the target because it's located on a small peninsula that juts out into the lake. I'd like you to fly up there tomorrow morning and test out the gun sight."

"All right, sir. Any special instructions?"

"Yes. There are always fishermen around the area despite the fact that the island and surrounding waters have been posted as a military firing range. They know they don't belong there so make a low pass and fire off a short burst as you overfly them. They'll get the message, pack up, and move on.

"After that I want you to make a number of high speed passes. Make sure you have the target properly lined up in the gun sight and let her rip. The trigger is the button on the end of the stick."

"Yes, sir. Will do. And thanks for the assignment."

"You're welcome."

Everything developed the following morning pretty much as Feranno had predicted. As Kelly was approaching the island she spotted a number of fishermen working the nearby waters. On her first low pass over the fishing boats she opted not to fire a warning burst, hoping instead that waggling her wings would get the message across and encourage them to move on. What she got instead were a number of raised arms with clenched fists as well as several middle finger salutes.

She wondered idly if their response would have been any different if they had known the pilot was a woman. It might have been worse Kelly decided. The hell with it, since they were not going to cooperate then she had no qualms about shattering the morning calm. After firing a warning burst, Kelly made a half a dozen runs on the target and as far as she could tell made a number of hits. When the pictures from the gun camera were developed they would tell the story about how accurate her firing had been.

If this was typical of the kind of test flights Feranno was going to assign her, Kirk's worries were unnecessary. Unless, of course, she ended up dying from boredom as a result.

As the holiday season approached everyone's thoughts were focused on the news from the Western front where the Germans had launched a major offensive in order to try and drive a wedge between the American and British forces, breach the allied line, and recapture Antwerp.

And at home the United States Supreme Court had declared the exclusion order unconstitutional when used as a basis for detaining loyal American citizens without cause. The wholesale incarceration of Japanese Americans in internment camps would soon be history.

At Wright Field there was no let-up in the testing schedule except for Christmas Day itself. But shortly after the beginning of the New Year, Major Feranno informed Kelly that her assignment at Wright Field would end on the last day of January. That same day the exclusion order was rescinded in its entirety. A few days later Kelly received a letter from Ami Takahashi stating that she and her mother and brother would be leaving the internment camp at Minidoka, Idaho, for Seattle within the week. They had heard from Mr. Takahashi, who had been held in another location somewhere in Montana, and expected him to get home about the same time as they did. The overall tone of the letter was joyous but there were undertones of anxiety, as well. Ami was worried about where they would be able to stay until the house could be repaired and made livable again. Although she didn't mention it, Kelly knew that Ami was also worried about her father's state of mind and whether or not he'd be able to adjust to life on the outside again. Kelly pondered the situation for a few hours then decided to stick her neck out and call her father to see if there's anything he could do to help or would be willing to do to help.

"Hi Dad! It's your favorite daughter calling to ask for a favor."

"Well, since my favorite daughter is also my only daughter, I guess I don't have much choice," he said in a playful voice.

"You haven't heard the favor I'm going to ask yet. When you do, you may not be so quick to give your approval."

"Go ahead–try me."

Kelly crossed her fingers, her arms and legs–even her eyes, until somebody walked by, glanced over, and gave her a strange look.

"I got a letter from Ami Takahashi today saying that they would be leaving Minidoka for home within the next several days. I just wondered if you could help them find a place to stay while they get their house back in livable condition. I know that's asking a lot, Dad, considering how you feel about the Japanese . . ."

"I still feel the same way towards the Japanese, Kelly, but I've been doing a lot of soul-searching. I finally got it through my thick head that Ami and her family are Americans and should be treated accordingly. Plus it helped to remember that your mother experienced some prejudice because she was part Indian. So this is what I've done.

"I paid my maintenance crew overtime to go over to the Takahashi's house, clean it up and make whatever repairs were necessary to make it livable. They've been going over after their regular shift for the most part–not without a certain amount of grumbling mind you–but they did a great job of fixing it up. And now that the war is winding down I was able to pick up a new refrigerator for our house so I had the maintenance crew move our old one over to the Takahashi's and take their old one to the dump. Shortly before they're expected home I'll stock it with food for them. It won't be Japanese food I'm afraid, but it will be good wholesome American food."

"Dad, that's fantastic! I'm so proud of you!"

"Thanks, honey, I thought you'd be pleased. And that's not all I'm going to do. I intend to offer Mr. Takahashi a job at the plant," he said.

"It has to be a real job, Dad. He's a proud man, and he would turn down anything that smacks of a handout."

"Don't worry, Kelly. I wouldn't pull that on anyone. If I'm going to pay someone to work for me, they'll be expected to produce something useful for the company. What I have in mind for Mr. Takahashi is a lower level job in the engineering department. To begin with anyway. As I recall, he had an electrical engineering degree. If he's as smart as I think he is, he can probably work his way up to a senior position in the department."

"I can't thank you enough for what you're doing, Dad." Kelly said.

"Just doing my part to try and make amends for the way in which they were treated, honey."

"Got to go, Dad. Talk to you again soon. Love you!"

"I love you too, Kelly. Bye."

✯ ✯ ✯

XXI

By the end of the first full week of February Kelly had wrapped up her affairs in Dayton, said goodbye to her fellow pilots, most all of whom wished her well in her new assignment with Northrop, and had arranged a hop for her to the Northrop plant in Hawthorne, California.

But two days before she was scheduled to fly out to California John Myers called to inform her that someone in the upper levels of corporate management had overruled his decision to bring Kelly onboard as the head of Operations Scheduling.

Myers was very apologetic but said that he had to limit the number of executive decisions he chose to challenge. Only those which were crucial to the success of his testing program were worth fighting to reverse.

Kelly, although disappointed, said she understood, and she did, having seen her father follow that same practice in his dealings with both his own board of directors and his suppliers.

The question that now entered her mind was whether Colonel Matthews would be able to make good on his promise to give her an opportunity to fly the German jet.

The allies were once again on the move after the setback at the Battle of the Bulge and the war could very well be over by the summer. If so, there would be plenty of male pilots back in the states looking for flying opportunities. And if that turned out to be the case, where did that leave her? She hadn't bothered to prepare a back-up plan, but after Myers' call, Kelly decided it made sense to go back home to Seattle and lend her father a helping hand in doing some preliminary planning on how to phase out of wartime production and gear up for reentry into the peacetime market. If Matthews did contact her, she could always break away from the plant and fly back to Wright Field.

In the meantime she hoped to be able to convince her father to purchase a company airplane and make her the company pilot. Rossiter's market for avionics equipment was already a national one and was likely to grow even more rapidly after the war was over and the airlines proceeded to update their aircraft fleets to handle the expected increase in business and personal travel.

Kelly arrived home on Valentine's Day to be greeted with a huge bouquet of lavender roses from Kirk. Along with a very loving note.

Dearest Kelly,

I'm not by any means a gifted writer so the words I use in this love letter (and that's exactly what it is) were penned by someone else.

I don't mean that someone else wrote this letter, only that my choice of words is not original.

The lavender rose has always signified a number of things. It's a symbol of enchantment and love at first sight. And despite the stormy beginning to our relationship there's no doubt in my mind that I fell in love with you as soon as I set eyes on you; that I was enchanted with you as soon as you made that explosive entrance into your father's outer office!

Lavender, as you are no doubt aware, is also the color associated with royalty.

And the way you carry yourself, the way you behave—all shout the same message: this is a unique woman: one who is a fount of innate class and dignity.

So my beautiful and classy wife, this is written with much love and appreciation for what I have in you—and what you bring to me!

Kirk

The lavender roses were absolutely exquisite and a nice change from the red roses that Keith had sent her the previous year on both her birthday and Valentine's Day. And the note from Kirk absolutely bowled her over.

The following Saturday she was sitting in the kitchen having a mid-morning cup of coffee with her father when the front doorbell rang. It was Ami Takahashi looking much better than she had at Minidoka.

Kelly invited Ami in and ushered her into the kitchen, relieved that she no longer had to worry about her father's cool treatment of her friend.

Rossiter rose to his feet and held out his hand to greet Ami.

"Welcome home, Ami," he said with genuine warmth in his voice.

Ami smiled and said, "Thanks, Mr. Rossiter. And my deepest thanks to you for what you have done for our family."

"My pleasure, Ami. I'm hoping that your neighbors will come to see things from a more balanced perspective too. Your neighbor across the street—what was his name?"

"Do you mean Mr. Diefenbaker?" Ami asked.

"Yes. That's who it was. One Saturday morning when I was there checking on how the work was progressing , he wandered across the street. A number of your other neighbors showed up when they saw us talking. At one point I asked Diefenbacker if he was German. He admitted that he was. He said that his grandparents had come to the U.S. back in the twenties.. So I asked him how we could be sure he wasn't an enemy of the United States. He bridled at that, of course, saying it was downright ridiculous as well as insulting.

"I kept pushing him, saying, 'How do we know you're not lying. Maybe the safest thing to do would have been to put all you Germans in a detention camp too. Then we wouldn't have to worry about any fifth column activity in our country.

"At one point I thought he was going to take a swing at me then I saw the look of anger slowly fade from his face to be replaced by a look of understanding."

" 'All right, buddy, you made your point,' " he said, somewhat grudgingly, before turning away and going back across the street to his own house."

"We really are indebted to you, Mr. Rossiter, in more ways than I imagined. Here is a small gift from my mother as a thank you for all your help," Ami said, as she handed him a box wrapped in decorative paper. I should tell you in advance, it's a traditional Japanese dessert called Botamochi. They're sweet rice balls, Mr. Rossiter. I hope you like rice," she added hesitantly.

"Like rice, Amy? Why my favorite dessert happens to be rice pudding."

At that announcement Ami breathed a sigh of relief.

"Dad has a real sweet tooth," Kelly said, speaking for the first time since she greeted Ami at the door. "You can never go wrong bringing him something that appeals to it."

"Hmmm. Sure smells good," he said after removing the paper and taking the lid off the box. "Think I'll try one right now. Have a seat, Ami. Can we get you something to drink?"

"I developed a taste for coffee at the detention center, so a cup of it would taste good if you have some already made."

"There's always a pot of coffee perking on the back burner of the stove in this house, Ami," Kelly said, as she poured a cup for her friend. "Dad likes his coffee almost as much as his sweets."

"More!" he said, with a big grin. "I can go a day or two without my sweets but only a couple of hours without my coffee. On a more serious note, Ami, how are your parents doing?"

"I'm afraid that my mother harbors a lot of bitterness, Mr. Rossiter."

Rossiter nodded his head. "I'm sure there a lot of Japanese-Americans who feel the same way. And who can blame them? The country did let you down, Ami. There's no doubt about it. Mass hysteria fanned by intemperate comments from senior military commanders—who should have known better—all the way down to those irresponsible journalists who deliberately set out to inflame the public's feelings against Americans of your ethnic background. I predict it will take decades, not merely years, to get this behind us."

Rossiter studied her reflectively for a minute or two. Then on a hunch he told her about his plan to offer her father a job in the company and asked what she thought of his idea.

"It may be just what is needed to give him a sense of purpose again, Mr. Rossiter. You see I've been a lot more worried about my father than my mother."

Kelly's father nodded. "I would think this whole experience has been more traumatic for the men of the family than for the women. Not that it's been easy for anyone," he quickly added.

"I see him as being mentally adrift," Ami said. "Work has always been the best therapy for him when he is troubled in spirit. And to be forced to sit around and pass the time away in some pointless, purposeless existence is the worst thing that could have happened to him."

"I understand that he has a degree in Electrical Engineering. Is that correct?"

"Yes, he graduated from Stanford in 1923, a few years after I was born." Ami said, after sipping the last of her coffee.

"He would have to start in a lower level position, Ami, but it would be an engineering assignment. Do you think he would be willing to accept a position like that?

Or would it hurt his pride?"

"I'm not sure he has any pride left to hurt. In answer to your first question, Mr. Rossiter, I do think he would be pleased at your offer."

"Good. One other thing I would encourage him to do is to take some night courses to get current in the field. There have been so many developments in recent years as a result of all the war-sponsored research."

"I know that it was always his intention to go on for a master's degree but the responsibilities of a young family forced him to postpone that. However, pursuing that degree while working in the field would be just the shot in the arm that he needs. At least that's what I think."

"Do you have a working phone yet?"

"No, Mr. Rossiter. And I have no idea at this point when we will be able to have one again."

"Did your father know that you were going to stop by here this morning?"

"Oh, yes. He did."

"Tell you what; why don't you tell him to contact me at the office early next week, and I'll take it from there. And we won't let on about this little conversation you and I have had. Okay?"

"That would probably be best, Mr. Rossiter."

After pouring a cup of coffee for Ami and a refill for her father Kelly had excused herself so her father and Ami could speak privately. She returned to the kitchen after overhearing what sounded like the end of the conversation between the two of them.

As she walked Ami to the door Kelly proposed they get together for lunch the following week.

"Where shall we go?" Ami asked.

"Why don't you take the bus down to my father's plant. We can have lunch in the executive cafeteria. They really put on a fantastic lunch there! That way we can sit and chat as long as we want to with no interruptions." *Or dirty looks or nasty cracks* Kelly thought, but left unsaid.

✯ ✯ ✯

XXII

Three days before the February meeting of the Executive Board, Kelly's father was discussing with her the need to expand the plant in order to provide space for the projected increase in productive capacity.

"Dad, it's time to take a close look at the way the existing space is being utilized," Kelly said. "There are some obvious inefficiencies that need to be corrected. And the pressure of meeting wartime production goals made those inefficiencies stand out in bold relief."

"I can't argue with you there, Kelly. But we're still going to need additional space beyond that which becomes available simply by reorganizing the existing production lines. Those new products that will be coming out of the research lab in the near future are going to need a newer, more modern production facility."

"But there's not enough room on the property to put up a new building—even a mid-sized one," she said.

"No, but there is a good size piece of land not very far from the plant, which, I understand, will probably go on the market within the next month."

"Oh? I can't think of anything nearby which fits that description."

"Yeah. It's there all right. And if you were thinking objectively right now, you'd know where it is and who owns it."

Kelly walked over to the window and looked out over the parking lot that abutted a choice piece of land her father had tried to buy several years earlier. Unfortunately, there was no clear title to the property. A series of claims and counterclaims had tied up the property in court for the past several years with no resolution to the dispute anywhere in sight.

Her mind made a three hundred and sixty degree sweep of the area surrounding her father's plant. There was no property of any size that hadn't already been developed except, of course, for Sal Locarno's farm. But Sal would never put the farm up for sale. He was too attached to it. Wasn't he?

Kelly turned around, leaned back against the window sill and looked at her father questioningly.

"From the expression on your face I'm guessing that you might have figured out which property I'm referring to."

"The only property I can think of that fits the description is Sal Locarno's farm, but I find it hard to believe that he would put it up for sale."

"Sal's been battling cancer, Kelly. He's no longer able to work the farm and he can't afford to pay someone else to do it for him. But he's not selling the whole shebang. Just an eight acre piece of it."

"The entire farm can't be much over that, dad."

"Twelve acres. That's how big it is. So, he plans on keeping the house and four acres. Which includes the barn and most of the outbuildings. I've already touched base with a real estate agent who's a member of the local rotary organization and who has a reputation for integrity. He's told me what the going price would be for that type and amount of acreage. I thought I'd offer Locarno ten percent above the market value."

"That seems more than fair, Dad."

"How do you think your husband will feel about this?"

Kelly shook her head. "Kirk will be disappointed that's for sure. I think he had hopes of buying out his uncle and operating the farm himself after he retired from the Army Air Force."

"That's a long time away to be attempting to do any realistic retirement planning now. There's no way he can possibly know at this point in his life what he's going to want to do in twenty-five or thirty years."

"You're right about that, Dad. He can't. I just hope that he'll buy that line of reasoning."

"I gather that you're not going to try and persuade me to look around for another piece of land, then?"

"No. I'm not because there isn't any other land that's close by and available. And I agree that there's no room for expansion in the existing space. So it seems to me that you have enough ammunition to make a strong pitch to the board Wednesday night."

"You've matured a lot in the last year, Kelly.

"How so?"

"Well, although you always had a strong intellect, your emotions would sometimes cloud your judgment and get in the way of you making a rational decision."

"And that's what you expected to happen this time?"

"Possibly, but not necessarily."

"Sorry to disappoint you, Dad," she said, with a quick grin and a playful punch to his shoulder as she passed him on the way to the door.

Kelly hadn't taken more than a half dozen steps when a thought suddenly struck her. "Are you going to bring my suggestion to purchase a company plane before the board?"

"I've been looking over your proposal, Kelly. Do you really think it's going to pay for itself by making business travel more efficient and less costly?"

"Definitely. Of course, this is all predicated on significant growth in the market for our products in the postwar period. But considering the fact that a lot of the suppliers and aircraft firms we deal with are located in the Los Angeles area, the Beechcraft Model 18 can get us there in six hours without having to stop en route to refuel."

"And you think we can pick up a used one for around thirty thousand?

"I'm sure of it," she said. Then as a clincher, Kelly decided to play her winning card. "Furthermore, Dad, Pratt and Whitney *Wasp Juniors* were adopted as the standard power plant for the aircraft shortly after production began."

"Good. Then I don't have to worry about those damnable Wright engines catching fire."

"That was a problem unique to the B-29, Dad."

"Yeah. And it almost did you in, Kelly."

Kelly noticed that her father's eyes watered with that last comment.

So he really does love me, she thought. And with that realization running through her mind, she went up to him, kissed him on the cheek, and hugged him.

The morning after the meeting of the board Kelly met her father in the company cafeteria for coffee.

"How did it go?" she asked.

"They okayed my proposal to purchase the Locarno property, Kelly, but a majority of the members want to hold off on the plane until there's a clearer picture of what kind of growth we're going to experience."

"But we're one of the leading avionics firms in the country, and we are going to have a number of new products available by 1945 or 1946, at the latest, so we're bound to experience significant growth in the postwar market."

"I agree with you, Kelly, but some of the board members felt we needed to proceed with caution. Plus, a few of them wondered if it was merely a ploy of yours to keep flying."

"It isn't! I was thinking of the transportation needs of the business. Mainly, anyway."

"I believe you. And it was a close vote, Kelly. So a number of the board members thought the same way we did."

"What was the vote?"

"Five in favor of, seven against, with two abstentions."

"The best we could have hoped for then was a tie," Kelly said.

"Yes, but it could have been worse, too. The vote could easily have been eight or nine against," her father reminded her.

Kelly was beginning to wonder if her flying days were all behind her. It looked that way unless Colonel Matthews came through with his offer to use her to shuttle German aircraft from Newark to Wright Field. *Damn it*, she thought, her *options to continue flying somewhere for someone, were rapidly evaporating.*

✫ ✫ ✫

XXIII

Kelly had only seen Kirk once since their honeymoon trip to San Francisco. He had returned from his assignment to the Pacific in early December and she had flown to Washington for a few days and stayed with him in the Visiting Officers Quarters at Bolling Field. There were a couple of brief phone conversations with him following that visit. Kelly, however, had been reluctant to bring up her father's purchase of the Locarno property.

But Kirk was flying West for a couple of days at the beginning of April to represent the Army Air Force at the ground-breaking ceremony for the new addition to the Rossiter plant. Kelly now regretted that she hadn't broached the subject before, so that he would have had time to digest the news and hopefully accept the fact that his uncle had no choice but to sell off a piece of the property.

Since Kirk planned to arrive the evening before the ceremony, that didn't leave much time to break the news to him. Kelly was pleasantly surprised, however, at Kirk's muted response to the news when she picked him up at the airfield on April 2nd.

"Look, Kell, I won't pretend that I'm thrilled with the news," he said. "But it was becoming increasingly clear that Uncle Sal wouldn't be able to work the farm much longer. And I know that his medical expenses have been piling up. So, if the property had to be sold and developed then I'm happy that it worked to the benefit of your father's business. So what else have you been up to lately in addition to being your father's number one business adviser?"

"Well, you should be happy to hear that I'm pushing hard to get the Board to approve the purchase of a company plane and name me the company pilot."

"Okay. I'd be comfortable with that type of flying assignment, Kell. But when is it supposed to happen?"

"I'm not exactly sure," she said. "They're studying my proposal to buy a used Beechcraft Twin." *Which wasn't quite true but it wasn't quite a lie either,* she thought.

In the meantime, I probably won't be doing any flying unless your old friend Paul Matthews gives me a call."

"You met Paul Matthews?"

"Yep! I had breakfast with him in Boston then flew him back to Wright shortly before I finished my tour of duty there. He thinks a lot of you, Kirk, and seemed genuinely thrilled at the news that you had gotten your first star."

"Yeah, that sounds like Paul all right. Not a jealous bone in his body. He's a real gem, Kell. A fine officer with a first class mind."

"He's going to be collecting examples of German aircraft to ship home to the states for testing and evaluation."

"That's his next assignment?"

"Yep. He told me that as soon as the allies began advancing into Germany his technical intelligence teams would follow along right behind them and as each sector was secured they would comb the area for German aircraft and aeronautical equipment."

"He's probably the ideal man for that type of job. A brilliant engineer and superb pilot who also happens to have finely developed diplomatic skills. Which he'll need when dealing with our British and French allies."

When they got to the house Kirk discovered that Kelly's father was hosting a small dinner party for them that evening. During the course of the evening Kirk was struck by how much better Kelly and her father seemed to be getting along.

"Well," she said, when he questioned her about it later that evening," I think we've both come to accept each other—foibles and all—and by doing so, are able to appreciate the underlying strength of our relationship. Plus, I discovered that he really does love me."

"You mean you actually doubted that?"

"For a while, yes. Oh, I knew that he was proud of my achievements but we clashed so much I was convinced that any affection he felt for me had long since been replaced by feelings of annoyance and frustration."

✧ ✧ ✧

The groundbreaking ceremony went off as planned the following morning. Kelly's father had invited Sal Locarno and assigned him a seat with the visiting dignitaries. Locarno was visibly moved at Bob Rossiter's gesture. Kirk had a chance to visit with his uncle before flying back to Washington and was pleased to discover that Locarno viewed the Rossiter Company as a good neighbor and felt that Bob Rossiter had treated him more than fairly.

A couple of days later Kelly was using her father's office while he was out of the plant at a meeting when his secretary buzzed her and said that she had a call from somebody by the name of Paul Matthews.

"Colonel Matthews?" Kelly said, when she picked up the receiver.

"Hi, Kelly! Yep, it's me all right."

"How are you, sir?"

"Fine. I'm about ready to head back overseas but I have some interesting news for you."

"Oh? What's that?"

"There's been a major shake-up at the Flight Test Division. Major Feranno's been promoted to Lieutenant Colonel and named head of the Fighter Flight Test Section and the Bomber Flight Test section has a new head also, Major Arvid Knudtson. I happen to know that Knudtson's sister is a WASP pilot and that he fully approves of women flying military aircraft. Anyway, here's what I suggest. Feranno has said he would be delighted to get you back."

"To make more administrative flights?" Kelly asked, apprehensively.

"No. But it's not exactly test flying either. For one thing, I'd like you to check out in the 190 before I ask you to shuttle any of them from

Newark to Wright Field. And as far as the YP-59 goes, as I said before if you get checked out in that jet, it will make it easier for you to transition to the ME 262.

"Knudtson can use you, also. The pilots in Bomber Flight Test have to make regular flights out to Wendover Field to keep Tibbets supplied with the parts he needs to keep his B-29s flying. Plus they're running other tests with the B-29 so you would be put to work as soon as you could get back to Wright Field. What do you think, Kelly? Can you help out?

"You're not going to have to ask me twice, Colonel Matthews."

"Good. I thought that would be your answer. By the way, I assume your husband would not be opposed to you doing this kind of flying?"

"No, sir. I shouldn't think he would be."

"Okay. Then how soon can you be ready to report there?"

"Can you give me a week to put things in order back here?"

"Of course. Tell you what, Kelly, give me a call a couple of days before you're ready to head back to Wright, and Colonel Feranno or Major Knudtson will arrange a hop for you from Boeing Field."

"All right, sir. Will do. How soon are you heading back to Europe?"

"Within the next several days but I should be back by in the states by late May or early June."

"Yes, sir. Stay well!"

✯ ✯ ✯

XXIV

There was only one problem. When Kelly got to Wright Field she discovered that Feranno had been given an overseas assignment and her old nemesis Peter Hellman had replaced him as acting head of the Fighter Flight Test Section. The other major change was in the Operations Office. Captain Simpson was gone and in his place was an officious young officer by the name of Logan Lafitte. Lafitte liked to introduce himself as Lieutenant Logan Lafitte from Lake Charles, Louisiana, taking great pleasure in stressing the alliteration in the phrase while pointing out that he was a direct descendent of the famous pirate, Jean Lafitte. Amanda Wilton was nowhere to be seen. Lafitte snickered when Kelly asked about her. He said that Amanda was now a special assistant to Major Hellman and with a salacious tone in his voice and a leering grin added that she was supposedly providing highly personal services to the Major.

Great, Kelly thought.

With the two of them in cahoots she didn't stand the chance of a snowball in hell.

But shortly after she arrived at Wright Field, Colonel Braithwaite, overall Chief of the Flight Test Division, told Kelly that he was temporarily transferring her to the Bomber Flight Test Section. In addition to transporting B-29 parts out to Tibbets at Wendover, they made several long distance flights while carrying a nine thousand pound weight simulating the weight of a new, highly-destructive bomb that was under development. Kelly was reminded of Kirk's comment about there being something in the wind which could bring the war in the Pacific to an abrupt end. And all of the pilots had heard rumors about the development of an atomic bomb. So putting two and two together, it seemed pretty clear what type of mission Tibbets was preparing for.

The best part of the assignment to the Bomber Flight Test Section, however, was the privilege that Kelly was routinely given of flying from the left seat on many of the missions in acknowledgment of her expertise with the B-29.

By early May, Hellman had been reassigned to Muroc Army Air Field in Southern California and Rob Latimer, now a major, was the new permanent head of the Fighter Flight Test Section. Latimer made a point of contacting Kelly to ask her if she would like to return to the Fighter Test Section. He assured Kelly that he would begin assigning her test flights on a regular basis if she did return.

Although Kelly enjoyed working for Knudtson, she jumped at the opportunity to return to the Fighter Flight Test Section, especially with Latimer at the controls.

A few days after returning to Fighter Flight Test she was given the chance to check out in the YP-59.

As it turned out, Amanda had followed Peter Hellman out to Muroc Field and was allowed to check out in one of the YP-59s assigned there.

So Kelly wouldn't be the first woman to fly a jet. But that didn't bother her in the least because she had never seen herself as being in competition with Amanda, or anyone else for that matter.

Latimer checked Kelly out himself. He climbed up on the wing and knelt down on one knee so he was at eye level with her as she sat in the cockpit.

After a review of those instruments and gauges which were unique to the jet, Latimer gave Kelly a couple of further warnings. "You can wring the bird out and see what you think of its overall performance but don't attempt any spin recoveries. And remember, once you're close to touchdown you're committed because the jet engine can't deliver the rapid acceleration needed for another go-around. That's the way it is with these babies." He hopped down off the wing and gestured to her to start the engines.

A few minutes later the tailpipes belched black smoke and red flame upon engine start-up. Kelly watched the gauge as the critical exhaust gas temperature came up to the point where she could began her take-off roll. As the aircraft gradually picked up speed, Kelly was struck by the fact that the whining of the jet engines was a lot more impressive than the amount of thrust they delivered.

After using up virtually the whole length of the runway she finally got airborne and began a gradual climb to cruising altitude. The engine noise was now behind her and the sensation was almost that of being in a glider.

The aircraft's handling characteristics proved to be generally better than average. The onset of stalls was gradual and the turning radius was excellent in tight turns. Since spin recovery was iffy, Kelly took Latimer's advice and decided not to check it out. Another drawback was the tendency of the aircraft to drift. The need to make continuous small corrections to keep it tracking properly would be a liability in combat when the pilot needed a stable gun platform.

All too soon the half hour was up and it was time to return to base. The landing was routine and as she taxied in from the end of the runway, her ears were assaulted once again by the banshee like screaming of the jet engines accompanied by clouds of black smoke.

It was May 8, 1945. A day that Kelly would never forget. Not only because she had been given the privilege of flying the first Air Force jet but upon returning to base and checking in at Operations, Latimer informed her that Germany had surrendered unconditionally the previous morning in Reims, France.

The spirit of jubilation in the Ops office was something to behold. Bedlam reigned. Kelly was immediately caught up in the impromptu celebration, and, if only for that brief time, was made to feel like one of the pilots. Latimer gave her a big hug, then handed her a bottle of beer. The rest of the pilots all gave her a slap on the back in a gesture of camaraderie which she was not to experience again for years to come.

A few days later, Major Latimer called Kelly into his office.

"Colonel Matthews told me to get you checked out in the 190 so you'd be prepared to help him fly them to Wright Field as soon they arrive in port.

The following week Latimer asked Kelly if she was willing to pick up a 190 at Pittsburgh airport and ferry it back to Freeman Field, which was only an hour's flying time away from Wright Field. Latimer didn't realize that she hadn't actually flown the Shrike yet.

Kelly agreed to do so based only on the knowledge she had acquired from a couple of readings of the flight manual. But that was how she had learned to fly the P-51, a fifteen minute survey of the flight manual while seated in the cockpit of the Mustang followed by a couple of practice take-offs and landings.

The flight to Freeman Field was uneventful until Kelly began her letdown. When she reached for the electrically operated elevator trim control, the result was completely unexpected and nearly disastrous as it cycled to a full-up position. The Shrike reacted by pitching up abruptly. What the devil was going on? Kelly tried to manually override the trim. No change! After backing off on the power she managed to find a power setting that would allow her to maintain straight and level flight while making some forward progress. She tried to correct the trim again but to no avail. It was locked in the full nose up position.

For the last few minutes she had been keeping an eye out for a place to land. Up ahead off to her right she spotted a small dirt strip. That would have to do!

Kelly started her letdown with more care than usual since she was nose high and tail low. Even with the tail dragging, her touch down speed was higher than called for so she immediately applied the brakes. That only made matters worse as the right brake promptly failed and the aircraft veered sharply to the left. The application of sudden torque caused the landing gear to collapse and the spinning propeller blades to dig into the ground. The whole propeller assembly was torn free and spun off to the right as the aircraft came to a stop on the grassy area adjacent to the strip.

Kelly slid the canopy back while the aircraft was still moving and was over the side of the 190 as soon as it came to rest. She hit the ground running. It was important to get as far away from the bird as possible in case there was an explosion and fire.

Amazingly, there was neither explosion nor fire.

✯ ✯ ✯

By the time Kelly got back to Wright Field there were reporters from the Cleveland Plain Dealer, Cincinnati Enquirer, Columbus Dispatch, and Dayton Daily News, as well as several other large daily newspapers, waiting to interview her.

Unfortunately, there was no way to avoid them. They were waiting at the gate and followed her vehicle up to the Operations building. As soon as it came to a stop they surrounded the car and, when Kelly got out, started in with the questions.

The onslaught might have been overwhelming for someone who wasn't used to dealing with the press. Kelly, however, had gained considerable experience dealing with demanding reporters when she had been in charge of public relations for her father's company. She had to handle a slew of difficult questions after a number of racial incidents occurred in the plant following the Pearl Harbor attack.

The reporter from the Dayton news managed to make himself heard above the cacophony of voices.

"Miss Rossiter, can you tell us what happened?"

"The elevator trim control malfunctioned and put the plane in a nose-high/tail-low position which I couldn't correct by overriding it manually."

"Would it have made a difference if an experienced pilot was flying the plane?" That from the Cincinnati Enquirer reporter.

"An experienced pilot was flying the plane."

"I meant an experienced male test pilot."

"I know exactly what you meant. I have experience as a test pilot but sorry—can't meet the qualifications for being a male."

That got a chuckle from most of the reporters. A short stocky man caught her attention.

"Ranalli," he said, by way of introduction. "Akron Beacon Journal. What kind of qualifications do you have for being a test pilot?"

"Eleven hundred hours of flying time. An engineering background. Experience with a number of America's first-line aircraft."

"But how many of those eleven hundred hours were accumulated actually testing new aircraft?" This question was from a tall lanky man who identified himself as a reporter with the Toledo Blade.

Kelly shrugged. "A couple of hundred."

"That's not many hours," Ranalli said. At that comment there was a general nodding of heads from the majority of the reporters crowding around Kelly.

"It's not just the number of hours," Kelly said, resisting the temptation to tell them all where to go. "It's the quality of the experience. If you guys had taken the time to do your homework, you'd know a lot more about my background and would be less inclined to take potshots at me—or maybe you wouldn't," she added, shaking her head in disgust.

"Excuse me Miss Rossiter—or perhaps I should refer to you as Mrs. Singleton—I'm Peggy Hull from the Cleveland Plain Dealer. I did take the time to do a little research on you."

A woman reporter! Kelly hadn't noticed her standing among the male reporters. But she had managed to work her way to the front row. Was she going to come down on Kelly's side or was she likely to be even more critical than the men? Kelly wondered.

"Among my discoveries was the reason why you happened to end up flying the B-29 that brought you the award of the DFC. Colonel Tibbets thought he had come up with a procedure for keeping the engines from overheating on take-off thus minimizing the prospect of having to deal with an engine fire. Isn't that true?"

"Yes. Essentially."

"Isn't it also true that he taught you and another WASP pilot to try this out first because the men were afraid to fly the new bomber?"

"Yes. That's also true."

"Well, Mrs. Singleton, alias Miss Rossiter, I can tell you from first-hand knowledge that your efforts really did pay dividends. I just came back from an assignment in the Pacific with the B-29 wings on Saipan and Tinian. The incidence of engine fires on take-off was lowered significantly. General LeMay is very pleased with the drop in the abort rate which he attributes primarily to this new take-off procedure."

Kelly nodded appreciatively, pleased that there was one friendly face among the group of reporters. She turned away and headed for the entrance to the Operations office.

Ranalli called after her. "One more question, Miss Rossiter."

Kelly stopped and turned back to face him. "Yes?" she asked, hands on hips.

"Are you going to attempt to continue your flying career once you finish your assignment here at Wright Field?"

"Attempt? No, Mr Ranalli. I'm not going to attempt anything. I will continue my flying career," she said, emphasizing the will so that there would be no mistake about what she was saying.

"What do you expect to do?"

"I don't know yet. But I'll find something. And you mark my words, Mr. Ranalli.

Eventually there will be women pilots and copilots on commercial airliners. I don't know how long it will take but it will happen."

After that parting shot she climbed the stairs two at a time and made her way into the Operations office.

First thing the next morning Colonel Braithwaite, head of the Flight Test Division, received a blistering phone call from General Franklin Kirby, commanding general of the Air Service Technical Command.

"Braithwaite, what in the hell are you doing over there? It's bad enough to lose one of the German fighters we recovered after taking the time and trouble to ship it back to the states for analysis and evaluation. But there'll be hell to pay if the press gets hold of the fact that it was a WASP pilot who pranged it in."

"They already know about it. A number of reporters interviewed her as soon as she got back to the field."

"Damn it, Colonel, the last thing we need is any negative publicity when we're trying to impress the public with the importance of maintaining a strong air force and drum up public support for a faltering jet program."

"Sir, it wasn't really Rossiter's fault. There's been an ongoing problem with the trim actuator. A number of the test pilots have encountered it. But nobody's bothered to document it because of the assumption that a test pilot should be able to handle unanticipated problems like that. Besides, Kelly Rossiter's not just any old WASP."

Kirby harrumphed. "I thought the WASP program had officially ended last December."

"It did, sir, but Kelly's on special assignment to NACA as a test pilot."

"How in the hell did she manage that?"

"I'm not sure. But her husband is a brigadier general on General Arnold's staff."

Kirby harrumphed a second time. "Well, I have some influence with General Arnold, too so we'll see who has more clout. In the meantime, I don't want her to do any more flying unless it's strictly an administrative flight."

"Yes, sir."

When Kelly heard the news she considered calling Kirk and asking him to intercede with General Arnold. But then, on second thought, it didn't seem fair to bother either him or General Arnold with the war at such a crucial stage.

✯ ✯ ✯

"Sergeant Ramsey?" Kirk was standing in the hallway outside of his office sipping a cup of coffee.

"Sir?"

"Is General Arnold in his office?"

"Yes, sir. He is."

"How busy is he right now?"

"Well, sir, he's studying the reports on last night's B-29 raid on Tokyo. And in another half hour he has to meet with Admiral King."

"Do you think I can squeeze in a ten minute visit with him?"

"If anyone can show up at his door unannounced and be invited in, it would be you, sir."

"Thanks for the encouraging words, Sergeant," Kirk said, as he started walking along with Sergeant Ramsey in the direction of General Arnold's office.

"It's the truth, General Singleton. I doubt if anyone–other than perhaps the President–has the same kind of access to the Chief."

"Methinks you exaggerate a little, my friend," Kirk said, glancing at Sergeant Ramsey out of the corner of his eyes.

Ramsey grinned at him. "Maybe, General Singleton, but if so, only a slight bit."

A few minutes later Kirk was about to knock on the partially open door to General Arnold's office when Arnold looked up and saw him.

"Come in, General Singleton. I'm glad you stopped by because I had a couple of things I wanted to talk to you about."

"Sir?" Kirk said, after Arnold had motioned for him to take a seat.

"I assume you knew about Kelly crash landing a 190 the other day."

"Yes, sir. She called me as soon as she could get to a phone to make sure I knew she was all right."

"Tell me, General, how do you feel about her doing this kind of flying?"

"Frankly, sir, I have mixed feelings. I made it clear that I was opposed to her doing any test flying. But Kelly insisted that she was fully capable of taking care of herself. When I reminded her that her run of luck couldn't last forever she told me in no uncertain terms that the reason she had survived two close calls was because of her superior piloting skills and that it had nothing to do with luck. Her final point was that I had only myself to blame because I was the one who got her the assignment to Wright Field."

Arnold tilted his head to the side, shrugged and grinned. "She's got you there, Kirk."

"Yes, sir, she does."

"Well, I'm taking a lot of heat from Kirby over in ASTC as well as my public relations staff. They're all saying pretty much the same thing."

"And what's that, sir?"

"There'll be a price to pay when word gets out that a WASP pilot was responsible for the loss of a captured German fighter. And, of course, it's out already. Did you read the report of the interview which Kelly gave to the Ohio newspapers?"

"Yes, sir. I did. I saw it after it was picked up by the Washington Post."

"What did you think of it?"

"I thought it was a measured response and that she handled it very well."

"I agree. But Drew Pearson has already sunk his teeth into it and is railing about how women have no place in military aviation especially now that there are large numbers of male pilots returning from overseas assignment. 'Send them back to the kitchen where they belong.' That was the way he ended his editorial."

"When Pearson gets up on his high horse an even-tempered response is about the last thing you can expect from him, sir."

"Unfortunately, that's true, General Singleton. However, from what I've been told, the incident with the 190 wasn't Kelly's fault. Apparently, it's highly unlikely that the result would have been any different had an experienced male test pilot been flying the aircraft."

"Yes, sir. I think that's true."

Arnold leaned back, clasped his hands on top of his head, and silently studied Kirk for a half a minute or so.

"Were you aware that your old friend from the plans section, Colonel Matthews, knew Kelly and was the one who offered her the opportunity to help fly captured German aircraft back to Wright Field before she finished up her flying career–her government-sponsored one, anyway."

"I knew that Kelly met him when she gave him a hop from Logan to Wright Field but didn't know he'd made her such an offer."

"He did. Furthermore, from a strictly personal standpoint I do feel that she should be allowed to continue her flying career at least for the next few months. I guess I can tolerate the heat from Congress and the Press. I've done it many times before.

"There are two people who I don't like on my case, however–three if you count George Marshall–but the only thing he and I typically disagree about is my failure to slow down and take care of my bum ticker. Anyway, when Mrs. Arnold applies the heat she doesn't let up until I give in. And, then, of course, there's Jackie Cochran. Both my wife and Jackie have told me in no uncertain terms that it would be totally unfair to pull the rug out from under Kelly now. Especially in view of the fact that Kelly's one of the best pilots in the service–of either sex–and a holder of the Distinguished Flying Cross to boot. Germany has their Hanna Reitsch; why shouldn't we have our Kelly Rossiter–that's the way Jackie put it."

"Yes, sir."

"The other thing in Kelly's favor is Mrs. Roosevelt's outspoken support of the right of women to pilot military aircraft. She's been the most effective advocate for the program so far. Primarily, of course, because she has the President's ear. But it also helps that she isn't strident about it like Jackie Cochran. So, I'm not going to intervene unless the pressure builds to an unbearable level.

"Anyway, there was a second thing I wanted to talk to you about. Now that the war is winding down I want to continue laying the groundwork for establishing the air force as an independent service. To that end, I've tapped a group of senior officers to form an ad hoc post-war study group whose specific responsibility is to come up with a plan for the best way to approach the issue. Fortunately, there are a number of things in our favor."

"What things, sir?"

"For one thing, Marshall feels the army air force matured enough during the war to merit being given its independence. And Eisenhower, who will most likely replace Marshall as army Chief of Staff sometime this fall, feels the same way. Eisenhower's tremendous popularity—with both the general public and Congress—should make him an invaluable ally in our drive for autonomy for the air force."

"What about the professional relationship between General Spaatz and General Eisenhoswer?" Kirk asked. "From what I've read in the papers, Eisenhower credits the army's success in the invasion of Europe in large part to the outstanding support they received from Spaatz's tactical and strategic air commanders—men like Vandenberg, Quesada, Eaker and Doolittle."

"Yes. Spaatz and Eisenhower have the highest regard for each other. And that also bodes well for the success of our effort.

"Spaatz will oversee the study group—primarily because he's likely to be my replacement when I retire so he'll be the one responsible for getting the infant air force up and running—or up and flying to use the appropriate metaphor. But Vandenberg will be in charge of the day to day workings of the group. I had planned on assigning both Norstad and Kuter to the group as well but I need them overseas. I also want you to be a member of the group, General Singleton."

"Me?"

"Yes. You. Since you've proven to be an exceptionally creative planner I want you to participate in their deliberations. And since I don't want you to feel like a junior member of the group I've recommended you for your second star."

For a long moment, Kirk was speechless. "Sir, I don't know what to say. Especially since it was just last September that I received my first star."

"Well, in light of the fact that Vandenberg is now a lieutenant general I was worried that you might feel obligated to defer to his rank and be reluctant to take a position contrary to his on a particular issue. Besides, although Vandenberg is a natural leader and a gifted commander, he's no match for you in the intellectual department."

"Yes, sir," Kirk said, shifting uneasily in his chair while wondering if his response had sounded arrogant.

"General Singleton, I know there are people on my staff and in the Pentagon who think that I play favorites with you. And it is true that I look upon you as a son but I'm not promoting you because I like you. Every assignment I've given you has been carried out in an exemplary manner, beginning with your work on AWPD-1 as a young major right up to your survey of B -29 operations in the Pacific last fall."

"Thank you, sir."

"Anyway, It seems that every time we have a chance to meet I have to cut it short and rush off to a meeting with Admiral King," Arnold said, with a passing smile.

"It does seem that way, sir," Kirk said, as he rose to his feet, saluted his boss and turned to go.

"By the way, soon to be Major General Singleton, the first thing I want you to do is sit down with Spaatz, then accompany Vandenberg as he meets with the other members. I've already alerted them to the importance of moving forward with this."

"Who are the other members, sir?"

"Generals George, Knerr, Bissell and Hansell. Hansell, being the junior man in the group, will serve as recording secretary. But I would like an oral report from you after each meeting so that I can be kept abreast of the group's deliberations."

"Yes, sir."

"And stop fretting about Kelly. That's one woman who is fully capable of taking care of herself."

☆ ☆ ☆

XXV

A few days after the crash landing with the 190, Kelly asked Major Latimer for permission to catch a flight to Westover Field in Chicopee Falls, Massachusetts, in order to pay a visit to her father's sister who lived in Northampton, Mass, a short distance from the Field. Besides, the base Flight Surgeon had recommended that she take a brief respite from flying.

Several days later she was waiting in the Operations Office at Westover for her return hop to Wright Field. While she was casually scanning some weather maps, Captain Fielding, the Operations Officer, appeared in the doorway to his office, paused momentarily then walked over to where Kelly was standing.

"Are you checked out in the C-54?" he asked skipping over any preliminary comments.

"Sort of."

"What's that supposed to mean?"

"It means that I flew as copilot on a C-54 that made a round trip to an Alaskan airfield. The A/C wasn't exactly the most generous pilot that I've flown with. He did give me a couple of landings and one take-off, but that's about it. Why do you ask?"

"Because the pilot of an inbound C-54 needs a copilot for a flight to Greenland."

"Greenland?"

"Yep."

"You mean he's been flying a C-54 without a copilot?"

"No. When he radioed in he said that his copilot is in bad shape—apparently suffering from a case of appendicitis. In fact, he asked for an ambulance to meet the plane as soon as they land."

Kelly nodded.

"I understand that you were awarded the DFC for a B-29 flight," Fielding said. "Is that true?"

"Yes."

"I didn't know that women were eligible to receive the award."

"Why wouldn't they be?"

Fielding shrugged. "I don't know. I never gave it any thought."

"You're not the only male who hasn't," Kelly said with a touch of sarcasm.

Approximately twenty minutes later a youthful looking Army Air Force lieutenant came into the Operations office. Kelly glanced up from her weather maps.

"My name's Clay Robertson. I'm the guy who radioed in asking if a pilot was available to take the right seat in my C-54." The pilot was talking to Captain Fielding while giving Kelly the once-over.

After the introductions were made and Robertson got over the initial shock of discovering he was about to acquire a female copilot, and a beautiful one at that, he gave Kelly a brief summary of the situation.

"A B-29 on a mission out of Ladd Field in Fairbanks ran into a severe storm over the North Pole and got lost somewhere over the icepack. They never did get a handle on exactly where they were but after running short of fuel made an emergency landing, thinking they were a few hundred miles northeast of Ladd. It turned out they actually landed near a frozen lake somewhere in Northern Greenland."

"What was a B-29 doing up there anyway?" Kelly asked.

Robertson shrugged. "Beats me.

"Anyway, another B-29 from Ladd pinpointed the location of the downed plane. And that's where we come into the picture. We're picking up some JATO bottles here at Westover which will be mounted on the fuselage at Thule . . ."

"What are JATO bottles?"

"Small jet engines that are used to give an aircraft an extra boost on takeoff. The powers that be figured we might need that to get off the frozen lake what with the extra weight we'll be carrying.

"First, though, we'll be making stops at Goose Bay, Labrador, and Sonderstrom Airfield, Greenland, to pick up arctic kits and survival equipment along with other supplies to drop to the stranded crew.

"There's no need to rush off immediately. The crew is in no immediate danger. There were no injuries, and they have enough food to last a couple of weeks. So we'll leave first thing in the morning. But right now I need a cup of coffee, then some food."

"I'll get you some coffee," Kelly said.

"And I'll arrange for transport over to the Officers Mess, Lieutenant Robertson," Fielding added.

"Thanks. To both of you."

"So tell me Miss Rossiter, have you had any experience flying in the north country?" Robertson asked as he took the cup of coffee Kelly handed him.

"Yes, sir, I have."

"There's no need to refer to me as sir. Call me Clay."

"And please call me Kelly," she said, returning his smile.

"All right, Kelly it will be."

"In answer to your question, Clay, I was the copilot on a C-54 that flew into Casco Airfield on Attu Island. That strip is mostly surrounded by mountains so the approach can be a little tricky. You come in at a fairly steep glide angle and maintain a nose-high attitude until you throttle back. By doing this, the wing acts as an airbrake and minimizes the use of the wheel brakes. That can be a big help if the runway is icy or has a snow cover."

"That same approach is going to be required to get down safely on the lake where the B-29 crash landed, Kelly."

She nodded. "I also made a couple of mid-winter deliveries to Yellowknife in the Northwest Territories. Yellowknife sits on the edge of the Great Slave Lake, which is frozen over for much of the year. So that's where I landed a ski-equipped C-47 on two separate occasions. The main difficulty was the problem with depth perception. It was hard to gauge exactly how far above the surface of the lake you were until seconds before touchdown."

"Well, it's apparent that you've had more experience with winter flying than I have. So I'm going to let you handle the landing on the lake. Are you okay with that?" he asked, putting his hands over his head and stretching.

"Sure."

✯ ✯ ✯

Thule Army Airfield, Greenland Thirty-six hours later

After accompanying the flight engineer on his preflight inspection, Kelly joined Clay Robertson up on the flight deck and began reading off the items on the *before starting engine section* of the checklist. As she read each item on the list, the responsible person—pilot, copilot, or flight engineer—carried out the required action while verbally confirming that it could be checked off as completed.

Next came the *start engine section*.

Robertson glanced over at Kelly and nodded. "Go ahead, Kelly."

By the time Kelly finished reading the items on the checklist all four engines were running smoothly. At this point, the battery cart was disconnected, the airplane battery switched on, and the chocks were removed in preparation for taxiing.

Kelly then handed the checklist over to the flight engineer freeing her up to concentrate on her taxiing duties. First she called the tower and received taxi clearance. While she was doing this Lieutenant Robertson operated the flight controls to make sure there was free movement of all the surfaces. After Robertson got an all clear signal from the ground crew, he released the parking brake, and began taxiing out to the run-up ramp. On the way Kelly held the control column forward to keep the nose wheel securely on the ground. She and Robertson also checked the operation of both the directional gyros and the turn and bank indicators. While the plane was being taxied the flight engineer moved the flaps through their full range to bleed the air out of the lines then returned them to full up. At the same time he also checked to make sure the movement of both flaps was in sync.

At the engine run-up ramp another series of checks were made to insure that oil pressure, oil temperature and cylinder head temperature were within limits for engine run-up.

This procedure was followed for each of the engines

Kelly then requested takeoff clearance from the tower.

As soon as it was received Robertson initiated the takeoff roll, advancing the throttles slowly and evenly, using the nose wheel steering wheel to maintain directional control. When the aircraft speed reached 85 mph, Robertson eased back on the control column to help get the nose wheel off the ground. Liftoff speed was reached at 110 miles per hour. At the pilot's verbal command the flight engineer raised the landing gear after the C-54 was airborne then moved the landing gear control handle to neutral.

When the aircraft reached 500 feet of altitude and an air speed of 135mph the pilot directed the flight engineer to raise the flaps. Robertson then told Kelly to reduce manifold pressure to 35 inches and the flight engineer to reduce engine rpm to 2350. Booster pumps were left on until cruising altitude was reached.

They climbed to 500 feet above their cruising altitude, reduced manifold pressure and engine rpm to required cruise settings, and gradually allowed the aircraft to lose the extra 500 feet of altitude. Leveling off at 10,000 feet, Robertson directed the flight engineer to close the cowl flaps. After trimming the aircraft to fly absolutely true, the mixture control levers were moved to the cruise control position. The C-54 was now flying in a tail-high attitude which enabled the aircraft to achieve optimum fuel efficiency. Their course was east northeast out of Thule. The lake was located about 300 miles away.

When they were about a half an hour out from their objective, Robertson turned the controls over to Kelly. They came in over the lake at an altitude of around 1000 feet. Kelly was dumfounded to discover that the B-29 was sitting on the lake about halfway down its length.

"What the hell is this?" she muttered under her breath. The B-29 was supposedly located adjacent to the lake, not sitting on it!

Meanwhile, Robertson had established radio contact with the B-29 pilot.

Kelly asked him to get an estimate as to the width and length of the lake from the crew on the ground. Also find out what the conditions were like on its surface.

The answer came back a few minutes later.

The lake was about a half mile long and 500 feet wide with relatively steep banks on either side. The surface was covered with from 2 to 10 inches of snow that had a wind hardened crust.

Kelly wasn't concerned about the snow since the C-54 was designed to land and take off in up to 10 inches of the white stuff. But the margin of error for the landing was pretty slim what with the B-29 partially blocking the runway halfway down its length.

"What's our wingspan, Clay?"

"Just under 120 feet."

"Okay. And the B-29's is 140. Since we only have 500 feet of width to play with, getting the C-54 safely past the B-29 is going to be something like threading a needle."

"Hopefully, you can get the C-54 stopped by the time we get to the B-29," Robertson said.

"That's my goal," Kelly said, as she banked the aircraft onto the downwind leg, "but the only chance I have of making that happen is to touch down at the extreme southern end of the lake."

Turning onto final approach Kelly brought the plane in over the hills south of the lake, then pushed the control column forward and established a steep glide angle. Moments later, she flared out, keeping the plane in a nose-high attitude, and made a flawless touch down at the southern tip of the lake.

Once on the lake, Kelly pulled the control column back in her lap. The tail down, nose high attitude kept the wing at an angle that produced a natural braking effect. It also enabled her to steer with the rudder until the plane slowed down enough to apply gentle brake pressure. But before that point was reached things began to go awry.

The plane was not slowing down quickly enough to stop before reaching the spot where the B-29 had come to rest!

Damn it, Kelly thought, *now I'm going to have to squeeze between the snow bank on the edge of the lake and the left wingtip of the B-29.*

She decided to try a cautious and somewhat tentative use of the brakes to reduce the taxi speed. It worked! Halleluiah! The B-29 crew, who were watching the spectacle from a safe distance, estimated the clearance between the two wingtips to be about two feet as the C-54 taxied by.

"Nice work, Kelly!" Robertson said.

Kelly smiled and thanked him while wiping the beads of sweat off her forehead with the edge of her hand.

"I never imagined I would break into a sweat in—of all places—northern Greenland!" she said.

"You may have been sweating, Kelly—and who wouldn't have been, confronted with a situation like that—but your actions were exactly right. You were cool as a cucumber!"

Kelly nodded as Robertson began reading the *after landing* items on the check list. In response to his queries the cowl flaps were opened and prop controls moved to high rpm by the flight engineer. Robertson then directed the engineer to raise the flaps and cut number 1 and 4 engines.

The B-29 crew had finished destroying all classified documents and equipment while Kelly's crew removed all non-essential equipment from the C-54. Kelly then taxied up and down the lake a few times from the point where the B-29 was sitting to make the surface as smooth as possible for their takeoff.

Robertson and the B-29 pilot estimated that there was about 1200 feet available to get the C-54 off the ground.

While the crew members from the B-29 were taken on board the C-54, the flight engineer, with the assistance of the B-29 flight engineer, activated the electrical connections to the four JATO bottles which had been attached to the fuselage at Thule.

As Kelly began her takeoff roll, the aircraft started to slide, but when the JATO bottles were ignited, the C-54 virtually leaped into the air after the sudden boost in power. Although the C-54 grossed out at an estimated 66,000 pounds it took less than a thousand feet to get the aircraft airborne. The JATO bottles made the difference.

The trip back to Westover was without incident. There was a two hour stopover at Thule where the B-29 crew members were checked out by base medical personnel and given a clean bill of health. Following that they were treated to a steak dinner in the cafeteria.

Robertson, noticing how tired Kelly seemed, suggested he fly the aircraft back to Westover Field. Kelly turned the controls over to Robertson shortly after they took off from Thule. It had been a long time since she'd felt that exhausted. Shortly after relinquishing the piloting responsibility she leaned back in her seat and closed her eyes to rest them for a few minutes. A half an hour later she awoke with a sudden involuntary movement startled to discover that she had dozed for that long and began apologizing profusely to Lieutenant Robertson.

"No apology needed, Kelly. You've done more than your fair share on this flight. Go ahead and doze off. If I need any help I'll let you know."

So she catnapped all the way back to Westover feeling a little guilty whenever she briefly returned to consciousness. But the last leg went without a hitch.

Before Kelly and Clay Robertson went their separate ways back at Westover, he was lavish in his praise for the piloting skill that she demonstrated in Greenland.

✯ ✯ ✯

XXVI

Mid-June, 1945

There was a message from Kirk waiting for her at the Westover Ops office. He wanted her to phone him as soon as she could find a private place to make a call. The number he left was the one for his Pentagon office.

After thanking Kelly for filling in for the ailing C-54 copilot, Captain Fielding offered her the use of his office to call her husband.

The call went right through to Kirk's office.

When he picked up she opened with, "Hey, handsome, missing me yet?"

"Always. No matter how busy I am you're always in my thoughts—maybe in the background if I'm really busy but then it doesn't take much to bring you up to the foreground. Guess what I miss the most?"

"Surely not the base sexual things. It must be the intellectually stimulating conversations we often have."

"That's it, beautiful," he said, smiling as he imagined the expression on her face. "Far be it from me to ever harbor a carnal thought."

"Yeah. You and every other flyboy. Your thoughts are always on the highest plane, right?"

"Was that an intentional, or unintentional pun?" he asked, laughing into the receiver. Anyway, to get down to serious business. Or maybe I should say to raise the level of the conversation several notches . . ."

"Yes?"

"Well, my darling wife, I've been given a new assignment by General Arnold."

"Really? What is it?"

"One with which you're going to be pleased."

"But you're not?"

"Let's just say I have mixed feelings about it. Although most people would probably look on it as a plum assignment."

"So, how much longer are you going to keep me in suspense?"

"Sorry!"

When he told her about being chosen to work with a number of other senior officers on the planning for an independent air force, Kelly's immediate response was,

"Does that mean you won't be heading out into the combat zone anymore?"

"Yes. Probably not."

"And you're not happy about that?"

"No, Kell. Because it's the commanders with combat experience who are going to get ahead in the new service. Not the administrative types."

"I'd hardly refer to your two month tour of B-29 operations in the Far East as being an administrative assignment."

"Maybe not. But it doesn't exactly qualify as a combat assignment either."

"Considering how heavily General Arnold leans on you, his ongoing support ought to insure you an important position in the independent air force, shouldn't it?"

"Not necessarily, Kell. For one thing, he'll probably be retiring at the end of the year–at the very latest."

"But won't his influence continue to be felt even after retirement?"

"There's a real question as to how much longer he'll live. He's already had four serious heart attacks. The likelihood of him surviving another one isn't very high."

"Who is his successor likely to be?"

"General Spaatz, probably."

"How well do you know him?"

"Not very."

"As a part of this study group you'll be working with him on a fairly regular basis from now on, won't you?"

"I'm not sure how often we'll actually meet with him. He'll probably expect us to work independently and report to him from time to time on our progress."

"Who else is going to be part of the group?"

"An old friend, Possum Hansell."

"Possum? What kind of a name is that?"

"It goes back to his teenage years, Kelly. He's got beady little eyes, a Bob Hope-like ski slope nose and thin facial features. His friends thought he bore a striking resemblance to the opossum, hence the nickname."

"It's interesting the way people acquire nicknames," she said, reflectively.

"Sometimes it's the person himself who encourages the use of a nickname because of the way he feels about his given name. For instance, the general who will be in charge of our group on a day to day basis is Hoyt Vandenberg."

"Vandenberg? Where have I heard that name before?"

"You probably saw it on the cover of *Time* Magazine back in January."

"I do remember seeing the picture of a youthful looking general but I didn't remember his name. One other thing I do recall: the secretaries in the steno pool at Wright Field were all drooling over his picture and bemoaning the fact that he was married."

Kirk chuckled. "I'm not surprised. The Washington Post once described Van as 'the most impossibly handsome man on the entire Washington scene.'"

"I can see where he might want a nickname with a given name like Hoyt. Whatever prompted his parents to choose a name like that I wonder?" Kelly asked.

Kirk shrugged. "Possibly because they knew that Hoyt comes from an old English word Hoit meaning tall and slender. And that's what Van is all right."

"But they couldn't possibly have known that he was going to turn out to be that way."

"Beats me, Kell. Maybe all the rest of the family was tall so his parents assumed he would be too."

"So who else is on this committee?"

"You wouldn't know the other members. They're all major generals with one exception."

"That's you, I presume."

"Not anymore."

"You mean you're now a two star general?"

"I soon will be, Kelly."

"But that's incredible. You were promoted to brigadier general less than a year ago."

"I know. Promotions come quickly during wartime, Kell."

"Wow! You are truly amazing, my talented husband!"

"Not really. I Just happen to be in the right place at the right time–and working for the right man. So, tell me what you've been up to lately."

"Flying, of course."

"Oh? Where to?"

"You won't believe me, Kirk!"

"Try me."

"Have you heard about the B-29 that was forced to crash land in northern Greenland?"

"Of course. What about it?"

"I was on the C-54 that flew the rescue mission."

"How did you manage that?"

"I happened to be in the Ops office at Westover when the C-54 pilot arrived there looking for a replacement for his ailing copilot. After hearing about my experience in the Aleutians and the Northwest Territories he asked me to handle the take-offs and landings in Greenland."

"I'm impressed, Kell, but I'm afraid the Chief is going to hit the roof when he hears about your little escapade."

"Why?"

"Do you remember what his reaction was when he discovered that Nancy Love and one of her WAFS pilots planned on flying a B-17 across the north Atlantic to Scotland?"

"Sure, I remember that he wasn't very happy about it. But it's not as though I was attempting to cross the North Atlantic like they were planning to do."

"Yeah, but you left the North American continent and flew over the North Atlantic. There would have been hell to pay if something had happened and you went down over the ocean."

"Well nothing happened. Kirk!"

"And what if it had? How do you think General Arnold would feel? And your father, not to speak of myself.

"What I want to know, Kell, is what you plan to do once your military flying career ends—as it's bound to do in the near future."

"Continue working for my father most likely."

You mean you're still on your father's payroll?"

"Of course. I'm probably his most trusted advisor—especially on technical matters."

"How much does he pay you, anyway?"

Kelly paused for a moment before answering, afraid of what Kirk's response might be. "Fifteen thousand dollars a year."

"Fifteen thou—," he said, virtually choking on the figure. "That's almost twice what I get paid," he blurted out peevishly.

"Yes, but my contribution translates into greater income for the company.

That response got to Kirk. "Are you saying your job is worth more than mine simply because you get paid more?"

"No, of course not."

"Well, it sure sounded that way to me!"

"*Dammit*, she thought, *How am I going to get out of this one.* "What I meant to say was our respective roles aren't really comparable because I work for a profit-making firm and you work for the good of the country. Or to be more accurate, the good of the world. And that's a priceless contribution, Kirk—literally and figuratively!

"Anyway, since I often accompanied my father on his trips to Washington I met most of the government people who he regularly deals with. And when he had them to our house in Seattle I was the one who played host to them."

"So what's your point?"

Although he had calmed down quite a bit, Kirk still sounded annoyed.

"Simply this," Kelly said. "Dad's been thinking for some time now that we should have a Washington liaison. Someone to keep track of any proposed legislation that could affect our business plus act as our on-site representative to the Defense Department."

"And he's proposing you play that role?"

"Yes. As I've already pointed out, in many respects I'd be perfect for the job."

"Maybe," Kirk granted, "except for the fact that being the wife of a senior officer would probably be considered a conflict of interests, Kell.

"I see what you mean," she acknowledged, reluctantly. Well, I would still continue as his technical expert."

"But that would mean flying out to the plant on a regular basis wouldn't it?"

Kelly hedged. "No. Just occasionally. Probably."

"Oh. Okay. So then you could focus your energies on being a full time service wife."

"How exciting."

"All right Kelly, you can skip the sarcasm."

"Sorry."

"You know, I'm now eligible to move into one of the Victorian homes on Generals Row at Fort Myer."

"Wow! Those mansions would make our home in Seattle look like a cottage."

"I don't think so, Kell. I remember my initial impression of your house with its large formal dining room. My first thought was it was too large to ever feel comfortable in."

"If you felt that way about my home, how are you going to feel about the quarters on Generals Row?"

Kirk shrugged. "I have to admit it's not exactly the house I would choose to live in but along with my rarified rank comes an obligation to do a certain amount of entertaining. And with you living there I'll have the perfect partner to help me host parties and other gatherings."

"When I moved out of my father's house I thought I was done with that kind of thing."

"You were the one who didn't want to marry a lowly lieutenant colonel, Kell. You got your wish, so stop complaining."

"All right."

✭ ✭ ✭

One hour later

General Spaatz' office

When Kirk approached Spaatz's office he saw that the door was open and the General was leaning back in his chair, feet propped up on his desk, talking animatedly to someone on the phone. Spaatz was the picture of nonchalance as he waved Kirk in and motioned for him to have a seat.

After a couple of minutes, the tenor of the conversation changed as Spaatz swung his feet off the desk onto the floor and sat up straight in his chair at the same time that his voice took on an edge. Moments later he ended the conversation and slammed the phone down on its base while muttering something about paranoid sailors.

"Ever have any dealings with the navy, Singleton?"

"Yes sir. Back in 1940 when I was working on AWPD-1. I swore at the time I'd try to avoid doing business with them in the future if I could possibly arrange it."

"Can't blame you, but unfortunately we're going to have to do business with them since they're likely to be the primary obstacle in our path to independence."

"Sir, I can work with just about anyone—including the navy—if I have to."

"Good. I'd like you to get together with Vandenberg today to do a little preliminary planning if his schedule permits it. Plus you can contact the other members of the group and set up your first full meeting."

"Will do, sir," Kirk said as he stood up, saluted and turned to go.

"General Singleton—"

"Sir?"

"Have you seen the ME 262 yet?"

"Only in a photo, sir, but Colonel Matthews promised me a ride in one after he gets them back to the states. That will make me the second member of my family to fly in one."

General Spaatz raised an eyebrow.

Kirk explained about Matthews's promise to Kelly.

"Oh, yes. I've heard a number of stories about your wife's flying skill. Wicked! Wicked!" Spaatz said, using one of his favorite phrases of admiration.

✯ ✯ ✯

XXVII

After the call to Kirk, Kelly placed a call to Major Feranno.

"Hi Kelly. I'm glad you checked in before catching a hop back to Wright Field."

"What's up, sir?"

"I got a call from Colonel Matthew's assistant. His name is Bob Stemple. Captain Robert Stemple. He's Matthews's frontman. Arrives in advance of Matthews to make sure things are going to go smoothly for his boss. He speaks with his boss's authority so you can be comfortable following his orders."

"Yes sir."

"According to Stemple the 262s are due in port in a day or two so Colonel Matthews would like you at Newark ready to transition from the prop jobs you've been flying to the jets as soon as he arrives. Which means you'd better catch a hop over to Newark ASAP."

"All right, sir. There's a C-54 leaving after lunch. I should be able to catch a ride on that."

The next day Kelly stood on the flight line chatting casually with Captain Stemple. Stemple informed her that Colonel Matthews should arrive the following day after flying a four engine German transport from Orly Field, Paris to the continental United States with only two stops, one in the Azores and another in Bermuda. The captured German fighters had been mothballed for protection and were brought back to the states on a British Aircraft Carrier which arrived in port several days before Matthews was expected to fly in on the giant German transport.

The process of removing the protective coating began as soon as the planes were delivered to Newark airfield. The first planes made ready for the flight to Wright Field were a pair of Shrikes, the famous Focke Wulf 190.

Stemple was about to ask Kelly to deliver one of the Shrikes to Wright Field but changed his mind when he remembered that she had to crash land one because of a malfunctioning trim actuator switch. Instead, he asked Lieutenant Jesse Hartwell, one of the original members of Matthew's Misfits who had not yet resigned from the Army Air Force, to fly it there.

Barely a half an hour later Kelly and Stemple watched in horror as a booby trap located in the left wing of the Shrike exploded shortly after Hartwell had broken ground and started to retract the landing gear. The force of the explosion blew off the wing and the plane flipped over on its back and dove into the ground, killing the pilot instantly. That was the first fatality among Matthews' pilots.

Kelly knew that it could easily have been her piloting the Shrike but Stemple's last minute decision to assign the mission to Hartwell had been her salvation.

✯ ✯ ✯

Matthews arrived exhausted from his cross-ocean flight only to be confronted with the news of the fatal crash.

When he discovered that the Shrike had been delivered to the port on a flatbed instead of being flown there Matthews concluded that the aircraft had not been checked for explosives. That was supposed to be SOP for each acquisition of an enemy aircraft. After looking around for someone to point the finger at, Matthews decided he had only himself to blame. He shouldn't have left Cherbourg until the last German fighter arrived and was thoroughly checked out for booby traps.

If anyone should be court-martialed for dereliction of duty, it was he. But no one said anything to him. There was an investigation, of course, but no charges were brought. It helped that Arnold had absolute faith in him and that Matthews had carried out his assignment to acquire examples of German aeronautical technology to perfection while managing to avoid antagonizing America's Western European allies.

While Matthews was recovering from his cross-Atlantic flight, Kelly was busy studying the operating manual for the Schwalbe, learning where the instruments and controls were located. After a few days she was blindfolded while sitting in the cockpit and informed that the aircraft was experiencing a certain type of emergency. She had to respond automatically by reaching for the appropriate controls and taking the steps needed to deal successfully with the emergency situation. This procedure was repeated for a variety of emergency situations which she might encounter in flight.

After a couple of day's rest Matthews began briefing Kelly on the idiosyncrasies of the Schwalbe. Just to satisfy himself about her knowledge of the Shwalbe's operating procedures he had a 262 tethered to the ground and made Kelly go through the cockpit routine including starting the engines, running them up, then shutting them down. This was the same procedure he had followed in Europe with each member of the misfits before letting them fly the jet aircraft for the first time. Of course, unlike Kelly, none of them had any previous experience in a jet.

"All right, Kelly. Let's talk about this bird. It's definitely a pilot's airplane. As you must have noticed, cockpit visibility is outstanding–as good as, maybe even better than, the Mustang."

"And from a combat standpoint, it helps that you're looking right down the barrels of the guns, right?" she added.

"Yes, because in a plane with guns in the wings like the P-47, for instance, the problem is estimating where three hundred yards is in the air–that's where the 50 caliber machine guns converge on a Thunderbolt. But that's nothing you need to be concerned with, so let's focus on the things you do need to know about."

"Yes sir."

"When you're on your take-off roll you need to hold the nose down on the ground. I made the mistake of elevating the nose first time I flew the bird but by half runway discovered that my airspeed was stuck at around sixty miles per hour. As soon as I lowered the nose the airspeed picked up and the plane popped off the ground before I reached the six thousand foot marker. That's one of the quirks of a swept wing aircraft.

"Another thing you need to be aware of is the leading edge wing slats. When these are deployed they extend the area of the wing and allow the plane to fly slower and land and take off in a shorter distance. They extend automatically at lower airspeeds and retract at high speeds. The slats make a hell of a racket when they pop in and out though, that's one reason why I'm telling you about them.

Kelly thought that Matthews looked and sounded far more stressed than he had several months earlier. There was a hint of impatience in his voice—no, more like disquiet—which she had not heard there previously.

"Are you all right with me flying this jet, sir?"

"I think so, Kelly. It's just that the loss of Hartwell has got me second guessing my decision."

"But from what I understand they've never found an Me262 that was booby-trapped."

"That's true. Furthermore, every one of them was gone over with a fine-tooth comb. All right Kelly. I'll and stop fretting.

"One of the most important things to keep in mind," he reminded her, "is that it takes a while for the turbines to spool up. If you back off on the throttle too much on your landing approach and find that you need to make a go-around you're going to be in trouble when you advance the throttle because you don't get the immediate response from a jet like you do from a prop job."

"In other words, it's pretty much the same situation I encountered with the YP-59."

"Yes. That's about it, Kelly. Oh wait a minute—there is one other thing."

Kelly suppressed a sigh of impatience. She was anxious to get the plane into the air. "Sir?" she said, cocking her head and wondering what more he could possibly have to tell her.

"You have to begin transferring fuel from the auxiliary tank to the main tank in front of the cockpit shortly after takeoff otherwise you'll quickly find yourself in serious trouble."

"All right, sir."

"Okay, Kelly. You can crank them up," he said before hopping down off the wing. As soon as Matthew's feet hit the ground Captain Stemple came running up to him with a message in his hand and a frantic expression on his face. Matthews scanned it at high speed to see why Stemple looked so flustered. The message was from General Arnold.

H.H. ARNOLD TO COLONELS MATTHEWS AND BRAITHEWHITE.

EFFECTIVE IMMEDIATELY KELLY ROSSITER/SINGLETON IS NO LONGER AUTHORIZED TO TEST FLY MILITARY AIRCRAFT, U. S. OR FOREIGN.

BY ORDER OF
HENRY H ARNOLD
COMMANDING GENERAL US ARMY AIR FORCES

Matthews turned around and glanced up at Kelly. He folded the message, put it in a pocket of his flight suit and motioned for Captain Stemple to follow him back into the hanger.

"Bob, has anyone, other than you, seen this message?"

"No sir, no one else."

"Good, let's keep it that way," he said, as he stood by the doorway watching Kelly taxi out to the end of the runway. As far as I'm concerned the Me262 is an operational aircraft so whoever's flying it is not by any means test flying an experimental plane," he added, glancing over his shoulder at Stemple.

"Your logic is irrefutable, sir."

"I like to think so Bob, nevertheless, I wouldn't care to defend my logic before the Chief. Understood?"

"Understood, sir."

Kelly's takeoff and climb to altitude were routine. She reached 9000 feet, leveled off and applied full power for slightly more than one minute, reaching over 530 mph true airspeed. After that brief burst of speed she backed off on the throttles and slowed down to a cruising speed of 350 mph. Since Kelly had been a test pilot and had flown the American jet, Matthews had authorized her to give the Messerschmitt a good wringing out. So she checked fuel consumption at different altitudes as well as determining that there was nothing out of the ordinary about the aircraft's stalling tendencies. Kelly also discovered that the leading edge slats extended at a speed between 150 and 160 mph depending upon the Schwalbe's angle of attack.

Her first attempt to land was unsuccessful because the aircraft was flying too fast even after pulling the throttles back to idle. It took Kelly two more tries to set it down on the runway. But once she had landed and taxied back to the hanger where Colonel Matthews was waiting for her, she shut down the engines, climbed down onto the tarmac and told Colonel Matthews that it was definitely a sweet plane to fly, putting the YP-59 to shame. Kelly said that she also agreed with the other pilot's assessment that the plane had no unusual quirks which could be the undoing of a new pilot.

When Matthews showed her the message from Arnold a few minutes later she simply shrugged, walked over to the hanger, sat down on the bottom step of the air stair, and contemplated what her next move should be. Since Kirk had supported her desire to fly the German fighters she assumed the decision was entirely Arnold's. It was prompted no doubt by his realization that if Kelly had been the pilot of the FW 190, her death, aside from the personal loss Arnold would experience, was likely to raise questions about his judgment and as a consequence might even lead to a call for his removal as Commanding General of the Army Air Forces.

A short while later Stemple came out of the Operations Office, walked up to Kelly and informed her that her husband was on the line wanting to speak to her.

When she picked up the receiver, Kirk started out by asking if she had been told about Arnold's orders grounding her.

"I wasn't grounded Kirk, just told that there would be no more test flying."

"Actually, Kell, it goes further than that. It basically means no more military flying even though it wasn't phrased that way."

"How do you know that?"

"Because Arnold informed me about his decision before he had the message sent out."

"Well, the message arrived after I was already airborne in the Me262."

"You're kidding!"

"No. I'm not kidding."

"Are you sure you and Paul Matthews didn't put your heads together and decide to disregard the message or simply pretend that it didn't arrive until you were airborne?"

"Yes. I'm sure. And I'm telling you the truth!"

"All right, Kell. I believe you."

"Well, you predicted that my military flying career could end at any moment. And you were right. But I guess I shouldn't complain because I flew much longer than the rest of the WASPs."

"That's for sure."

※ ※ ※

Kelly called her father later that day to tell him the news.

"So what do you plan to do now, honey: stay in Washington with your husband and try to fit into the role of service wife?"

"Not right away, dad. Not if I can help it, that is. Although that's what Kirk wants me to do, of course."

"I probably shouldn't tell you this but there's a flying job waiting for you out here if you want it."

"Dad! You mean the Board approved the purchase of a company airplane!"

The prospect of having a plane to fly—even if it was primarily a matter of transporting company executives to meetings in various parts of the country—was an exciting thought.

"Whoa, honey. Don't go jumping to conclusions. I didn't say anything about a company airplane, did I?"

"No. But what else could it be?"

"Just this. Do you remember your first flight instructor—Phil Halliburton?"

"Of course. He was the one who said I was ready to solo after only four hours of dual instruction."

"Well, I ran into him at the Towne Diner a couple of days ago. Over the past year he's been edging his way into the crop dusting business to supplement the income he gets from instructing. There's a big time dusting operation in Arizona run by a guy named Bill Marsh. Marsh's business has been steadily expanding into other western states. In fact, he's got a sub-station here in Washington now in the Skagit Valley. When he heard about Phil's one-man operation Marsh contacted him and asked if he'd be interested in overseeing the Washington operation."

"He asked him just like that—out of the blue?"

"I'm sure he did some checking first, Kelly. After he discovered that Phil was not only a top notch pilot but also a successful businessman that's when he probably made the offer.

Part of Phil's responsibility is to hire additional pilots to help handle the increased workload. So, of course, he thought of you right away. He asked if you were close to finishing up your military flying career.

"I told him I thought so. And that's when he asked if I had any idea whether you might be interested in flying for him."

"Kirk's going to have a fit but I'd like to give it a try, dad. The Stearman is still my favorite plane to fly. So next time you see Phil tell him I'm definitely interested."

"Okay, honey. When do you expect to be heading back this way?"

"How soon does Phil need my help?"

"ASAP, Kelly."

"All right. Tell Phil I'll plan on heading back no later than the week after next."

"Will do."

"Good!"

When Kelly called Kirk back and told him what she planned to do there was complete silence on the other end of the line.

"Are you still there or have you hung up on me?"

"I'm still here–for the moment, anyway," was his curt answer.

"You're upset. I can tell."

"Damn right I'm upset! What did you expect?"

"Look Kirk, It's a lot safer than test flying."

"The hell it is! You spend most of your time flying only a few feet off the ground at a speed of over a hundred miles an hour. And crop dusters face plenty of hazards in a typical day: trees, storage tanks, telephone wires and power lines. Plus you're going to be breathing in all that poisonous stuff you spread on the crops.

"That's no longer the case. Crop dusters use respirators and wear gloves."

"No excuses, Kelly. Besides, I need you here helping me out."

"Can't you postpone any major entertaining–you know like large cocktail parties or formal dinner parties–until the fall? That way I can be there to play the hostess role."

"Possibly, but I'm still opposed to you doing any crop dusting. Look Kelly, If you want this marriage to work you'd better get your butt down here to Washington pronto. Do you understand me?"

After a long pause she said, "Yes. I do. I'll be there sometime next week."

"The last time you said 'I do' your tone was very different, Kelly," Kirk said before hanging up.

She had no answer to that.

✯ ✯ ✯

ACKNOWLEDGMENTS

Special thanks to authors Chandra Prasad and Marc Wortman who took time from their own busy writing schedules to read my novel and write pre-publication endorsements for it.

Special thanks also to Jerry Painter, Chief Pilot of *WILD BLUE AVIATION*, for reading the novel, reviewing the flight scenes for accuracy, and for writing a wonderful endorsement of the book.

I'm indebted to Patty Clauser, an old friend, who, in the midst of a very busy life, found time to read the novel chapter by chapter, critiquing both the plot and the characterization. I also wish to express my appreciation to Noel Higgins for her initial editing of the manuscript as well as her suggestion for a title.

My thanks to Chester Marshall, a co-pilot on a B-29, who read an early draft of the novel back in 1999 and advised me on all aspects of the operation of the B-29. I am indebted to a friend, Skip Miller, who, through his membership in a pilot's roundtable, was able to help me make contact with Charles Chauncey, another B-29 pilot. Charles "Chuck" Chauncey, who flew 35 missions over Japan and is now associated with the Commemorative Air Force, was good enough to check my final draft and catch a couple of errors that had slipped into the text. More recently, John Cox, the aircraft commander on the same B-29 on which Chester Marshall flew as copilot, read and commented favorably on the final version of the novel.

My sister-in-law Karen Kukil, editor of the Sylvia Plath Journals, provided valuable input by reviewing the chapters, a few at a time, as I finished writing them. Her husband, Bo Kukil, read my manuscript in its entirety once it was finished and made some specific suggestions about how the novel could be further strengthened.

A final review was carried out by Mary Datillo, a professional editor and published author. Many thanks for her recommendations on further improvements that made the novel more reader friendly.

I also wish to thank another friend, Margaret Mann, a published novelist in her own right, for reading an early draft of the first half of the novel and pointing out, in a very tactful way, all the amateurish mistakes I was making. She gave me some very practical advice on how to correct the mistakes and avoid making similar ones in the future. She also found some positive things to say and strongly encouraged me to keep writing—that she was looking forward to reading it when it was finished. So here it is Margaret: finally finished eight years later!

APPENDIX

The following non-fiction books about the WASP program were used as sources for a number of the adventures that Kelly experiences in the novel.

Those Wonderful Women in their Flying Machines by Sally VanWagenen Keil

On Silver Wings by Marianne Verges

Women Pilots of World War II by Jean Hascall Cole

A WASP Among Eagles by Ann B. Carl

Clipped Wings: The Rise and Fall of the Women Airforce Service Pilots (WASP) of World War II by Molly Merryman

I also drew on an incident from *The Lucky Bastard Club: A B-17 Pilot in Training* by Eugene Fletcher